18/13

Holding My Breath

Dear Joel
with many
thanks!
Sidura

Holding My Breath

Sidura Ludwig

**Tindal
Street
Press**

First published in 2007 by Key Porter Books, Toronto

First published in Great Britain in February 2008
by Tindal Street Press Ltd
217 The Custard Factory, Gibb Street, Birmingham, B9 4AA
www.tindalstreet.co.uk

A CIP catalogue reference for this book is available
from the British Library

ISBN: 978 0 9551 384 7 8

Typeset by Country Setting, Kingsdown, Kent
Printed and bound in Great Britain by Clays Ltd, St Ives PLC

FSC
Mixed Sources
Product group from well-managed
forests and other controlled sources
Cert no. SGS - COC - 2061
www.fsc.org
© 1996 Forest Stewardship Council

For my grandmothers

Holding My Breath

I

When my parents, Goldie and Saul Levy, got married in 1947, there was no gown. My mother wore a simple white dress, and my father wore the first suit he had ever owned. They didn't get married at the Royal Alex Hotel, and there was no ballroom luncheon. Baba, my grandmother, hosted the wedding at the house with the *chuppah* in the living room. Everyone stood around them while they were blessed like their forefathers before them. It was August, and Goldie, even though her dress was knee-length, almost fainted from the smell of musty suits, alcohol, cigarettes and cologne. Saul almost fainted, too, but that was out of disbelief. He held his own hands behind his back, while under the chuppah, to stop himself from reaching out to touch my mother. Her face glistened with sweat; her hair up off her face was damp where it met her neck. Nobody else thought of her as a doll except for my father, who wondered the entire ceremony what she was doing standing beside him.

The chuppah was one of my grandmother's tablecloths, which she planned to give to the couple for their *Shabbos* table. My parents didn't want a religious wedding, but Zaida, my grandfather, had insisted on the chuppah, which was at least traditional. He made the poles himself, treating the wood and sanding it in the backyard for two weeks before the wedding day. He made dowels for the poles,

3

too, and carved little Stars of David on each one. On the wedding day, four men – two uncles, a cousin and a neighbour recently bar mitzvahed – held the chuppah up over the couple's heads so that neither of them could see the stars. My *zaida* thought of them as bits of God watching over the marriage without my mother and father knowing.

Unfortunately, God forgot to watch over the chicken soup Baba had intended to serve for lunch. On the hot August day, with the house packed with melting guests, the soup stayed out too long and nearly boiled in the heat alone. When my father broke the glass and everyone clapped around them, Baba ran to the kitchen to get the soup ready in the bowls. She lifted the lid off the pot, and the soup almost jumped out and grabbed her nose. That was the smell: rotten dill, grey chicken. It was enough to make my iron-willed grandmother the third almost-fainting casualty. She had other food to serve. That wasn't the issue; it was having her soup spoil on a day meant to be as sweet as the first *challah* dipped in honey that upset her. She did not believe in omens, and she felt that the *dybbuk* and the evil eye were for women from the Old Country who refused to leave. She was here, in Winnipeg, Canada, at her oldest daughter's wedding. She did not let a single tear drop when she poured the liquid from the soup down the sink. Drops of her sweat mixed with it instead.

'*Yichud!*' Zaida called because everyone was crowding around the new couple. Religious or not, my parents were permitted their first few moments alone as a married couple and my grandfather attempted to usher them up to their room. The room had been my Uncle Phil's and was recently converted slightly to accommodate a double bed (which my zaida also made) and new curtains – white with embroidered yellow daisies, a gift from a cousin in the United States. My parents would live in that room for the first five years of their marriage until my father managed

4

enough savings to get them a small apartment. Until then, they were to live on Alfred Avenue, in the two-storey, three-bedroom house with white stucco and blue shutters. They would eat dinner at my grandparents' dark-stained dining-room table with matching hutch, and they would share the one small, pink bathroom on the top floor with everyone else. And at night, they would lie in bed, in their room, sandwiched between my grandparents, my aunts, Carrie and Sarah, and the ghost of my mother's recently dead brother, Phil, the war hero.

My Uncle Phil died during the Second World War in a plane that crashed somewhere in North Africa. Growing up, I didn't know anything about Africa, except that it is a long way from Winnipeg and that there are deserts. Somewhere in one of the deserts, there is a plane buried in the sand with my uncle's bones beneath it.

He died two years before my mother and father got married. At the wedding, no one talked about the presence they felt, each in their own way. For my grandfather, it was the extra pair of hands holding the chuppah he had made himself. He couldn't deny that, leading up to the wedding, he felt as though another hand guided his own while he sanded the poles for the canopy. He kept this to himself, partly because if he told anyone about his son's ghost, they would think he was crazy; but also, he liked to think that he was the only one who felt it.

For my grandmother, it was the feeling that someone was sitting at her kitchen table while she poured her soured soup down the drain. Someone with long legs, wrapped around her wooden chairs. Someone chuckling softly, kindly, at her mishap. That laugh, like a whisper right by her ear, kept her from crying.

For my parents, it was the pair of eyes they could both feel, if not actually see, when they stood together, alone, for the first time as husband and wife. My mother, who for her whole engagement had wanted nothing more than for her older brother to be alive and celebrating with them, couldn't understand why right then she wished him far away. She just wanted to be alone with my father, for once, without feeling guilty and without worrying that if she kissed him, everyone would be whispering about how they had behaved so inappropriately. That afternoon, my mother closed her eyes, leaned her head against my father's chest and said goodbye to her brother. It was then that Phil's eyes, his long legs, his hands, they all disappeared and no one even noticed him leave.

'Will it always be like this?' Goldie whispered to Saul. They heard the voices of the guests downstairs, eating sponge cake instead of spoiled soup. My father laid his wife's head on his shoulder. They had sat this way many times before, dreaming of their future, worrying about the present.

'Not always,' he promised her. And then he told her about the house they would have one day, the one on McAdam Avenue that she had her eye on – three storeys with an eat-in kitchen and a covered, screened-in porch in the back. He promised her a tomato garden and lilac bushes, and he told her that when (not if) they bought the house he would fix up the garage himself (they always commented on how it was crumbling to pieces; how some people just don't know how to take care of what they've got). The more he talked, the more my mother's back muscles relaxed, followed by her face and then she looked up and all over again fell hopelessly in love. It happened like that – my father telling her her dreams and my mother living in them long enough that she saw everything through her dreaming eyes. She pulled his face toward hers and kissed him deeply, only concentrating on her lips entirely feeling his. She wanted only to breathe him in and to ignore this house, which was starting (even upstairs) to smell like fifty guests, sweaty and nearly spoiled like the chicken soup. My father smelled like everything she thought she wanted in her life – the McAdam Avenue house, four children, a membership to *Hadassah*. If my grandfather hadn't knocked on the door right then, they would have undressed so that they could feel each other, and their dreams, all over their bodies.

I have grown to understand that expectations can develop very early in a person's life, even before they are born. This scene – my two parents newly married and out of breath with excitement, desire and anticipation of their unfolding future – is the beginning of my life, even though it happened long before I was conceived. I see them sitting on that bed and the promises they are making to each other. They know, should they not fulfill them, then their children will, and that is nearly as good. Of course, they didn't have children. They only had one child. Me. But on that afternoon, those promises got packaged up and stored away like love letters at the back of a spare-room closet, to be taken down periodically, reviewed, adored and then stored away again.

2

I feel as if I have spent my life piecing things together – stories I have heard, conversations I shouldn't have. I have become my family's narrator; I take everything I know, and I make this framework of a puzzle that when completed is my family's story. (And therefore, I guess, mine.) And then I fill in the middle with my imagination, with the details no one was willing to share but need to be there for everything to make sense. Isn't that how we create modern myths? And yet, to me, none of this is myth. Everything is real, everything is truth, because I have strung all of these disconnected stories and details, and made them flow in a narrative that I can understand. Somewhere, at the end of all of this, I should emerge a full and complete individual, someone sure of where she's going because she knows where she came from. This is what I am waiting for.

To really understand my mother, you had to know her right after I was born. This was when she changed. Before then, she was a dreamer and defiant. She wanted a life they could barely afford to fantasize about, let alone attain. My father wanted it too, but more because my mother was so desperate to be not only wealthy but respected. In our community, if you had money and you were seen to spend it well (that includes offering your fair share to *tzedakah* to support the community), then you were looked up to by your neighbours. You sat on committees. You were asked to chair synagogue boards. You led groups building community centres, headed symphony fundraisers, and organized money-making activities, like trips to the art gallery and Sunday afternoon teas at the local Jewish day school. Without money, you weren't so much looked down on as pitied. People left you alone to make do. Sometimes they quietly rallied to get you out of immediate debt, and your parents were left to present you with a cheque, the source of which they would not explain.

My father ran a pharmacy just off Main Street, and people came in and out of it because they knew he needed the business. Friends of my grandparents who moved to the South End of Winnipeg would still come north for their prescriptions because there were no Jewish pharmacists yet in their neighbourhood. They would come into the store and find my parents behind the counter in their white coats, my mother with her hair pinned back so that it didn't get in her eyes, and in those last months bursting at her middle because of me. My father would hand her the orders, and she would pack the medication into little brown lunch bags. These people walked away after they had made their purchases before my father could hand them the change. He would call out after them, but only so loud. They had a box under the counter for these tips, and my mother used the money to buy things like kosher meat for the weekend and fresh fruit.

Women told her she looked beautiful, all pregnant and round. Goldie had grown thin after getting married, leaving home and moving above the pharmacy. In the summer, the upstairs apartment took in all of the heat from the sun, and then the added heat created by the activity on the street below. Children raced each other on bicycles on the sidewalks. Girls played jump rope games and called out nonsensical rhymes. Boys rolled around with each other under sprinklers and tried to spray water on screeching girls. With all of this around her, my mother didn't cook that whole summer in their first apartment. They ate bread and butter for supper with a glass of milk. And while her other married friends seemed to put on an extra layer of flesh just by having a husband, my mother had shrunk so much that people remarked how hard it must be for such a young couple to make a go of it these days. When she finally got pregnant, everyone told her how healthy she looked, and my father glowed, thinking they meant he was doing a good job keeping her well.

The pregnancy gave Goldie licence to dream in a way she hadn't since her wedding night. When she wasn't helping Saul in the store, she made lace curtains for their apartment and hung them in their bedroom and kitchen. She used leftover lace to decorate a bassinette for me, which she kept by the bed in the last couple of months before I was born. She knit, of course, often behind the counter when there weren't too many customers and my father had forbidden her from bending down and lifting things in her condition.

'You will have your fair share of lifting when the baby's born,' he told her. 'Save your strength.'

Men picking up prescriptions for their wives joked with my father about these pregnant women and their moods. One man told him his wife made him run out five times one Sunday morning until she made up her mind that all she was really craving for was homemade pancakes (which she made herself). My father laughed at those stories but stole a glance at my mother who smiled softly in a way which he knew meant 'count your blessings.' He did.

As the pregnancy wore on, every night she fell into a deep sleep while he rubbed her feet and her shoulders. And then, when she snored slightly against her pillow, my father ran his fingers through her hair and told her things he could never say when she was awake.

'You are my life,' he whispered. He led his finger down her face to her shoulder and then over her swollen belly. 'I am lost without you.'

He took to falling asleep with his hand resting on her stomach because this was as close as he could get to me. My mother would wake up in the middle of the night (strapped to the bed by the weight of my father's arm) and place her hand on top of his. She didn't whisper things to him while he was sleeping. She rubbed his hand and watched the ceiling, blue from the lamplight outside their window, following the cracks with her eyes, erasing each of them and building instead the house she dreamed of for her children.

I was born on a Tuesday afternoon in September, 1952. My mother's waters broke while she was mopping the store floor early that morning, and, had it not been for the cramps, she would have kept on mopping, pushing the fluid to the corner of the shop where all the dust gathered, making the cheap tiles glow. For a moment, all she did was marvel at how clean the floor looked every morning before customers started filing in with their dirt and troubles. She was thinking of that when the water poured out of her. It was only when the cramps came that she remembered she was having a baby, and she called out to my father to get her to the hospital.

My parents rode by taxi, holding each other's hands, not sure which one was supporting the other. I was born in the St. Boniface hospital where there is a cross on every wall, and the nurses bless each baby quietly in the name of Jesus Christ himself. I came out in the end, but I fought it each and every push. My mother, ever so patient, told the doctor I was stubborn like her youngest sister, Sarah, who took thirty-six hours to be delivered out of my grandmother.

I didn't take that long, but it was as if I had my hands pressed against the sides of my mother's womb, stopping me from tumbling out into a world I didn't know. When I did finally come, my mother held me against her chest and said, 'There now. It wasn't that bad, Bethy. There will be times when things get a lot worse.'

I was named Beth for Zaida – who was Binyamin Rabino-witz in Russia but Ben Rosen in Canada – who died from a heart attack the year before I was born. My grandmother found him in the backyard, slumped over a table he was building for her. She kept the table in her house exactly as she found it – barely sanded and partially cracked from where he fell. I think my mother thought that when I was born, I would bring them the money they needed to move into a house and out of the bug-infested apartment (there were ants in the kitchen) above the pharmacy. I think she thought I could bring her a backyard with a tire-swing hanging off of a crabapple tree. She thought she would be making jam and baking blueberry coffee cakes, because she would be drinking a lot of coffee with her lady friends.

All I came with, though, was a red, angry face that glowed in the middle of the night and tight, tiny fists, which I hit against her breast when she tried to feed me. Her milk must have tasted sour because when I was hungry I would take her nipple in my mouth and then spit it out, howling, grabbing at her skin, my cries mixing with her swallowed yelps of pain and devastation. At night, only my father could calm me down. He walked with me around the apartment front room, and then stood in front of the window so that we were cast in lamplight and the head-light of the occasional passing car. The sound of his low, tuneless voice lulled me into tiny hiccups before he could pass me to my mother's arms. Once she had fed me and I was asleep at her breast, she laid me in my bassinette and cried silently, but viciously. She hated my father (who was also asleep) and, against her instinct, hated me as well. Then she curled up and cried even harder, falling asleep finally on her side of the bed.

She left us once, my mother. It was very unlike her, but it didn't last more than an afternoon. She had taken to having me in the store with my father because if I cried, he could settle me down. He couldn't afford to hire someone to help him, so my mother took customers while my father was taking care of me. People did speak about it (strange that this young woman would prefer to sell shampoo than to be with her baby girl), but only once did anyone say something to her. It was that afternoon, in fact, when my colic was really bad and my father was singing loudly out of tune to keep me quiet. Mrs Slonin, my grandmother's friend from the Propoisker Society, was buying some bath soap, and as my mother handed her her change, she said, 'Your baby wants you. Be grateful.'

She left my mother shaking and still holding the change. My mother, always poised in public, threw the change on the floor and ran out of the store. She swung the door open and the bell rang loudly, as if telling on her. My father saw her running down the road. It was raining, and the back of her coat was spotted with wet dots. He didn't run after her, only watched her, knowing so well that she ran lopsided when upset and that, as poised as she could seem, she was never really graceful. She disappeared around the corner and he thought (with me finally quiet in his arms) of how much he loved her like that, a bit unpredictable, even to herself.

My mother, not really knowing why she was running, landed at my baba's house. Sarah was at school. Her other sister, Carrie, was sewing blouses for a small factory on Princess Street. Baba was in the kitchen making borscht for Carrie and Sarah for when they got home. Their two-storey home was almost hidden from the street by the three evergreen trees on the front lawn, the ones which miraculously survived the flood two years before and whose branches hung heavy, but determined and stubborn from the rain collecting on the needles. Had my mother stood beneath one of them, she would have stayed dry. But instead, she stood on the doorstep of the house, not sure whether to knock on the door, walk in, or stay there and dissolve. My baba was a practical woman and this scared my mother because she knew as hard as she tried, she could never be as level-headed.

It was my grandmother's practicality that led her to open the door first and bring my mother into the kitchen when she saw her out there, wet, on the porch.

My mother drank a hot bowl of the beet soup, its pink colour dripping down her chin as she shivered.

'You expect too much,' Baba told her in Yiddish. 'Life is not there to give you everything you want just because you want it. He is a good husband and you have a beautiful baby. That's it.'

Mum drank a cup of tea as well, no milk or sugar, and Baba brought her a blanket to keep her from catching pneumonia, or worse, polio.

'You need to be responsible now,' she went on. 'Too many people getting sick. You can't be sick with a baby.'

Baba wasn't the type to tell people that it was so much tougher in the *shtetl*, but my mother knew a lot of what she wasn't being told. Lots of women lost babies in Russia because their homes were burnt to the ground. In Canada, no one came after you because of your religion. And no one tried to kill your children. Russia, my mother imagined, was like a frozen ancient Egypt. Then, of course, there was the guilt of having run away from a perfectly wonderful life to her mother's home, which had seen the loss of both a husband and a son. Baba would never speak of either of those deaths, but this is what hung in the air while she stirred her soup and my mother calmed down.

'One day you'll have a house,' Baba said. 'For now, at least the roof doesn't have holes.'

3

My Auntie Carrie was not at my fourth birthday party. I have gone over the photos, and there is no trace of her, not even a sleeve. I have pictures of myself with a wide grin, fat cheeks, wispy hair and a party dress with a crocheted smocking, sitting on my grandmother's lap (who also had fat cheeks, but no grin, which was the immigrant Russian way). Then there is the three-generation shot of my mother, my grandmother and me, and finally another shot of my youngest aunt, Sarah, who is fourteen years old and dressed up as Snow White, tickling me and making me laugh with my mouth wide open in a continuous howl. There are also pictures of the small folding table my mother decorated with food (party sandwiches, spreads and cut-up vegetables), which seemed overdone for the small number of guests, mainly children. But there is no sign of Carrie. And it only struck me as I got older to wonder where she would have been when all the rest of us were together for a celebration.

The only photo I have of my Auntie Carrie as a little girl, on her own, shows her with her hair cut short, almost to the scalp. She is in my Baba's kitchen, sitting on a chair, looking at the floor, which is covered in hair. I have never seen anyone look as sad as she looks in this shot.

Carrie had a skin condition on her scalp when she was younger. Her head was itchy a lot, and she lost patches of hair. Sometimes, she would wake up and handfuls would be left on her pillow. The doctor told my Baba to cut her hair short.

And so she did – in the kitchen where it was easy to sweep the floor. She sat Carrie on a chair away from the table. The chair had one leg shorter than the other, and as Baba cut her hair, pieces fell like feathers and landed softly in piles on the floor, and the chair rocked side to side. Carrie told me that she was worried she would be lopsided.

'Mummah,' she said in a whisper, 'isn't that enough?'

My grandmother's thick, fleshy arm brushed the side of Carrie's face. She cut and cut, and Carrie thought she hadn't heard her, until Baba said, 'You cannot be with disease.'

And so she kept cutting, and Carrie cried because she never realized how much hair she'd had. The doctor asked for photos for some kind of research he was doing. Uncle Phil owned a camera and took three photos, giving the doctor two and keeping this one for himself. Later, while my grandmother swept the hair from the floor, Phil stayed upstairs with Carrie in her room, playing cards with her on her bed while she decided not to speak a word for each strand of hair she lost. Somehow, while playing Fish, she calculated that would amount to two years of silence.

It's funny that people called Carrie 'the Silent One,' because when I think about it, she's the one I listened to the most. When I was a preschooler, she watched over me while my parents worked in the store. We played Queens and Princesses in the apartment upstairs, wearing long scarves on our heads for the thick, blond hair neither of us had. For someone who rarely spoke, Carrie had a vivid imagination, and it only served to inspire my own.

'Pretend you're getting married,' I'd say.

'Right,' she'd say back. 'I'm going to marry the handsome Prince Philip.'

'The hero,' I'd tell her.

'That's right,' she'd say back. 'The hero.'

Carrie made us dresses out of bed sheets and safety pins. The linen fell far past my toes, so I had to gather the material in my hands when I walked. When my Auntie Carrie marched up the aisle to her pretend wedding, I followed behind, throwing imaginary rose petals, adored by the thousands of imaginary spectators.

'Okay,' I told her. 'Prince Philip says he's ready for the wedding to start.'

Carrie turned around and looked at the wall. We both saw my uncle, in a lopsided crown, looking back at her.

'Okay,' she said. 'I'm ready too.'

After we had discarded our bed-sheet dresses, Carrie would make me lunch (usually hot cottage cheese and macaroni noodles). While I ate, she told me stories about when she and my mother were girls and about Uncle Phil. Once, he climbed a tree in the park to retrieve Carrie's ball that got stuck in the branches, and then he fell, reaching for it, and broke his arm in two places. Later, she sat by his bed and held his 7UP for him to sip from, and he teased her about having a terrible pitch.

'Carrie, you're never going to make it in the big leagues by throwing balls into trees,' he said.

'Your uncle,' she told me, 'had a funny smile and a loud laugh. He didn't care that his arm was broken. He just loved that he could tease me. And I didn't care about the teasing, because I loved to hear him laugh.'

And so it came that my uncle, who was dead to everyone else, came alive to me through my silent aunt and my ever-hungry imagination. She told me about his love for astronomy and the constellations, and how they would lie outside in my grandparents' backyard staring at the sky, drawing pictures with the stars like connect the dots. She showed me some of the drawings she had kept, and as I fell asleep on her lap, I traced the diagrams on the page, sometimes wondering if God ever did the same thing with real stars from up in Heaven. Sometimes I just imagined my missing uncle, floating amongst the stars he drew, invisible. I had photos of him, but still I had trouble imagining his face. I pictured him like the cartoon drawing of Prince Charming in my Cinderella book, always smiling, forever determined. Long before any of Carrie's stories turned to Philip leaving for war, he was for me a hero, a brilliant budding scientist and an ever-loving brother who never believed that someone who was silent had nothing to say.

People say that Carrie never had a romantic relationship because of her looks, but for as long as I can remember, Carrie has said that she never wanted to marry. She was not pretty. It's true. Her brown hair turned grey in uneven patches when she was in her mid-twenties. Her large chest made her seem boxy. She wore stiff clothes, and her glasses always looked as though they needed cleaning. My mother would often say, 'If she would only let people know her the way we do, she probably would be married.'

When I was younger, I understood this to mean Carrie acted in a way that made men not interested in marrying her. The line stuck with me, making me frightened that I too could be acting in a way, unbeknownst to me, that could turn people away from me for good.

The odd time, if Carrie was sick, I stayed with my parents behind the store counter. The floor had gold specks, and I pretended they were stars and I was floating amongst them. I lay on the floor and closed my eyes, waving my arms and legs beside me, like I was making a snow angel. When my mother asked me what I was doing, I said I was playing with Uncle Phil, in the stars. We were making somersaults and watching everyone from Heaven. She pulled me up by my armpits and took me to the backroom where we had some picture books.

'I don't want you to play that anymore. I want you to read some books instead.'

'But I want my stars!'

She spoke to me in a tight whisper. 'Beth, it's not time for those kinds of games right now. I want you to play nicely here instead.'

She left, and I flipped through the pages of a picture book for a while. There was a cartoon lamb in a meadow. He seemed to be floating through the grass. His blue eyes looked out of the pages, glazed, and eventually I just closed the book.

Soon, I lay down on the floor and closed my eyes again. I could play my game no matter where I was. In the storage room, I floated and tumbled through the heavens and raced to catch up with my uncle who was spinning wildly in front of me.

The next day my mother took Carrie into the bedroom and told her to stop filling my head with stories and ghosts.

'You're upsetting her, Carrie,' my mother said. 'She wakes up at night with nightmares. She has temper tantrums. She doesn't need to know about all the things you talk about.'

'She likes my stories,' Carrie replied.

'I don't,' my mother answered.

Later, when my mother left to go downstairs, I said to Carrie, 'I never have nightmares.'

Carrie kissed my cheek and said, 'I know. But your mum wants us to pretend you do.'

Carrie had left her job at the factory and now worked as a dressmaker at the back of the store when she wasn't my babysitter. Her clients, women from around the neighbourhood, brought her outfits they could no longer squeeze into. Carrie added darts, or took out seams, or moved the buttons – she called it 'letting the clothes breathe.' I would sit beside her sewing stool and watch the women turn around and around in front of her while she pinned them. They came in holding their breath so that their buttons wouldn't pop; they left breathing freely and their clothes transformed their bodies so that they looked like queens.

'You are a miracle worker,' they told her.

'It's wonderful fabric,' she might say back, instead of thank you. And then, 'Wear it in good health.'

From where I sat, I would see my aunt's thighs bulging over the stool from under her navy dress. Nothing Carrie wore ever made her stop to look at herself in the mirror. Unlike these women, who turned around and looked over their shoulder at the full-length mirror resting in front of them against the back wall, Carrie never looked up even to move her hair from her eyes.

My Auntie Sarah would often come to Carrie to have her clothes fixed. One day, I remember she came to have a party dress altered to make way for her growing bust. It was Carrie who thought to check that the door to the main room of the store was closed when Sarah pulled her top off. The other women got changed behind a screen, but Sarah stared at her body in the mirror while Carrie repinned the dress before giving it to her to try on.

'Sarah, do you have to stare at yourself in your underwear?' Carrie asked her. Sarah had thick, dark auburn curls that rested on her milky shoulders. She tossed her hair back three times. I tried to do the same thing, but my hair was too thin and too short to have the same effect.

'I have nothing to be ashamed of,' she said, still staring. Sarah wasn't yet ready for a bra, but her breasts were beginning to swell beneath her undershirt. She placed her hands on the small of her back and arched it. I got up and copied her, which made her laugh.

Carrie shook her head. 'Stop it, Sarah. Beth is too young for all this.'

'Gawd, Carrie. Stop acting like an old fart.'

I giggled. Sarah was the only one I knew who could get away with saying 'fart.' Carrie stayed seated with her shoulders hunched over, her cheeks flaming. When Sarah tried on the dress, like all the other women, she walked around the small back room as if she were royalty. We watched her, and sometime later when we would go back to playing pretend, I think Carrie and I both mimicked that walk slightly. In the meantime, I realized that I knew of no one who could fix Carrie's clothes so that she walked like that.

Sarah was the closest I came to knowing royalty. So, for my fourth birthday, when I said I wanted a visit by a real princess, Sarah dressed up like Snow White and descended upon us. I had six girlfriends there, plus my mother, father and grandmother, and Sarah turned my grandmother's basement into our Enchanted Forest. Each of us wore a party dress, mine a gift from Carrie, which she left for my mother to give to me. My dress was royal blue with a white crinoline and a red and white sash. Carrie left me an extra bit of ribbon to wear as a headband. The sleeves were puffed and in the same material as the sash. On the collar, she stitched little red hearts and my initials, BL.

I would only try the dress on downstairs in Carrie's back room with the full-length mirror. There I turned around and around – the blue skirt billowing out like waves.

'You look very beautiful,' my mother said. 'Maybe later you'll draw your auntie a picture to thank her.'

'I'll thank her at my party,' I said.

'Auntie Carrie's not going to be at your party, dear,' Mum said. 'She had to go away.'

And that was all.

My mother sat us all in a circle in Baba's basement. The carpet was burgundy, and against the back wall there was an electric fireplace, which she turned on for the special occasion. It glowed orange-red, the light pulsating from behind the pretend logs. Cheryl Moss sat beside me. Her mother had pinned her honey-coloured ringlet curls up behind her ears with pink barrettes. I wanted those barrettes. My father snapped pictures of us awaiting our princess, and in each shot, you can see me reaching for Cheryl's hair, Cheryl squirming away, my mother behind us with her hand on my wrist pulling my open-wide hand away from Cheryl's beautiful head. I was only allowed to wear headbands because my hair was too thin for barrettes and elastics. My mother feared I would become as bald as Carrie. Pretty girls wore barrettes – that's as much as I knew. Cheryl and I were howling at each other, and my mother looked close to tears by the time my Auntie Sarah came bounding down the stairs.

'Help, help!' she cried, and we all stopped to watch her. 'My name is Snow White, and I am lost in the forest. Who can help me?'

'Me! Me!' the girls cried, including Cheryl, who ran away from me and my mother to sit in front of Sarah at the other end of the room. I watched my girlfriends crowd around my aunt's feet. She wore black, shiny Mary Janes and a red and yellow dress with white puffed sleeves. She had powdered her face and painted her lips bright red. Her teeth were shiny against her dark lips, and when she smiled, it was her teeth, not her skin, that seemed as white as snow.

'Go sit with the girls,' my mother urged me, pressing her palms against my back.

I shook my head and instead went to sit at my grand-mother's feet. Baba was sitting in an armchair in the corner of the room. While Sarah entertained my guests, I picked at the carpet by Baba's feet and listened to her laboured breathing. She smelled like pea soup and sweat, and I leaned into her legs to rest my head against her leathery skin.

'I don't want Snow White,' I said, still thinking of Cheryl's barrettes. Baba placed her hand on my head. Her nails were clipped short, and I only felt her pudgy finger-tips as she took off my headband and combed through my hair with her fingers. Somewhere, deep in the Enchanted Forest, Sarah had chosen Cheryl to act as one of the dwarfs, Happy. My father was Prince Charming, my mother the Wicked Witch. When Sarah pulled out a bright red apple from her basket, my grandmother muttered, '*Esn nicht.*'

She ate it anyway. She took one large delicious bite. The juice from the fruit ran down her chin and dripped twice onto her dress.

After my father awoke Sarah with a kiss on her forehead, and after Sarah took a deep bow while everyone applauded, my mother called us over to the card table, which was covered in a white paper tablecloth printed with red, blue and yellow balloons. I sat at the head of the table, on a lawn chair decorated in streamers and real balloons, and forgot all about the barrettes while everyone sang 'Happy Birthday.' My father caught me in a photo with my eyes closed and my cheeks puffed out, just as I was letting go of my breath and making my wish. It had something to do with becoming pretty.

With the attention off of her, and all of us busy eating chocolate cake covered in coloured sprinkles, Sarah sat down on the floor, away from everyone. She unpinned her hair and leaned back on her hands with her face tilted up toward the ceiling. Baba, still sitting in the armchair, never having moved, called over to her. But she had to call her several times before Sarah snapped, 'What!'

Baba held out an empty paper plate and waved it at her. Sarah stood up and rolled her eyes.

'You could get it yourself if you weren't so lazy,' she mumbled as she walked behind me. She was loud enough for my mother to hear, and my mother caught her by the arm as she passed by.

'Show some respect, Sarah,' Mum said. 'She's your mother, and she's not well.'

Sarah shook off my mother's hand and rubbed her arm. 'She's always not well. None of my friends have parents as old as she is. She's been getting old since the day I was born.'

'Bite your tongue,' my mother whispered. Sarah did. She stuck out her tongue and bit down on it, showing my mother all of her snow white teeth.

I wouldn't take my dress off when it was time for bed. My mother, exasperated from tidying Baba's house before we left, lifted her hands and let me do as I pleased. I lay in bed, with my hands folded over my stomach, pretending I was Snow White, sleeping peacefully until my Prince Philip Charming came to kiss me awake. When my father came to tuck me in, I was already half asleep. He kissed my forehead and said, 'You were the most beautiful princess there.'

In my dream, I lifted up my arms for him to carry me away.

Sometime in the middle of the night, I woke up and climbed out of bed. My dress was wrinkled, and my legs were itchy from the crinoline. The apartment was bathed in silver light from the street lamp. Instead of going to my parents' room, I took my blanket and headed downstairs for the store.

My father's store sparkled at night, and I felt like I was floating underwater as I walked up and down the aisle. He carried hairspray in silver containers and packages of pink plastic rollers. They were schools of fish at night in a rainbow of colours. At the end of the aisle were some hair clips, and I took a package of pink barrettes and clipped them in my hair. Then I swam my way to Carrie's room at the back of the store.

My parents found me there the next morning. Mum cried that she had been looking everywhere for me. I had frightened her to death. What if I had wandered outside into the cold to freeze? My father cradled me in his arms, although I was too big to be held like a baby, and asked me to please never run away again.

'I wasn't,' I said, rubbing my eyes. When I had finally fallen asleep on the floor, by the mirror, I dreamt not of the ocean but of the night sky and thousands upon thousands of stars.

'What were you doing down here?' my mother asked, reaching for me.

I climbed out of my father's arms and into hers, putting my head on her shoulder. I said, 'Waiting for Carrie.'

When Carrie came back, maybe weeks later, maybe months, she brought me a black and white photo of a cityscape at night. Tiny stars dotted the black sky and a crescent-shaped moon hung over the city, almost in a smile. She taped it on the wall above my head.

'You went away,' I said. 'For a long time.'

'But I came back,' she answered. 'You knew I was coming back.'

I sat in her lap and leaned my back into her pillowed chest. She breathed heavily behind me, and I wondered if she wanted to be in that picture, looking up at someone else's sky, somewhere else, far away from all of us.

4

While I spent my days playing pretend with my aunt, my parents worked to save up for my mother's dream house. My father drank his morning coffee in the kitchen and he slept beside my mother at night, but otherwise he lived in the store either behind the counter or in between the stocked shelves. My mother joined him after I had finished my cereal in the morning, and Carrie arrived to take over. Mum stayed downstairs until 4 p.m., when she would climb back up to make our supper. She stood over the stove to boil pasta or potatoes, shifting her weight from foot to foot and holding one hand by her lower back where she massaged around her tailbone.

On Wednesday mornings, Carrie took my mother's place at the pharmacy and my father sent us out on errands. In the winter, my mother put me in a red wool coat with wooden buttons. She wrapped a green scarf around my head, and when I breathed through the woollen mesh, the air was damp and warm. We would walk up and down Selkirk Avenue with the wind pricking our exposed skin like little needles. I would cry if my mittens slipped down my hands and my wrists were left unprotected. My mother held on tightly to my wrist, and our boots crushed the dry snow like cereal. You heard us squeak with every step.

We bought fresh baking from Gunn's and washing detergent from Oretzki's Department Store (which had everything;

you could buy washing detergent, underwear and a frying pan in one visit). If my father didn't need us back right away, my mother took me to the Greek diner across from the Palace Theatre, and she fed me hot chocolate with a spoon so that she could blow on it first. We would sit by the frost-covered window and watch cars driving by, blowing freezing exhaust that would hang in the air and then fall to the street on the tire tracks. If clouds could fall, that's what they would have looked like. This is what I mean about the cold: everything was heavier.

Before going home, we would cross the street and stop in front of the Palace Theatre to see what was playing that week, and my mother would sigh and say it had been so long since she had seen a film. Beautiful women like Marlene Dietrich and Grace Kelly stood tall and thin on the posters beside the theatre doors. I have in my memory a vision of my mother and me going into the theatre and sitting in the red plush seats, no one around us, just her and me watching a film with a five-cent box of popcorn and a Pepsi-Cola. In this memory, my feet don't touch the floor, and my mother leans over to get some tissue out of the shopping bag so that she can wipe her eyes. Marlene dies a glamorous death in the arms of a man with dark eyebrows. At the end of the film, my mother and I would head home to real life, but it felt as if time stood still while we were in the theatre.

My parents never went out to see films. There were lots of things they didn't do: they didn't go away in the summer for vacations, never went to the symphony, didn't eat in steak houses or downtown restaurants that served veal. My mother's migraines and backaches from being on her feet all day kept them away from community functions, to which they sent anonymous donations of no more than five dollars. Instead, they took dancing lessons from Estelle (which my mother paid for in baking) in her South End basement. There were four couples who did this every week. My parents took a ride with the Silvers who lived in the North End (Anita and Marvin were natural dancers, and my father – who wasn't – often wondered if they only came to show off). Estelle had a record player and travelled to Florida and Arizona in the winter where she learned how to foxtrot and waltz. Determined to raise the profile of the Winnipeg Jewish community, Estelle offered dancing lessons to young couples so that one day they could host charity balls. My mother and father only went twice, and Estelle spent both lessons holding my father's waist from behind while he danced with his wife.

'The foxtrot is just like walking,' she said, her bum swaying her skirt while she took the steps on the spot. 'One, two. One, two. Saul, you need to move your hips.'

My father muttered that he was sure his dead father-in-law would not approve of him dancing with two women at once. My mother gripped his hand and closed her eyes, imagining the synagogue social hall with soft gold lights, a live band, and herself dressed in a sequined gown (she with a bit more muscle and my father a bit taller). By the second lesson, they managed to trot around the basement in a circle by themselves. But, in a bid to get my father to 'move his tush,' Estelle pinched his bum. My parents walked out of her house before the record finished.

I slept in what should have been our living room. My bed was pushed up against the wall, under the window. Head-lights from cars driving down Main Street would shine over me like a spotlight, and sometimes I hid from them under my blanket. My parents often stayed up arguing in the kitchen – my father telling my mother to go to sleep if she was so tired, my mother snapping that there was too much still to do. If he wanted his books balanced, he needed to leave her alone. Often, I couldn't fall asleep until my mother shut the kitchen light and closed their bedroom door, where from my side of the wall, I could hear their mattress squeak as my father shifted to rest his arm across her stomach. If I still couldn't sleep, I would climb out of my bed and take my blanket to my parents' room where I would sleep on their floor. Sometimes, I could hear my father whispering.

'Remember the porch lights?' he'd say to her. 'Remember how we want paper lanterns? And pine cupboards in the kitchen?'

My mother lay beside him with her eyes closed. She would be stubborn, biting her lip to keep from crying, breathing deeply into her pillow. He'd stay like that, holding her, even if she didn't speak. He'd run his hand along her body so that she knew, even if she was angry, he thought she was beautiful.

Late one night, the phone rang, waking us all up with a start. I remember vividly because I was starting kindergarten in three weeks' time.

Sarah was on the line in tears. Baba had fallen down the stairs and couldn't move. She was crying out that her back was breaking. Carrie was trying to soothe her. She brought her a cold cloth for her head, which she had bumped. But Baba threw the cloth away and said to her, 'Get me Goldie.'

So we all walked over to my grandmother's house. My mother wanted to go alone, but my father refused to let her walk by herself. She said, 'But someone needs to stay with Beth.' And so they let me walk with them in my nightgown and loafers. I carried my blanket with me, and it dragged along the sidewalk picking up dead twigs and leaves. We walked on Main Street, which was wide and empty in the middle of the night. People talked about Main Street being rough, but it seemed everyone in the city was asleep except for us. I pretended we were pioneers out to find our new home in a new land where no one else lived. We were going to build a farm with horses and chickens, and I would help my mother every morning by retrieving fresh eggs. We passed by the Ukrainian Ortho- dox Church with the rounded black pillared roof and tall crosses. The black pillars made the church look like three men in large black hats. I wondered if God and his angels were hiding there, watching us. The street lamps distorted and elongated our shadows, like ghosts floating before us and then behind us. We passed a boarded-up ice-cream stand advertising three flavours of soft ice cream. I wanted some, but I could feel with my mother's tight grip that I shouldn't ask. We passed three Jewish-style delicatessens, and even at night, they smelled of fried salami. I began to take deep breaths to swallow the taste. My mother stopped and asked me what was wrong.

'Nothing,' I said. Then, the rest of the way, I held my breath to see how long I could go without letting it out.

When we got to my Baba's place, I sat on the couch and pulled at all of the dirt my blanket had collected on the walk to make it clean again.

'She needs to go to the hospital,' my mother said.

'No!' my grandmother insisted, still lying on the floor. 'No hospital. No ambulance.'

'Mummah, don't be ridiculous. You may have broken something,' my mother told her. Sarah sat on the stairs, watching from above, her arm wrapped around the railing. Carrie had wet the washcloth again and was wiping my grandmother's face, which was covered in sweat.

'No doctor,' my grandmother said, this time wincing.

Goldie stood up and shook her head. 'This is ludicrous,' she said. 'Absolutely crazy. You're lying on the floor. You can't move, and you are in pain. Three very good reasons to get to the hospital and fast.'

Slowly, and with great control, my grandmother turned herself over and sat up against the wall. She held her breath the whole time – as did all of us. When she was sitting against the wall to support her back, she said to Saul, 'Put me in bed.' Her face was grey, and there was a large bruise forming on her upper arm.

'Why don't we put her in bed and call the doctor to the house in the morning,' my dad said, bending down to lift her.

'You are as crazy as she is,' my mother replied.

Carrie moved to help him as he got my grandmother onto her feet by supporting her under her arm.

'Better,' Baba said, not convincingly. 'This better.'

'I'll call Dr Duboff in the morning,' Carrie offered. 'There's no sense waking him now.'

My mother shook her head. 'You are all barking mad.'

I slept in Sarah's bed that night, with Carrie in the bed next to us. My parents took the room they had when they were first married. We all lay silently, each of us listening for Baba, for her moaning and the sharp intake of her breath that sounded like knives were stabbing into her back. She wouldn't let my mother stay by her bed, so Goldie made her keep the bedroom door open. The rest of us kept ours open too. On top of my grandmother's noises, I could hear my parents in the next room, whispering, shifting in bed when neither of them could sleep. The voices floated out of the rooms to mingle in the hallway. It was like we were airing out the upstairs of all the sounds.

Sarah lay facing away from me, and I thought she was sleeping until she said, 'Why don't they just say she's dying?'

Carrie answered, 'Don't talk like that, Sarah. Especially not in front of Beth.'

'Is that how people die?' I asked them. 'When their back hurts?'

'No,' Carrie said. 'And Baba's not dying.' She leaned over from her bed and kissed my hand. 'Go to sleep and have good dreams.'

I concentrated on good thoughts until I heard Sarah say, 'Why is everyone so afraid of telling the truth?'

Dr Duboff came early the next morning. My mother followed him into the bedroom, and I watched from the doorway. They didn't notice me when he lifted Baba's nightgown from the back and studied the dark lesions covering her skin. I almost stayed quiet enough to hear him tell my mother that there was nothing he could do, except try to make her more comfortable. Only when Baba yelled out in pain as he felt along her back, I gasped. When my mother saw me at the doorway, she told me to go outside and play. Then she shut the door.

The rest I heard later when I was supposed to be outside, but instead I hid up in Carrie and Sarah's room. Carrie met Mum downstairs in the kitchen after the doctor left, saying he was sorry, and to call if they needed him. I stayed upstairs by the railing, where Sarah had been the night before.

'We'll stay here,' Mum told Carrie. 'Don't worry, you won't have to go through this alone.'

'I wish I could run away,' Sarah said from behind me. She had come out of the bathroom and was sitting on the floor, cross-legged.

'Please don't,' I whispered.

She hugged me from around my waist and kissed the back of my head. 'I won't. Don't worry. I just wish I could.'

I never went back to sleep at the apartment. That night my father brought over all of my clothes and toys, and I moved into the bedroom with Sarah and Carrie. Sarah and I shared her bed, but we slept head to foot to save room. I slept with my head at the foot of the bed, where there was more light from the hallway, and I could stay up looking at books. Carrie cleared out two drawers for me from her dresser, and we stuffed all my underwear, pyjamas and socks together. In the morning, the drawer got stuck when I tried to open it, and Sarah complained I was making too much noise getting dressed and stuck her head under her pillow to drown out the sound.

Carrie, it seemed, was always awake. If I woke in the middle of the night to use the washroom, she would be lying with her eyes open. If I woke early in the morning, before anyone else, she'd still be lying there, looking at the ceiling. Sometimes she'd end up on her side, facing us and the window. I asked her once in the middle of the night and in a whisper if she slept with her eyes open.

'No,' she whispered back. 'I just don't sleep. I haven't slept in months.'

'Why?'

'I guess because I'm sad.'

'Can I make you happy?'

She smiled at me. In the dark, it reminded me of the half moon in the postcard, which we'd left at the apartment and I never saw again.

'I'm very happy that you're here. I'm less lonely now.'

'Me too.'

We lay quietly and listened to everyone breathing. Sarah breathed out of her mouth in little sighs.

'Auntie Carrie, what do you do if you're not sleeping?'

'I think,' she said.

'About what?'

'About the people I love who are no longer here.'

Baba did not leave her bed again, and my mother took over her kitchen, wearing her aprons. In the morning, she

34

laid out bowls, spoons and cereal boxes with cut-up peaches. My father ate first and left early to open the store. Carrie ate next, sometimes two bowls' worth and a whole orange. My mother also made her a lunch to take to the store and eat in the back room, in between fittings. Sarah took her bowl and ate in the living room on the couch. She sat slouched in her pyjamas, the milk from her spoon dripping onto the cushions. The first morning, I followed her to the couch and sat beside her, trying to balance my Cornflakes on my lap. I failed, and they spilled all over the teal carpet, just as my mother walked in.

'Beth! You know better than to eat in Baba's living room. Go get the vacuum and clean this up. Then you come back to the kitchen and eat your breakfast properly.' She turned to Sarah, who had not looked up from her cereal. 'That goes for you too.'

'I'm okay here,' she said, finishing her cereal and setting the bowl carefully on the floor.

'I didn't ask whether you were okay. I said that I want you to eat in the kitchen with your niece. Show a good example, Sarah.'

Sarah stood up and rolled her eyes. 'Gawd, Goldie. Who died and made you boss?'

My mother froze for a moment, and I stood between them, watching and waiting.

'Don't speak like that,' she said finally, in a whisper. 'You'll bring on the evil eye.'

Sarah laughed and picked up her bowl. 'Can't you see that it's here already? And it didn't even ask your permission.'

My mother brought my grandmother weak tea with sugar and pureed vegetable soups. She sat by her bed and fed her from a spoon. Baba looked like a baby bird waiting for food. Each day she seemed to grow smaller. My mother covered her in blankets when she shivered in bed, and sat with her after she finished eating until she fell asleep. Baba slept propped up by pillows with her mouth open and the tip of her tongue at the side of her mouth by her lips. I never went into the room, but I sat on the floor by the doorway until my mother saw me and told me to play.

'I don't want to,' I told her.

'Beth, it isn't good for you to be here. Please go away.'

Some days, when Carrie wasn't busy at the store, she would come home and take me to the park. She pushed me on the swings, and we pretended I was in a rocket ship, flying to the moon. School was starting in just under a week, and my hair was cut short in a bob. As I swung up and down, I felt the wind lift each strand off of my head and then fall back into place again against my skull.

'Your Uncle Phil wanted to be an astronaut,' she told me. 'He said that when he got into space, he was going to find a star and name it after me.'

'I'm going to do that,' I told her. 'I'm going to fly into space and name all the stars.'

She pushed me higher, and it seemed I was swinging far above the rooftops. I wore my new penny loafers, even though Mum had told me to put them away until school started. I kicked my legs out and reached for the sun.

'Make sure you name one for him,' she said. 'And then maybe me. But it's more important for Phil.'

'There's tons of stars, Carrie,' I said back. 'I'm going to find one for everyone.'

That summer, when my Baba fell ill, and my mother made herself into a nurse and my father stayed away to run the store all by himself, I'd think about my uncle and I wished he was around so that I could ask him about the Big Dipper and the planets and how they all revolve around the sun. Why was Earth the only planet that had water and plants and animals and humans? Since her wedding

36

night, my mother hadn't talked about Phil, and when I asked these kinds of questions out loud, she came over to me, closed my children's astronomy book.

'Space is not for little girls, Beth. You're starting school soon. You don't want to busy yourself with his nonsense.'

Carrie, on the other hand, (when my mother wasn't around) would tell me that Phil was a genius.

'He could have changed the world,' she said once when I was looking at my astronomy book in bed before going to sleep. 'Sometimes I found him in our backyard at night, lying back and staring up at the sky. I would sit with him like his assistant, and he'd say stuff like, "After the war, I'm going to be a space explorer. I'll be waving to you, Carrie, from beyond the heavens."'

'Maybe he's waving now.'

'Oh, I'm sure he is,' she answered. It always amazed me how Carrie could talk about Phil without crying, and yet with so much love. 'There are nights when I unfocus my eyes, and I look upwards and something about how the stars and clouds form together, I think I see him there.' She paused and then said, softly, 'And there were nights when he used to promise that he would come back from the war and we would move off together to study space. Now, I was never really interested in all that, but I would have gone anywhere he did.'

Then she took my book from my hands and handed me a worn-out red leather journal.

'Your mother doesn't want to read this, but one day I think you should. Your uncle was a quiet man, but he had some very interesting things to say.' Leaving me with the book lying in my open palms, she said, 'I meant it when I said he could have changed the world, Beth. And I think you could too.'

Thus began my obsession with the beige pages that were my uncle's notes and musings before he went to war. That night when I began the journal, I was only interested in his drawings of the night sky. Diagrams I had previously only seen in library books, he had drawn on his own, like a proper scientist. A real author. I wanted to experience the same movements of his hand, so I traced his drawings onto my own paper and hung them on my wall. By then, I already knew how to print my ABCs. So while I skipped over large sections of his writing, I studied and memorized the curve of his vowels, the way he dropped his g's at the end of a word like a mouse tail. I tried to copy his writing and wondered if someone could come back to you if you repeated something he did in exactly the same way.

Distance from the Sun: Mercury–36 million miles,
Venus–67.2 million miles, Earth–93 million miles,
Mars–142 million miles, Jupiter–483.6 million miles,
Saturn–885 million miles, Uranus–1.78 billion miles,
Neptune–2.8 billion miles, Pluto–3.7 billion miles.
If I flew to the sun in an airplane, I would be over thirty years old when I returned. No one would recognize me.

My aunt never told my mother about the journals, and I was careful not to let her find out. My nighttime ritual included my mother tucking me in first, then my aunt reading to me from sections of the journal. Sarah often didn't come to bed until much later, sometimes after I was fast asleep. It meant that Carrie and I could sit alone in bed, surrounded by the sounds of my mother cleaning up in the kitchen, scrubbing pots in my grandmother's porcelain sink. With each page we read, my uncle grew more and more animated like a cartoon we made come alive by flipping through the pages.

People misuse the term meteor. A meteor is just the flash of light, the shooting star, when a small object enters the Earth's atmosphere. A meteoroid is the small object. A meteorite is an object that falls to the surface of the Earth.

For the days leading up to the start of school, I walked around the neighbourhood with my head bent down, scanning the ground for meteorites. Sometimes I picked up pebbles from the pavement and pretended they were dust particles from space that my uncle had sent specially to me. By the first day of school, I had collected over two hundred pebbles, different colours and sparkly, and I kept them in a pencil case. When I spread them on the floor of my bedroom, I would arrange them like the constellation maps my uncle drew. This was as close as I could ever come to speaking to him directly.

Some nights, while Carrie and I were reading, Sarah would be getting ready. She wore deep red lipstick and painted her eyelashes with dark mascara. She put her hair up in a high ponytail that swayed back and forth when she walked. She went out with her friends at night, and when my mother asked her to be home by ten, she'd laugh and say, 'I'm fifteen and you're not my mother, Goldie.'

Carrie was in the middle of one of her stories for me, when Sarah put down her makeup on the dresser and turned around.

'Jeez, Carrie! It's enough already. You are always living in the past. Phil's never coming back.'

'Just because someone dies, doesn't mean they have to disappear,' Carrie answered.

'Yes it does,' Sarah said back. We were all mindful that as she spoke, my grandmother could have been taking her final breath in her room. 'When someone dies, they're just gone.'

5

On my first day of school, my mother came into our room to get me dressed. She brushed my hair in front of the mirror that Sarah used to put on her makeup. My hair stood up from the static, and my mother had to spit on her hands to pat it back down. I pretended I could have a long ponytail, longer than Sarah's, one that reached my back, tickling the base of my neck. My mother had not played with my hair in a long time. Instead, she sponged my grandmother's deteriorating body, her hands shaking with exhaustion and maybe fear. As she played with my hair, they shook as well.

'Now,' my mother said to my reflection, 'I'm going to walk you to school this morning, and then I want you to wait on the steps at lunchtime for me to come and pick you up. Please don't run around in your new dress. This is special for your first day. It's not to play in the mud.'

She did not notice the scuffs on my loafers from the park gravel.

'And most importantly, you have to behave in class. I want to hear that you are listening to your teachers and being nice to the other kids.'

'I'm always nice,' I said, raising my arms so that she could put on my undershirt. Then she took out my lime-green sundress with the embroidered daisies on the skirt. Carrie made me a matching sweater that had ribbon along the collar and pearl buttons. I insisted on wearing it, even though Mum thought I would be too hot.

On the walk to school, I held my mother's hand. We walked along Salter Street and passed by the pet store that had hamsters in the window, running on their wheels. She said there was no time to stop and look. There were three synagogues on Salter, situated very close together, and as we walked by them, men came out carrying their briefcases and wiping their faces of poppy seeds and bagel crumbs. In one of the synagogues, there was a Talmud Torah school, and lots of Jewish kids were climbing the steps to go inside. Some of the boys wore velvet or silk *yarmulkes* that slid off their heads as they ran up the stairs. I could not ever remember, nor imagine, seeing my father in a yarmulke.

'Is that my school?' I asked as we passed it.

Mum kept walking. 'No, that school's not for you. Your school is coming up soon.'

We passed the small perogi restaurant, and I could smell fried onions and potatoes. When my mother makes us perogies at home, they are always boiled. In the restaurants, they come crispy fried with browned onions and sour cream in a small plastic cup. I preferred the ones in the restaurant, but I could never tell my mother that. The whole way to school she talked about her first day walking this very same route, holding my Baba's hand.

'And I remember being so frightened to be away from my mother for the first time. But she said to me, 'Big girls don't cry like kittens."

'I'm not frightened.'

'Good,' she said.

After we took a few more steps, I said, 'Meow.'

My mother laughed. I hadn't heard her laugh since we moved into my Baba's house. 'Meow,' I said again, and curled my fingers up like claws.

She looked down to me and cupped my chin in her hand. 'Big girls don't cry like kittens,' she said, her eyes beginning to tear. So I stopped.

I wore the sweater all day even though it was hot, and I felt sweaty around my neck. Cheryl was in my class, and we ran to each other and promised to be best friends for the whole year. Two other girls came to join us while we played with the wooden puzzles at the back of the room. Norma and Marilyn were first cousins and lived two blocks over from me. The four of us took apart a puzzle of Humpty Dumpty, and then took turns adding pieces to put him back together again.

Our teacher had us sit in a circle to introduce ourselves to the rest of the class. We had to say our names, and then what we wanted to be when we grew up. There were two Davids, three Miriams and three people with the last name Rosenberg who were not cousins. Lots of the girls said they wanted to be mummies or teachers. Norma said she wanted to be a nurse. I thought about the night before when I could hear my grandmother throwing up and my mother rushing to change the linen on her bed, and then filling a basin with warm water because Baba was too weak to get into the tub to clean herself up. I wrinkled my nose. I did not want to be a nurse, ever.

'My name is Beth Levy, and when I grow up, I want to fly into space and be an astronaut.'

'Well, now,' my teacher said. 'It sounds like you have quite an imagination.'

'No,' I said. 'I'm going to do it for real.'

She smiled and moved onto the next child, someone named Andrew who wanted to do something boring like drive a bus.

Cheryl whispered to me. 'Yours sounded like fun. Maybe I'll come with you.'

I nodded back. 'Sure. I'm going to ask for a telescope for my birthday. You could come over and see it.'

'Neat,' she said. Already, I imagined Cheryl as my assistant.

Sometime that morning, probably while I was writing out my ABCs, my grandmother died. She was surrounded by blankets, pillows and her two oldest daughters. I didn't know this until much later, but Carrie told me that my mother had crawled into bed with Baba after she took her last breath. She laid her head on her mother's shoulder and wrapped her arm around her stomach. It took both my father and Dr Duboff to get her off that bed, and then into her own, where she fell asleep for the rest of the day.

Almost everyone's mother was waiting for them outside the school at lunchtime. Marilyn walked home with Norma's mother because their mothers were sisters and they were going to take turns doing lunches. Cheryl went home with her older sister and brothers. She turned around to wave to me from the end of the block. I sat on the steps and waited for my mother, like I was told. My stomach growled, and I wondered if she would make me a grilled cheese sandwich for lunch because that was my favourite. I put my chin on my knees and looked at the ground for pebbles. I spotted three, which I would pick up only once my mother came to get me. I waited some more and the school bell rang to say it was noon. No one else was left waiting, and the bell echoed across the empty playground and over all the houses. I looked as far as I could down the street, and I could not see her coming. I looked in the other direction, just in case, but I only saw a man walking his dog. When he came past me, he asked if I was all right. I nodded my head, but kept my chin on my knees. As soon as the man was far enough away that he wouldn't look back, I started to cry.

After a while, I walked home on my own. I didn't pick up any pebbles, and eventually, I took off my sweater because I was too hot. I did not stop to look at the pet store, and when I passed the restaurant, my stomach growled. When I got close to my street, there was a Catholic church with many steps leading up to the heavy wooden doors. Two nuns stood outside the doors, talking. The one holding the door open called out and asked if I was lost. I shook my head, but I didn't look up. My hair was a mess and my barrettes had fallen loose and were hanging in my eyes. I walked slowly as if I were carrying that wooden door on my back.

When I walked inside our house, Carrie was sitting on the couch with her hands in her lap.

'Where's Mum?' I asked.

'She's upstairs. Baba died this morning, Beth. Your mum's lying down.'

'No one came to get me.'

'I was coming,' she said, softly. 'But you did the right thing by walking home.'

'I'm hungry,' I told her and she nodded. She brought me into the kitchen where I ate a bowl of cereal. When I had almost finished eating, Sarah came running into the house and bounded up the stairs. A few minutes later, she came running down the stairs and back out the door, slamming it shut behind her. No one went after her. My aunt put her head in her hands and started to cry, her face crumpled and red.

'I don't want to go upstairs,' I said.

She dried her eyes and took a deep breath. 'That's fine.'

'I want to go play with Cheryl.'

'Okay. Come home for supper.'

'You'll tell my mum?'

She nodded. I heard someone moving around upstairs, opening the door to my grandmother's bedroom, and then walking out. Carrie heard it too and walked toward the staircase.

She turned to me. 'Come straight home. Don't dilly-dally.'

'I won't,' I said as she ran up the stairs. I tried to pour myself some orange juice but it spilled on the kitchen counter. Instead of cleaning it up, I ran out of the house like Sarah, running down the steps and all the way to Cheryl's house. My throat tickled for the whole afternoon.

When I got home, I went upstairs and lay down beside my mother, and even though she was asleep, I told her everything about my day – about meeting Norma and Marilyn, about the puzzles, about knowing how to read better than anyone else in the class.

'I'm sorry, honey,' she said, with her hand over her nose and mouth, and her eyes closed. 'I'm just so tired.'

'That's okay,' I said. I kept talking while she slept. When I finished telling her everything, I took a breath and then started again from the beginning.

6

Men from the neighbourhood came in and out of our house every morning and evening for the next week while we sat *shiva* for Baba. In the mornings, they wore limp prayer shawls and black *tefillin* boxes wrapped tightly around their arms and heads. I was not allowed into the living room while they were praying. Sometimes my father led the services, standing in front of a tall candle in a long glass case that would stay lit for my grandmother for the whole week. I didn't know that he knew how to pray so well that he could be a leader. I didn't know that he could speak Hebrew. My father chanted musical phrases while swaying, and the men answered him back, also swaying. I watched them from upstairs by the banister, and it sometimes looked as if the whole living room was rocking back and forth with them. Their prayer shawls all had fringes on the bottoms and long strings hanging from the four corners. When the men swayed, the shawls moved as if there were a gentle breeze.

Every morning that week, I got myself dressed, made my own breakfast and walked myself to school. I collected 187 sparkly pebbles and kept them in my drawer with my pyjamas, underwear and socks. I came home on my own and ate leftovers for lunch from whatever meal one of the neighbours had brought. One day it was cold beet borscht. Another it was meatloaf. I really wanted a grilled cheese sandwich, but I was not allowed to use the toaster myself, and my mother was told by the rabbi that she had to spend the week sitting on a low chair in the living room letting other people do things for her. That is exactly what she did. Same with Carrie. Sarah, on the other hand, refused and went to school instead. She showered, dressed, brushed her shiny hair and made up her eyes.

All of the mirrors in our house were supposed to be covered with bed sheets while we were mourning. Sarah refused that too. When Carrie left our room in the morning to take her seat downstairs, Sarah tore the bed sheet off our dresser mirror with such flair, it was as if she were doing a magic trick. And I guess it was, because during this time when everything seemed heavy with sorrow, even the walls of the house seemed to sag, Sarah painted her face every morning so that it shined. It shined when she ate her cereal standing up by the kitchen counter, and it shined when she bounded out the front door, my mother watching her from her low chair, staring at her swinging ponytail as it bounced away down the street.

One night, my mother came into our bedroom and asked Sarah if she would stay home just one day this week because people were asking about her.

'I'm not going to participate in this. It's not for me,' Sarah replied. She was lying on our bed, reading an Eaton's catalogue.

'It's not a question of whether or not you want to. It's a question of doing what's right. Our mother has died. This is how we show her respect.' My mother spoke as if she had written the manual on Right and Wrong.

'Goldie, stop bossing me around! You are not my damn mother.'

'Don't swear,' my mother said. 'Not in front of Beth. And certainly not now.'

Sarah put down the catalogue and stared at Goldie from her bed.

'Dammit,' she said in a low whisper, not breaking my mother's gaze. 'Dammit to hell.'

My mother was growing pale. Her hands were shaking, so she crossed her arms under her chest.

'I'll wash your mouth out,' she said back, but her voice shook like her hands.

Sarah leaned back on her pillows and picked up the catalogue again. She smiled.

'You wouldn't dare,' she challenged.

And we sat there, waiting. I'm not sure what for – maybe waiting for my mother to come charging across the room, grab Sarah by the wrist and haul her off to the bathroom to eat a soapy washcloth. I knew she wouldn't, Sarah knew she wouldn't, but my mother looked like an animal sizing up its competition, and then realizing it didn't stand a chance.

'I will,' she said, but she was backing away. 'If I catch you talking like that again, especially in front of Beth, I most certainly will.'

Sometime later, after the shiva, I was angry at my mother and I said, 'Dammit to hell.'

It took no time for my mother to have her hand wrapped tight around my forearm and for her to drag me to the bathroom where she did indeed wash my mouth out with cold, Ivory soap water. We both cried while she did it, and afterward she hugged me for a long time. Since then, I have often thought that my tears tasted less like salt and more like a washcloth that has not been rinsed out properly.

Shiva was only supposed to last for a week, but the mourning in our house seemed to go on forever. About a week after the shiva ended, Carrie got up, went down to the kitchen to have some coffee, took one look at the calendar, and then ran back up to our room, where she shut the door and wouldn't let anyone in.

'But I need my book!' I told her from the hall. My mother came up behind me and knocked on the door, loudly.

'Carrie, open up! This is ridiculous. It's not the time for this. You have to learn to let things go and move on.'

She didn't answer. I heard her bed creak, as if she were turning over, under the covers.

'Mum, I really need my book,' I said. 'For school.'

'I know. Your aunt is being silly.' She knocked on the door again. 'Come on, Carrie. Be reasonable!'

'Is it because of Baba?' I asked.

'No,' my mother said. Then, loudly enough for Carrie to definitely hear, she added, 'It's because your aunt has difficulty moving on from what's past. We all have to learn to leave bad things behind and to move toward the good.'

I liked how strong she sounded. She sounded more awake than she had since we moved into the house.

'Maybe we can break down the door?' I suggested, just when Carrie opened it and handed me my book. Before either of us could come in, she shut it and locked the handle.

My mother shook her head and muttered, 'What does she think? Once a year the world will stop?'

She took me downstairs and said to leave Carrie alone. I did, but when I came home from school, I went to play outside in the backyard. We had a crabapple tree that grew just outside our bedroom window. I took my shoes off and climbed up until I could see in and watch her through our gauzy curtains as she lay on her bed curled up and facing away from the window. It was a hot day outside, but she stayed under the covers with her small rotating fan blowing stale air around the room. She wasn't sleeping. I watched her toss in her bed, and I saw her wipe tears away from her face. At one point she turned to face the window, and I think she saw me. There was a split second when our eyes met. But then she rolled back onto her side, away from me, and for the rest of the time I was there, she didn't move.

Two weeks later it was the anniversary of my Uncle Phil's death. The only time my parents mentioned my uncle to each other was on his *yartzeit*. Even then, it wasn't so much about him as it was about remembering their obligations. Mum would say to Dad, 'Are you going to *shul* this evening? For Phil's yartzeit?'

Or Dad would say, 'Did you buy the candle? For Phil's yartzeit?'

They would both nod because neither of them ever forgot.

That year show and tell fell around the time of Phil's yartzeit. Most people brought their favourite toy to school and told some silly story about why they named their ratty stuffed dog Sugarplum or Rover. A couple of kids wanted to bring their pets, but we weren't allowed to have animals in school, so they had to show us a drawn picture instead. Norma did this. She drew a picture of her cat, Cleo ('CleoCATra,' she said. 'Instead of CleoPATra. Get it?'), and she told us about how she found the cat under her dad's car one night, and he said she could keep it. She said that Cleo was her best friend. Except for Marilyn. She had to say except for Marilyn, otherwise Marilyn would have told her mother on her, and Norma never liked to get in trouble.

I wanted something special for my show and tell. My parents had refused to get me a telescope for my birthday. ('It's too expensive, Sweetheart,' my father said. 'You're a little girl,' my mother added. 'You don't need one.') By this time, I had a total of 421 pebbles in my drawer, and they rattled whenever I opened or closed it. Sometimes I laid them out on the floor in the hall outside our room and

I made constellations, following the diagrams in my library books or even from the drawings Phil had made himself. I constructed the night sky across the floor with the pebbles I had collected, and then I squinted my eyes to see if I could make out his face. Sometimes I could. When my eyes were unfocused enough that everything was fuzzy, sometimes his face was the only thing that looked clear.

When my dad left for services that evening, and Mum got out Phil's yartzeit candle, I went into the closet in our room. I pulled out six sheets of black construction paper and white glue. I sat in the hall and pasted rocks onto the paper until they shone under the hall light and became stars. Then there were the photos. I found a shoebox of photos of my uncle hidden in the basement behind some Yiddish books and beneath a dusty portrait of a city street in the rain. He was handsome, pale and thin, but he looked strong. One photo must have been taken when he had enlisted in the air force. He was sitting a bit on an angle, and his pilot's hat was tilted down just above his eyes. He looked out at the camera and smiled without using his teeth. I showed the photo to Cheryl. She told me he looked mysterious. Cheryl had a way of talking about men as if she were older.

I pasted the photos onto the black cardboard. There are pictures of Phil with my mum, with my grandparents, and even one with my Auntie Sarah when she was a baby. I made up a story for each photo: where it took place, what was going on when it was taken, who the people were I didn't recognize. My uncle was the oldest child, and in the photo, which was taken before he left to save the world and then die in the North African skies, he had his long arms around my mother and Carrie, and Sarah was on his shoulders. My mother rested her head on his chest. They all looked like they had been laughing, and Sarah, who was a baby, had her mouth open wide and was looking up to the sky.

After my mother and Carrie lit the candle in the kitchen and went to sit in the living room to watch the news, I went over to the stove where the twenty-four-hour candle in its glass holder was burning in the centre. I laid the sheets of stars all over the floor and counter so that it looked like the candle was one of them. Then I put the photos up behind the candle so that the flame reflected a bit on their faces and all the people were tainted light orange. Cheryl told me it was going to look like a séance. But I thought it looked more like something out of a museum.

'Mum! Carrie!' I called. I stood on the spoon of the Big Dipper. With my arms out, I spun around on that one spot. 'Come and see what I've done!'

'What do you mean?' Mum called back. I could hear both of them getting up from the couch in the other room, the quick creak of the springs as they rose. Mum walked slowly to the kitchen because of how tired she could get in the evenings. Carrie followed behind her.

Mum came into the kitchen first while I spun around. I saw her twice before stopping and wobbling on the one spot.

'Do you like it?' I asked her. It was my heaven. Mine and Phil's and hers, if she wanted.

She looked around the room at the stars and then the candle and the photos. She squinted her eyes, and I wondered if she saw Phil.

'What's all of this?' she asked, staying by the doorway, her arms folded tight beneath her chest. She kept herself wrapped up in her green cotton housecoat.

Carrie stood behind her. 'Oh,' she said, and she smiled. She didn't say anything else, but she put her hand on her chest, close to her heart.

'It's for Uncle Phil,' I told them. 'To remember him.' I sat down on one of my stars. 'I've made a collage, and these are the stars he would have liked. I'm going to take it to show and tell tomorrow.'

Carrie was nodding. My mother wasn't.

She came over and started to pick up my papers. 'Beth, I wish you would stop this with these stars. You need to think about what you learn in school, not planets and the sun and how far away the moon is. This isn't healthy.' When she had all the sheets but the one I was sitting on, she looked up at the photos. 'And these were put away for a reason. You should know not to take things without asking.'

She pushed me off the paper so that she could get to it.

'I thought photos were to look at,' I said as she tried to put them in a neat pile. Some of the pebbles started to fall off of the papers.

'Don't be sassy with me,' she warned. When she reached for the photos behind the candle, I could feel tears just behind my eyes. It hurt my throat and my cheeks trying not to let them fall.

'Please keep them up,' I asked her. 'So that I can show Daddy.' I leaned over to take the photos away from her reach, but she grabbed them from my hand. She lost her balance, and stumbled just overtop of the candle. Her bare arm grazed the flame and she cried out, dropping the photos.

Mum ran to the sink, sticking her arm beneath the cold tap. Carrie ran over and held Mum's arm under the water while my mother gasped. I stood in the doorway, feeling a million feet tall and wide. It was very obvious I was standing there, doing nothing.

'Do you need a bandage?' I asked her.

'You can leave me alone and get yourself ready for bed!' she snapped. 'If you had listened to me in the first place, this wouldn't have happened.' She spoke with a tight voice, and I wondered about the words she wouldn't let off of her tongue.

'I just wanted to show you what I made,' I said.

'And I just want you to do as you're told!' she answered. She whipped around and I saw tears at the corners of her eyes.

Carrie turned around. 'Beth, dear. Go get ready for bed like your mother asked you to.'

I grabbed the papers and went up to bed. I left them the photos so that they could put them away in the basement where she wanted them to stay.

7

My grandmother's house was better than living in the apartment, but that was all. It was not like living in our own house. We kept all of her furniture exactly how it was: the mint green candlestick phone on the wobbly table in the front hall; the blue itchy couch with the wine stain in the middle, from my grandfather just days before his heart attack. My grandmother had not been an emotional person, but she couldn't stand to clean that stain, and so she left it to fade into the fabric, to get lighter from the sunlight and almost, but not quite, disappear into the blue.

After the shiva, my mother vacuumed, but she did not move chairs or planters to get at the carpet underneath. She moved the upright vac across the floor, and when she was done you could see the path of the vacuum cleaner across the carpet like sand after a gusty wind. In the mornings, we ate in the kitchen off of my grandmother's milk dishes, and on Friday nights, we used her china for Shabbos dinner.

Mum lit Baba's Shabbos candles on behalf of all of us. She wore her mother's aprons, which still had oil stains from when Baba was well enough to make her own gefilte fish and *griven*, crispy fried onions and chicken skin. One Sunday, my mother walked around the house in my grandmother's slippers. She managed for a whole morning in them until Sarah, staring at her ratty, pink, fluffy feet, said, 'Aren't those Mummah's slippers?'

'Oh, they are?' my mother answered, as if her feet had walked into them on their own. She took them off and put them in the front hall closet. The next week, my father gave her money to buy new slippers from Oretzki's Department Store on Selkirk Avenue. My grandmother's slippers didn't come out of the closet until we were packing to move years later.

The door to my grandmother's room stayed closed after she died. My parents slept in Phil's old room. I shared a bedroom with Sarah and Carrie, even though Sarah complained that I kicked in my sleep.

'This is crazy,' she said when my mother wasn't around. 'I don't understand what they're waiting for. There is a perfectly good room we could be using, and then at least all of us would have our own beds.'

'I don't need my own bed,' I said. I liked sleeping with Sarah. We still slept head to toe and at night I would study her feet. They twitched like butterfly wings when she was sleeping soundly.

'If you're really bothered,' Carrie said. 'I don't mind sharing a bed with Beth.'

'That's not the point,' Sarah answered, but she knew she couldn't win this one. In the end, I moved over to sleep with Carrie, who whispered stories to me at night, let me lie against her chest and ran her fingers through my hair until I was sleeping.

My aunts shared a bedroom, but nothing else. Carrie did not wear makeup and could never fit into Sarah's clothes. Once she picked up one of Sarah's fashion magazines, and I watched her flipping through it.

'This stuff is fluff,' she said. 'All these women are doing is looking pretty for the camera.'

'It's just like the clothes you make,' I said. 'Your clothes could be in a magazine.'

She closed the magazine and tossed it onto Sarah's bed. 'No, my clothes are for real people. Not mannequins.' Then she turned to me: 'If there's one thing my brother taught me it's not to waste my brain. And that is exactly what your other aunt is doing.'

Carrie shook her head and waved her hand at Sarah's makeup and jewellery scattered across our dresser. 'She never got the chance to know him,' she said. 'And he loved her so much. He used to call her his baby.'

Her eyes got all teary. I was so tired of people crying. 'Please don't, Carrie. Don't cry.'

She blew her nose and took a deep breath. 'It's just so sad when a baby has to grow up not knowing someone who loved him.'

'You mean her,' I said.

She nodded and wiped her nose again. 'Yes. Her.'

My mother took walks on Sunday afternoons (when the pharmacy was closed, and I was playing with Cheryl Moss) just so she could stand outside her dream home on McAdam Avenue. I followed her once. She walked along Main Street, past St. John's Park with the drooping willows, then past the ten-cent movie theatre, where Sarah hung out on Saturday nights, and the Salisbury House restaurant next door that always smelled of coffee and bacon. She walked down Matheson Avenue, toward the synagogue, and then she cut through the parking lot, which was empty on a Sunday, but would have been full the day before for someone's bar mitzvah. She went down the small grassy hill, along the quiet street, which, because of the synagogue, was not attached to Main Street, and then there it was.

I stood behind a tree and watched my mother staring at the three-storey home with the screened-in front porch.

There were crabapple trees in the backyard, and because the house was on the corner close to Scotia Street (where very wealthy North Enders lived), everything was a little bit bigger: the yard, the steps, the window in the living room framed like a picture. Children ran in and out of each other's backyards. No one's fences needed fixing. There were snowmen with red scarves and matching hats and imprints from angels beside them. My mother would have sat herself on a park bench right there if she could have. She would have sketched the house and hung the picture in our tiny living room, if she knew how to draw. The best she could do was walk down to McAdam while my father was busy restocking the store and spend each Sunday memorizing another part, so that when she closed her eyes before sleeping, she saw it all before her as if it were real.

Sarah turned sixteen that winter. When Baba died, my parents were left the house, its contents, and Sarah. She talked about going to university to study theatre and then becoming a famous actress. She let me lie on her bed with her at night, looking at movie star pictures in her magazines, long after I should have been asleep. The space age and the space race had begun with the Russian launch of Sputnik, but Sarah showed no interest. Space was not pretty. Planets could not smile coyly from the glossy pages of her magazines. My father clipped newspaper articles for me, but after a while they just lay under my bed, hidden in the shadow of my comforter. Instead I would lay my head on Sarah's stomach and then fall asleep no longer dreaming of real stars, but of Marlon Brando and Elvis Presley in close-up shots with squinting eyes. Sarah stayed sitting upright for a long time. Her bed was closest to the window, which faced the backyard and the lane behind the fence. Once, while I was falling asleep, I asked her if she would stay with us forever.

It took her a long time before she answered, 'I don't know.'

Then, when she kissed my head and put me back in my own bed, she said, 'But I'll always love you. Don't worry about that.'

Carrie finished getting changed and then got into bed with me. She said, loud enough for Sarah to hear, 'I'm not going to leave you, Beth. Family sticks together.'

Sarah had her hair in curlers. She lay curled away from us on her side, facing the window. She did not pull the blinds down and instead looked out at the tree, its branches silvery from the snow and ice. As I fell asleep, I thought I heard her crying.

I tried to share Phil's journal with Sarah, but she only leafed through the pages, skimming his writing. When I said, 'Carrie says he was a genius,' she answered, 'It doesn't matter now. Because he's dead.'

'Of course it matters! He's still important.'

Sarah gave me back the journal, closed. 'When someone dies, they're gone forever. You can't bring them back. I prefer to concentrate on the living.'

My aunt was very alive. Even after Baba died, she walked into a room with a wide smile. When she spoke to people, she looked them in the eye and followed their gaze so that they felt they had her hanging on their every word. People walked away flushed after being with Sarah. On the other hand, my mother and Carrie seemed to be sinking and disappearing. People walked away from them and sighed out of pity and relief. Of course, I wanted to be more like my aunt, who floated in and out of rooms like everyone's fairy godmother. So when Sarah closed away Phil's journal, so did I, and for weeks, I didn't read it.

In the springtime, my father came home one day and said he wanted to take us all out for dinner. We never went out for dinner. If we were having a treat, my mother bought TV dinners wrapped in tinfoil that she heated up in the oven and we could eat on folding trays and tables in the living room. But we never went out as a whole family. My mother wondered aloud what she was supposed to do with the food she had already cooked for us. Carrie sat on the couch and said she wasn't feeling well. Only Sarah jumped up and kissed my father on the cheek before running up to our room to get changed.

Saul looked at Goldie and Carrie and said, 'Come on. I really think we need to do this.'

He put his hand on my mother's shoulder and she sighed, putting her hand on top of his. 'I suppose you're right.' Then she held out her hand to Carrie, 'Let's go.'

And so we did.

Dad took us to a family restaurant where they made fried chicken and served everything in wicker baskets with red-and-white checkered napkins. We all had chicken and fries, except for Carrie who ordered onion rings. Sarah was the most animated at the table, peeling the skin off her chicken and then cutting it into little pieces with her knife and fork. She talked the whole time about school, her English teacher who was 'amazing,' and her friend Patricia whose family was going to Europe that summer. Since we all moved in together, I couldn't remember a time like this when Sarah acted like she wanted to be with us. The rest of us ate with our fingers and listened to her. I wondered if we looked like a happy family to anyone who glanced our way.

One of my mother's friends came over to us and put her hand on my mother's shoulder.

'Goldie, how are you doing?' she asked.

'Susan, hello! Oh, I'm fine. Really. We're all doing very well.'

My father wiped his hands on his napkin and reached over to shake hers. She took his hand with both of hers and said, 'Saul, so good to see you out. I know what a trying time this has been for all of you.' She looked back at my mother. 'We all think it's so admirable the way you've stepped in to look after your family.'

Sarah looked over at me and rolled her eyes. I tried to do the same, but couldn't. I just managed to lift my eyebrows. Sarah retaliated by crossing her eyes to look at her nose. I laughed out loud and my mother shot me a look.

'Beth, dear,' she said, and I covered my mouth. I wanted to keep laughing forever and ever. Carrie looked up and winked at me. I tightened my hand around my mouth and felt a laugh bubbling up my throat, threatening to explode out.

'Thank you for coming over, Susan,' my mother continued. 'And for your concern. Really, we're managing just fine. Please drop by one evening for coffee. I'd love to catch up.'

Susan patted my mother's shoulder again and walked back to her table. I heard her say, 'They're doing just fine,' just as I took my hand off my mouth and let out a loud fast laugh, like a burp.

Carrie was the first to finish her meal. She chewed on her chicken bones and sucked out the marrow, which she said was the best part. When she was finished, her basket was a pile of stripped bones and batter crumbs from her onion rings.

Sarah looked over at her. 'That's disgusting,' she said and pushed her half-eaten meal away.

'I enjoyed my food,' Carrie replied, dipping her napkin in a glass of water so she could wipe her face and hands. Then she reached into her basket and pulled out a Y-shaped bone and held it across the table at me.

'Beth, make a wish,' she said.

'How do I do that?'

'You make a wish and then pull on your end of the bone. I'll make a wish too, and whoever has the bigger piece, their wish will come true.'

I grabbed one end of the bone and closed my eyes. Sarah had turned to my mother and was telling her all the details of Patricia's trip. She was saying that one day she planned on seeing Europe, and Asia, and South America. It all sounded very far away. Sitting in this restaurant, where the tablecloths matched the napkins, and with my whole family around me, I feared my family getting smaller.

'Did you make your wish?' Carrie asked me. I squeezed my eyes tight and wished for a baby sister to fill in the gaps of our shrinking family. When I opened my eyes, I was holding the bigger piece. I don't know what Carrie wished for, but she said, 'I hope you wished carefully and didn't waste it.'

'I didn't,' I promised, and then I waved the bone at my mother. 'Mummy, look! I won, I won!'

'Beth, dear,' she said, as our waiter approached. 'Put that down. We don't play with our food at the table.'

When we got home, I followed my mother up to her room and watched her undress. She wiped her makeup off with a lotion on her vanity, an old desk that had been my uncle's which she transformed by putting a doily across the top. She sat in her bra and underwear, her tummy bloated from our indulgent supper.

'I don't miss Baba,' I said.

She brushed her hair out and it turned fluffy. 'Your feelings are your business,' she said. She looked closely in the mirror and pulled at a grey hair from her temple. 'What's important is that you remember the people you love.'

'Is Baba with Uncle Phil now?' I asked.

She said yes, quietly, and I wondered if that was the moment that her face changed. She turned around from her vanity and told me to go get my pyjamas on. She had lines on her face I hadn't noticed when we were out for dinner. I wanted to crawl onto her lap and run my finger along them. They ran down the side of her face from her eyes, lightly over her cheeks and then disappeared by her chin. They were there now even when she didn't smile. The skin under her eyes was dark, like a shadow, and she looked like she could fall asleep any minute and not wake up for weeks.

I went to Hebrew school on Sunday mornings with Cheryl, Norma and Marilyn. We had classes in the basement of the synagogue on Matheson. That year, the basement had new carpet and in the spring, we left our rubber boots by the back door so that we could chase each other in our socks to give electric shocks. On the walls in the classrooms there were plaques with the names of Jewish children who were the smartest in their Hebrew School classes. Cheryl's oldest sister got her name on one of the plaques the year before. She had her *bat mitzvah* that year and had an essay published in the *Jewish Post*. When my mother read it, she said, 'That girl is going to go places.' It made me wonder about where there was to go outside of Winnipeg, and why only some people got there.

In our class, Norma always won the *Menschlichkite* Award, which meant she was nice to everyone. On Sunday mornings, her mother ironed her dirty blond hair so that it was straight and shiny, and she wore it half back in a ribbon to match her tunic dress (pink, denim blue or sea green). Norma would sit with anyone who needed help – even two or three of the boys who looked like they refused to bathe, ever.

Marilyn didn't win awards at Hebrew School, but in our public school, she sometimes got ribbons on Sports Day for things like long jump and the ball toss, but never for running. Where Norma was thin, Marilyn was chunky. Not fat, but she had thick leg muscles that made her look swollen in her tartan skirt, which her mother made her wear to Hebrew school. Marilyn carried a pair of her older brother's jeans in her backpack and she would change as soon as our class finished. She walked differently in jeans. She took longer strides, and we had to race to keep up with her.

Cheryl was going to be like her sister. She was much better at reading Hebrew than I was. The principal of our Hebrew school wanted to move Cheryl up into the next grade, but she wanted to stay with her friends, so they let her remain with us and be at the top of our class. Cheryl studied hard at home and sometimes spoke Hebrew to herself as she went to sleep, to practise. When we would have sleepovers, she always said we should speak in Hebrew, like a secret language. But I couldn't get my tongue around the foreign sounds. I was better in Yiddish, but Cheryl came from a family of strong Zionists who said that Yiddish was the language of the old country and would die out in a couple of generations. Hebrew was the language of the Jewish future. Cheryl sometimes talked about going to Israel and living on a *kibbutz*, which is what her sister was planning to do instead of university.

'Wouldn't it be neat?' she'd say. 'Working in the field? Like real farmers!'

It sounded dirty and hot to me, and I knew that any real Israeli would laugh at the way I pronounced the letter *chet*, which, to me, sounded like I was coughing up phlegm. So while Cheryl dreamt of our Promised Land, I would lie there not able to picture anything farther away than the backyard of my mother's dream house.

I didn't get awards in either school. In public school, I was not the fastest or slowest at anything. (Although once I made it to the semifinals in a bow and arrow competition during a Victoria Day celebration. But some boy who said he had family actually from Nottingham, England, won that one. He also told me, with his bow and arrow in hand, that his ancestors captured Jewish Christ-killers and ate them for breakfast, back at the time of Robin Hood. I didn't much care about winning a stupid competition after that.) At Hebrew school, I was nice enough, but Norma was always the first to offer to help out those who needed extra review in our class. She was very patient and never noticed when some of the boys teased her behind her back for being a bit of a schoolmarm.

My mother tallied up awards and accolades in her head. She would never say to me, 'Why can't you be more like Norma/Cheryl/Marilyn?' when it came to awards days and sports events. But she would say, 'So how did everyone do?'

And if I answered, 'Fine,' she might push me a little for details.

'Tell me how everyone did.'

And so, I would have to recount each award, or ribbon, and who was the winner. My mother would nod her head with each entry, and when I finished, she'd say, 'That's all?'

I know she thought I was saving myself for last. I know she hoped she was raising a modest girl who didn't boast about her achievements, and I know she lay in bed thinking of all the things I would accomplish that she didn't.

'That's all,' I'd answer.

She'd nod her head and go do something else. Over the ironing, she'd review the lists of names I brought home and in her mental filing she'd count, 'Three awards for Brocha's daughter, four for Millie's, two this year for Gertie's . . .'

*

After school, Cheryl, Norma, Marilyn and I played on the swings at Luxton School. We had contests to see who could swing highest. Cheryl had smooth curls, and her mother let her wear her hair back in clips with plastic flowers. Her ringlets lifted up in the breeze as we swung. Our mothers had warned us not to swing too high, or else boys would see our underpants. We swung so high our skirts blew in the air like wings.

We jumped off to see who could land the farthest, and Cheryl won. We landed in the snow and it fell into my boots, melting against my stockings. My mother still had my hair cut short because it was so thin. I don't think it lifted at all. While Cheryl was busy winning, her hair was looking very bouncy and she danced around the school-yard singing the Hebrew alphabet, which she knew I hadn't managed to memorize.

'I want to build a snow fort,' I said to them as they headed back to the swings. I was preparing to build the world's most intricate fort, with tunnels and three towers.

'Let's race,' Marilyn said, while I imagined shaping knights and horses out of sticky snow.

'No, I don't want to,' I said. Marilyn wasn't any good at building forts. Her fort would look more like a lumpy pyramid. Norma's would be neat and square. Cheryl would lose patience and end up helping me with mine.

'You chicken that I'll beat you again, Beth?' Cheryl asked. I rolled my eyes. Cheryl had two older brothers, as well as her sister, and they were always competing against each other. She used me as the younger sister she never had.

'I'm not chicken. I'm just saving my strength.'

We got to the field and I started rolling the snow into a boulder.

'Saving your strength for what?' Norma asked. I went onto my knees and got my coat wet. Norma stayed standing with her hands in her pockets. She hated getting wet or dirty.

'You can't tell anyone.'

'What? Is it a secret?' Cheryl asked.

I took a deep breath, for effect. Telling the girls made it real. I hoped that God was listening. 'My parents are going to have a baby soon. I'm going to be a big sister.'

I expected their full attention. Norma squealed and her eyes went wide. Marilyn wrinkled her nose because she hated babies. Cheryl didn't look up and kept digging into the snow like a rabbit.

'Why do you need to save your energy? You're not going to have the baby,' she said.

'If I'm going to be a big sister, I'm going to have to run after my little sister or brother. My mother is counting on me to help her out. I'm going to be very important.'

The more I said it, the more I believed it. I knew that if my parents had another baby, my mother would end up being very delicate. I would have to learn how to cook because my father would need to be in the store for long hours to provide for us. Sarah might have to work there too, because certainly my mother wouldn't be able to. I would have to learn how to make tea, and how to carry her lunch on a tray up the stairs without spilling it. When the baby came, I would fetch it from its crib when she would need to nurse it. And I would lie in bed with her then, feeling the top of its downy head. My mother would tell me stories about when I was that age, and how good I was to her. How beautiful I was.

It worked, all this talk about the baby. Cheryl forgot about all the contests she had won that day.

'You're so lucky, Beth,' she said. 'I don't think my parents are going to have any more kids. They always say four is more than enough. I'm always going to be the youngest.'

'Babies are a pain,' Marilyn said. 'And they smell.'

'They're gorgeous!' Norma argued. 'I wish my mum was having one.'

Norma had one brother who was just one year younger than us, so she didn't remember when he was a baby.

By then, I had immersed myself in my vision of our new family. I almost told the girls about the wishbone, in case they didn't know about it already and how to use it. Then I stood up and wiped the snow off my coat. Maybe I could keep one secret to myself.

'I need to go home,' I told them. 'My mother really needs me already.'

When Norma asked me if she could help too, I told her no because to help you had to be a part of our family.

That night my father put on a Jewish comedy record, and we all sat in the living room to listen, even Sarah. My mother decided to start a summer sweater for me, and while she knit, she managed a smile at some of her favourite jokes. Carrie giggled. She covered her mouth whenever she wanted to laugh, as if she wasn't supposed to. The man on the record spoke with a New York accent and made jokes about his mother-in-law pulling a guilt trip on God. My father sat in his armchair with a glass of Scotch and kept one eye on my mother while he laughed and laughed. Sarah shook her head while he let his voice roar out, but even she knew it was the best sound any of us had heard in ages.

When the phone rang, and my mother went to answer it, I crawled onto my father's lap. It was definitely going to happen, I had decided. This baby. We were all going to be happy like this for a long, long time.

'We are very lucky,' I said out loud. I smelled the mix of Scotch and wool from my father's breath and his cardigan. I put my nose to his chest.

'Come again?' he asked. His cardigan was warm against my cheek, and I felt the heat melting my insides from my face downward. I almost told him about the baby. The wishbone, my praying, everything. Like a prophet, I nearly told him how I knew our lives were about to change.

My mother came back into the room, her face with its lines again, and her eyes very small.

'Beth, that was Cheryl's mum,' she said, and I kept my head by my father's chest.

'She was calling to wish us *mazel tov* on the new baby,' she continued.

My father leaned over to put his glass on the floor. 'The new what?'

My mother didn't answer him. Instead she asked me, 'Why did you tell Cheryl we were having a new baby?'

But you are, I wanted to say. *You just don't know it yet.*

Now it was Sarah's turn to cover her mouth and giggle. My mother turned away from me and pointed at her. 'You're no better!' she said. 'Does everyone need to know my *tzuris*? Does everyone need to rub it in my face?'

Sarah dissolved into a fit of giggles again. The record played in the background and somewhere, an audience laughed at my mother as she sobbed, sinking into the couch. My father eased me off his lap and pulled my mother to his shoulder. Everything stuck at the back of my throat – my wish, my certainty, everything. The sound of my mother crying so freely was grating, like a knife cutting ice.

Sarah took me up to bed and helped me into my nightgown, even though she knew I could dress myself. After I brushed my teeth and used the toilet, she sat in bed with me and told me again about her plan to finish high school and then move to New York to become a famous actress.

'You could come with me,' she said. 'Be my assistant. We could live in an apartment near Central Park, and we could go to the zoo all of the time. Wouldn't you like that?' she asked. 'To live so close to the zoo?'

Down the hall I could hear Carrie running the water in the tub and my father helping my mother undress. Carrie bathed her while she cried in the tub, her high-pitched voice echoing of the bathroom tiles. It made my skin turn cold, and I put my head under my pillow and said the *Shema* prayer over and over until I could hear the water draining from the tub. Once she had her in bed, Carrie came into our room and lifted the pillow gently off my head.

'Babies aren't something to joke about,' Carrie said.

'I wasn't joking.'

She kept talking, like she didn't hear me. 'People want babies so much it can make them crazy. It can make them feel crazy things, like someone tearing out their heart.'

'I didn't mean to hurt her heart.'

She went on, but she was looking past me at the far wall. 'Don't talk about babies anymore to your friends or anyone. It's not fair to your mum.' And then quietly she added, 'Or to me.'

'But Carrie, it's what I wished for. The wishbone. That was my wish.'

She hugged me and said, 'I'm sorry, Bethy. You weren't supposed to wish for that. That can never come true.'

After that night, I didn't speak to Cheryl. When she came over to play with me at recess, I walked the other way. Soon, I got some of the other girls from our class to follow me (but not Norma, who hated being mean and taking sides). I told them that Cheryl wet the bed whenever she had sleepovers. We made up stories about seeing her in diapers. When she came near us, we made baby noises and sucked our thumbs. It was the same as spitting, and she knew that. When we made her cry, I turned the other way and felt my insides turn to stone.

I learned to play at home, by myself. I played Mummy and Babies with my dolls. Although I had stopped speaking to God (because He obviously wasn't listening anyway), I still imagined our house filled with babies, their powdery breath and milky cries filling the silence. Sunday afternoon, after Hebrew School, I came straight home and took out my dolls with their clothes, laying everything out on the living-room floor. I dressed them in the outfits they would wear for Friday night dinner, and then I undressed them when it was time for bed. I made them cribs out of throw pillows from the couches. When they were having their naps, I went into the kitchen for a glass of milk.

I could never have known that after I was born, the doctor told my mother she must never have more children. I could never have known that she bled so much having me that they thought she was flushing out her insides. My father spent the night I was born worrying that he was going to lose his entire life and be left as only a shell of a person to care for a baby girl. So when my mother did wake up, and the doctor told her she needed to make sure never to have another baby, my father cried out of relief that he would never have to almost lose her again.

My mother cried, too, only hers were bitter tears. She had a carefully constructed dream of her future with my father, and it included her McAdam Avenue house along with four children, each neatly spaced in age by no more than two years. She wanted a recreation of the family she grew up with, or at least, she wanted one son to replace the brother who had been stolen from our family without her permission. She wanted the messy kitchen floor from dozens of muddy shoes, and the maze of wooden blocks and toy trains her ever-smiling children would play with.

I could never have known how she lay in her hospital bed crying more ferociously than I was in the nursery, and then refused to see me when a well-meaning nurse brought me in thinking a young mother could get joy from nothing else. I couldn't have known any of this when I was getting my glass of milk and I left my baby dolls on the couch, sleeping, as my mother came down the stairs, deciding for the first time in weeks that she would take her Sunday walk.

In fact, I had forgotten about my dolls altogether until Auntie Carrie came in over an hour later with her arm around my mother's waist. I was drawing pictures in the kitchen when I heard Carrie send my mother up to her room.

'I'll be right with you, Goldie,' she said. 'You go lie down.'

Then she came into the kitchen. Carrie's cheeks were pink from the cool evening and her nose was running. She knelt down so that her face was the same height as mine. She had my baby doll, which had been wrapped in blankets, and even still it radiated the cold air.

'Beth, your mum's gone up to rest now,' she said. 'She's tired from her walk.' Carrie handed me my doll. 'You need to put these away now so that your mum doesn't find them again. Okay? I want you to put them somewhere so that they don't bother her anymore.'

I hid the dolls in the basement, close to my Uncle Phil's pictures, because I knew she never looked there. I also took the journal from my nightstand drawer and buried it within the picture box, so that my mother wouldn't find it accidentally. There were times in my life when I wanted my uncle's ghost to guide me. And then, like this time, there were moments when I wanted to bury him away, so that my mother could rise again.

The people from the McAdam Avenue house came over that evening to tell my father that my mother needed help and that if this happened again, they would have to call the police. Sarah and I stayed in our room and left the door ajar so that we could listen.

When they said they would have to call the police, she said to me, 'They're not Jewish.'

My mother stayed in bed for the whole of the next month. What I didn't know was that all she had done was walk into the McAdam Avenue house so that she could make her way to its back porch, which was only meant as a summer room. There, in the heaviness of the winter air, she sat on the wicker furniture in her wool coat and laced-up boots. She rocked my baby doll and told it that this was their home, and wasn't it pretty. When she spoke, her words came out in white, cotton breaths hanging in the damp air.

The British woman who lived in the house with her husband had been upstairs cleaning their bathroom. She found my mother an hour later, pale from the cold and a room meant only to be visited when the flowers came out. The woman knew my Auntie Carrie because she had once altered a suit for her, and so she called her right away. When Carrie came, my mother got up and walked out without even saying sorry for dragging mud onto the woman's summer porch.

On their walk home, Carrie put her arm through my mother's and said, 'You have to be better than this, Goldie. This isn't what Mummah would want.'

My mother didn't answer her but handed Carrie the doll. For a moment, Carrie held the doll as if it were her own. This doll was intoxicating, its pale blue eyes like a newborn's. She imagined it squirming. She imagined holding it for as long as she wanted without anyone taking it away. Carrie nearly ran away with it herself, maybe to an apartment she could call her own, where she could lie there, stroking its hair, and saying all the things she held onto, all the things she would never have the chance to say. But then, as quick as a breath, she placed it by her hip and turned to my mother.

'At least you have Beth,' she said.

'I want more,' my mother responded. 'Many more.'

'So did I,' Carrie said, and she reached out her hand to guide my mother back home.

8

By the time I was nearly eight I had forgotten all about the constellations and, for a while, about my Uncle Phil. Instead, I wanted to be Esther Williams. My Auntie Sarah had photos and annuals with Esther Williams from when she was younger, and she gave them to me when she was clearing out her drawers. Esther could hold her breath under water forever. She never got water up her nose, and somehow she could smile and keep her eyes open under water without using goggles. Esther always looked like a swan, or a dolphin floating along, making ballet, her toes pointed and her bathing suit sparkling.

But next to Esther, I wanted to be my Auntie Sarah. I wanted Sarah's rose lips, her white, straight teeth. She was eighteen and had the longest legs – and I really wanted those legs. My mother called them dancer's legs, the kind that men couldn't stay away from. Mum always said she got the brains and Sarah got the beauty. And I did want to be beautiful.

Every day that summer, Sarah took me to the swimming pool in Kildonan Park. She wore a white straw hat with a floppy brim and dark oval sunglasses. I couldn't see her eyes, but I knew she was watching everyone watching her. She walked slowly except that her legs were so long it took me three steps to keep up with her one. She swung her hips carefully like a grandfather clock pendulum, back and forth in time with her steps. Sometimes I copied her and for the first few steps I felt eighteen, not seven. I had her long legs, her strappy high-heeled sandals and a wrap-around skirt to cover my curvy bathing suit. And then someone would catch sight of me, little Beth Levy, wiggling and tripping beside her grown-up aunt. They'd start giggling. I'd have to stop and watch all of my beauty melting away.

Sarah had lots of friends, women who'd crowd around her in the changing-room and tell her what a beautiful figure she had. I'd change into my bathing suit and be flat as a sandwich board. Once, I saw Sarah in the changing-room mirror. She was putting on her bra, adjusting her breasts into the cups. She saw me watching and told me that one day I'd have breasts and hips too.

'Will they make me beautiful?' I asked.

'Hmm,' she said, 'sometimes.'

That summer it was very hot in Winnipeg. Too hot. We listened to the radio only to find out it was going to be 90 degrees again. My mother said things like, 'It's another Great Depression,' and she walked around the house slowly as if the air was thicker. The heat made you feel like you were choking all the time. It was like being under a hair dryer all day. And it was even worse in the house, especially in our bedroom. I couldn't sleep next to Carrie anymore. Her body heat was like a blanket I couldn't kick off. I moved around a lot at night, and even Carrie, who was always patient, would sigh and say, 'Beth, please stay still. We're all suffering here.'

Finally, I went downstairs to sleep in the living room with the windows open on all sides so that the wind could pass through. But it had been so hot there wasn't any wind, only mosquitoes, one or two buzzing and tickling in my ear as I tried to sleep on the couch.

Even though God hit us with such heat, at least we could thank Him for the pool. When the mayor found out

76

that it was going to be hot and dry, he announced, 'The summer of '60 will be a summer of clean, wet fun.'

He made all the park pools open seven days a week, and he brought us lifeguards. That's how we got Jonathan. Jonathan was from Toronto. He was very tall and never wore a shirt in case he had to jump into the pool and rescue someone. He had blond hair, but it was really the colour of sand, which I figured made sense because he was a lifeguard. When he sat up in his lifeguard chair, the sun made his hair sparkle like he was wearing a crown.

In real life, Jonathan was not a king or a prince. He was a lifeguard and my swimming instructor, which meant he made me swim when I was tired, and he wouldn't let me come out of the pool for even a minute, even when I was cold. In the changing room, Sarah and her friends said things like, 'He's just a dream,' and 'I'd be in heaven if he'd just smile at me.' He smiled at me plenty, and I never did enter heaven.

But always after my lesson he'd bend down and ask me to call my auntie over. She did her walk, wearing her shiny black bathing suit (the one that glimmered in the sun when wet), to his side of the pool, and he stood up by the wall, leaning on his elbow. She walked right up to him, so close they could whisper by the noisy pool and still hear each other. That's when she gave him one of her white smiles, and he looked like he was ready to go run a marathon.

My mother once said to me: 'Your Auntie Sarah is very powerful. But sometimes that can be dangerous.'

My mother and Sarah had one thing in common at least: they were both striving for an image. My mother owned many aprons, and when she was not working with my father in a lab coat, she would stay in her kitchen dressed in one of her aprons, usually the one with purple flowers and a little ruffle sleeve. She wore slipper shoes in the house, and when she thought no one was looking, she practised smiling while she was doing the dishes or vacuuming. Those smiles were real, but frozen, as though she was a snapshot, a picture in a magazine of a modern-day Venus, lovingly cleaning her shell.

Sarah also looked like a model in a picture, but from a different magazine. She wore wide-neck sweaters to show off her beautifully tanned neck and chest. She walked around with a half-smile, her freshly painted lips full and closed as if hiding something. Sarah would never wear an apron; she would never help my mother bake or make jam. Instead, she cut out pictures from fashion magazines and the Eaton's catalogue and pasted them along our walls and ceiling. When we lay in bed at night, we stared at a different set of stars than the ones I had pasted out of stones what felt like eons before.

My aunt read Harlequin romance novels at night, when we should have been asleep. She sighed in her bed beside mine, flipping the pages of her paperback, lazily. The women on the front covers of her books wore off-the-shoulder nightgowns, and they carried candelabras, the flames from the candles and their blue eyes piercing through the illustration. One night, I waited until she fell asleep and then took her book from off the nightstand. The women had names like Eloise and Margarite. They seemed to float through the pages like ballerinas. Their men, muscular, brooding (named Noel or Bradford), did not just embrace them, they swept them into their arms and carried them away into a brilliant sunset. When Noel kissed Eloise passionately on her neck, I had to close the book so that my own heart would stop pounding.

My parents did not look at each other with that kind of desperation. Surely my grandparents never could have. I watched my aunt sleeping and, as I placed her book back on her night table, just as she had it before, I wondered if she was dreaming of this technicolour love. I wondered if she dreamt of being carried away.

It took Sarah a while, at first, to convince my mother to let her take me to the pool. Mum was still nervous about public swimming pools even though we'd had the polio vaccine for five years. She didn't want me to end up like her friend Sonia's daughter – paralyzed in her legs and never able to walk again.

'Lighten up, Goldie!' I heard Sarah say to Mum one night at the beginning of the summer. They were in the kitchen, and they thought I was asleep on the couch. I lay with my eyes open and listened to their voices as if they circled above my head.

'She's a little girl. Let her have a bit of fun,' Sarah continued. 'You can't keep her cooped up in this house all summer.'

My mother put down the pot she had been drying and it banged against the counter.

'What I don't need,' my mother said, her voice as sharp as scissors cutting paper, 'is for my daughter to be learning tricks from you.'

She said the word 'tricks' as if spitting it as far as possible onto the floor. It made Sarah go quiet, and I heard my mother turn the tap water back on. I wondered about those tricks that Sarah knew and maybe my mother never learned.

'I won't be like that,' Sarah said in a different voice than before, a quieter one. 'I'll look after her.'

'Really. Tell me something. What am I supposed to do when my neighbours tell me that they've seen you all over some boy at the theatre? Do I need to subject my daughter to something that disgraceful?'

Now Sarah's voice got tight. 'Tell your neighbours to mind their own business.'

'It is their business, Sarah! Don't be so naive. If you can't be careful enough to keep your private life private, then what do you expect people to say?'

'At least I'm not a meddling gossip who has nothing better to do than to sit around making comments about other people's lives! You're just envious, Goldie. You wish you were young again. And you're taking it out on me and Beth.'

'Don't tell me how to raise my daughter!'

'Don't tell me how to live my life!'

My mother went back to washing the dishes, and after a moment, Sarah left the kitchen.

The next morning, at breakfast, I pretended I hadn't heard the two of them fighting the night before, and I asked Mum if Sarah and I could go to the pool that day.

'If you'd like,' she said, sipping her coffee. I smiled but watched her watching Sarah without blinking.

When I finished my breakfast, I went upstairs to find my bathing suit. My mother came into my room while I was changing. She had finally allowed my hair to grow, and that morning she stood behind me to pull my hair back into pigtails. I tried to wiggle away from her hands, but she tugged at my hair through her fingers and pulled the elastics tight.

'Mum,' I said, 'I don't want it like this.'

'Beth,' she answered, 'I want you to remember your manners when you're out. You know that wherever you go, you represent the family. I don't want to hear of any nonsense about you from anyone.'

She let go of me and I took down my pigtails. My hair wasn't as long as Sarah's, but it fell right at my shoulders. And someday I imagined it would grow past them, tumbling over my skin, resting on my breasts like hers.

'Sweetheart,' Mum said, this time softer, 'when you're out with your auntie I want you to remember that you are only seven years old. That means no matter what your auntie is doing, I want you to only be doing things that are right for seven year olds. Do you understand?'

I nodded. But if my mother was trying to draw me away from Sarah, she was failing. Conversations like that only made me more fascinated and determined. If God Himself had come down and told me right then that I had to decide between being a well-behaved seven-year-old, or growing up to become like my aunt, well, there was no question.

Sarah rushed me to get ready, and we walked quickly to the pool. That is, Sarah walked – I ran. She had high-heeled sandals on, and they clicked beneath her in perfect time. My shoes pounded like a two-year-old's toy drum. Also, she never sweat. Not even on her upper lip.

It was a long walk to the pool. We had to cross Main Street, go past St. John's Park, and then walk all along Scotia beside the really fancy houses that backed onto the Red River. I had been inside one of those houses only once. It had a gazebo in the back and an orchard of crab-apple trees. The girl who lived in the house went to my Hebrew School and invited me over to see the secret passage that led up to her attic. It wasn't so much a secret passage as an old rickety staircase, tucked away beside their linen closet. I was much more curious about their bathroom, which had a matching toilet, bathtub and something they called a bidet.

'What's it for?' I asked her.

'For cleaning your bum.'

'Why can't you just use a washcloth?' I asked.

She shrugged her shoulders. 'My dad likes this better.'

From then on I realized that rich people had all kinds of things, like dishwashers, to make their lives easier.

When we finally got to the pool, Sarah stretched her neck to spot Jonathan and usually he was doing the same. She smiled once she caught his eye and took a deep breath.

'Go and get changed,' she told me, never breaking his gaze.

'Aren't you coming?'

'Soon,' she said.

By then, Jonathan was coming toward us and I ran into the changing room. But when I turned around from the doorway, he had his hands on her waist and she was looking up at him with her head tilted, as if he were crooked.

When I came back from the changing room, Jonathan said he was going to teach me how to tread water. He sat on the edge of the pool while I held on to the wall.

'You know how an egg beater works?' he asked.

I nodded.

'So that's what I want you to do with your legs. Make like you're an egg beater.'

He moved his legs in little circles in the water, and I tried it holding on to the ledge. When we tried it in the water together, he held my hands so that I didn't sink under. I swung my legs around and around and tried to keep my chin above water.

'Hey,' he said, 'no drowning. You have to keep your head up.'

'It's hard.'

'I know,' he said. 'So talk to me. That will make it easier.'

'Can I show you how I hold my breath under water?' I asked.

'Later,' he said. 'Right now I need you to show me how you stay above water. If you do that, I'll get your auntie over here and we'll both watch you hold your breath.'

And before I knew what I was saying, I asked, 'Are you going to marry my aunt?'

He stared at me a bit and then laughed.

'We're a little young for that, don't you think?'

My chin sank under so I pushed myself harder with my legs.

'But you like her,' I said.

'Sure I like her. But that doesn't mean we'll get married.'

'She'd marry you if you wanted,' I said. I didn't know this for sure, but I said it anyway. 'I bet she'd marry you any day.'

He laughed again.

'That's certainly good for me to know.'

Sarah came over to our side of the pool then, and I stayed under water for ten seconds. They clapped for me when I came up, and Jonathan said, 'You're just like Esther Williams.'

I went under again to keep my cheeks from burning. I did a somersault, and the water swirled by my ears like I was floating. I wondered if that's what heaven feels like.

The more time I spent with Sarah, the less time I had for Carrie. At night, Carrie still wanted to tell me Uncle Phil stories.

'Have I told you the one – '

'Yes,' I cut her off. 'You've told me all of them.'

'A good story can be heard over and over again, you know.'

I lay on the couch with Sarah's hand-me-down *Seventeen* magazines. Carrie sat beside me. There were pictures of teenaged girls at the beach, tossing blow-up balls and Frisbees. Tanned boys cheered them on. *These are their boyfriends,* I thought. I wondered, if I were in the picture, which one would be mine?

'I'm tired of stories,' I told Carrie. Carrie did not dress well for summer. She wore long sleeves and pants, and she was always sweating under her arms. I wished that she would put on a sundress, or wear a pair of sandals, or even a navy blue bathing suit and lie out in the sun on a lounge chair. Carrie hated the sun. She stayed inside, hibernating all day, with her desk fan blowing the hot air around and around at her face. The only time she ever went outside was at night, when the mosquitoes were out, and she would stand in the backyard looking up at the sky, not caring that she got bit up and down her back.

'Well,' she said, finally. 'You just come and find me when you've stopped being tired.'

In the middle of August, the pool hosted a late-night swim because we'd had two weeks without any rain. Sarah asked me if I wanted to go. I had never swum in the evening before, and the poster promised a bonfire on the grass with marshmallows and hotdogs to roast once it got dark. I wanted to roast my marshmallows until they were crispy on the outside and the inside was gooey all over my lips.

From our bedroom doorway, I watched Sarah sitting at our dresser, putting on makeup. She had her hair pinned up, and she looked like a movie star. She wore her bathing suit under her blouse and blue pleated skirt. She had a blue cashmere sweater to match, which hung on the back of her chair.

I ran over to my bed to be closer to her.

'Hi, Sweetheart,' she said. My stomach jumped again. There was nothing like being Sarah's sweetheart. She had mascara on so her eyelashes curled up and made her eyes wide. When she smiled at me, the skin at the corners of her eyes folded up and looked like stars. I knew I was getting too big for this, but I crawled onto her lap anyway.

'Hey, big girl. What can I do for you?' she asked.

I watched her hair in the mirror all piled up on her head like a ballerina. I wished I could grow mine longer.

'Can I have some lipstick?' I asked.

'Your mum would kill me,' she whispered.

'I won't tell! I won't even look at her when we leave. Please?'

She picked up a round, pink container and rubbed her finger in the paint.

'As long as you don't say a word!' she said as she put her finger to my lips and spread the colour over my mouth. It felt smooth like honey, only it wasn't sticky. I watched myself in the mirror as my lips seemed to jump off my face. I made kisses in the air and this made Sarah laugh.

'You look very glamorous,' she told me, lifting me off her lap. 'The pool won't know what hit it.'

On our way out the door, we passed by Carrie sitting on the front steps.

'There's a bonfire tonight, Carrie,' I said. I jumped from the second step on to the ground. Then I ran back up the steps to see if I could do it again from the third.

'So I hear,' Carrie replied. She looked at me, and then at my lips, before slowly turning to Sarah.

'You're going to look after her?' Carrie asked.

Sarah adjusted the bag on her shoulder and then put her hand on my head. 'Of course. I always do.'

'I can look after myself,' I said, feeling bold and grown-up.

Sarah laughed, and we started to walk away.

'You know,' she called back to Carrie, 'Beth is growing up. No one wants to admit it, but it is happening.'

Carrie shook her head. 'Don't you make her grow up too fast.'

Sarah held my hand and walked with a very straight back away from the house. I talked a lot, asking things like how big would the bonfire be? Would it be very hot? How many marshmallows would I be allowed? Every time I moved my mouth, I felt the lipstick on my mouth.

'Do you think Jonathan will be there?' I asked.

'Umhmm,' she answered.

'Will I have to take a swimming lesson, then?' This made her laugh.

'No, silly. It's a free swim. You don't need to worry about him at all.'

'I'm not worried, I was just wondering,' I said. Then I took a breath. 'I don't like him.'

This made her stop. She turned to me.

'What makes you say that?'

I shrugged my shoulders. I don't know what made me say it. I just did. But the look on her face made me want to grab my words back and swallow them.

She bent down so that her eyes were the same level as mine. She smelled like vanilla and cocoa butter.

'We're just getting to know each other. I like him a lot and that's all. When two people like each other, they like to spend a lot of time together.'

'I didn't mean it,' I said, quickly. 'I really like him. Really.'

Sarah smiled. 'You just don't like it when he makes you swim too much.'

I smiled back, and we began walking again.

When Sarah and I got to the pool, Jonathan was slouched in his lifeguard chair with his chin in his hand. When we walked out of the changing room, he sat up fast. Sarah was wearing her new green bikini. She looked like a model, and everyone was looking at her. They couldn't believe someone like her was at the pool in Kildonan Park. The bikini was like satin, shiny and the colour of grass after a rainy day. Sarah's friends oohed over her swimsuit, and she said lots of thank-yous. One friend sighed, 'If only I had a body like yours.'

None of them did, though. Sarah's friends either had fat legs or really skinny arms. She was the only one who was perfect.

Jonathan came over to us and stared at Sarah as if he'd never seen her before.

'Look, Jonathan,' I said, hopping on the spot, pretending I was tap dancing. 'Look at my lipstick.'

He looked over at me and raised his eyebrows. 'Very sexy,' he said, and all of Sarah's friends laughed. I blew kisses in the air, and this made them laugh even more, until Sarah told me to stop because it was inappropriate.

I went to play in the shallow end and did some Esther Williams handstands. I breathed out of my nose to keep the water from rushing up my head. I was practising how long I could hold my breath. I also wanted to keep my eyes open, but the chlorine stung, so I closed them.

One banana, two banana . . .

I got as far as ten, and then I rushed to the surface to grab more air. Sarah sat on the side of the pool with Jonathan behind her, his arms around her neck.

'Auntie Sarah, count how long I can hold my breath!' I called to her.

'All right,' she said, and I heard them laugh as I dove back under.

One banana, two banana . . .

This time I counted up to twelve.

'That was ten,' Sarah said when I came up for more air. Jonathan made tiny kisses on her shoulder.

'Was not! I counted twelve,' I argued. 'You weren't paying attention.'

'Try it again,' Jonathan said. 'This time we'll watch more carefully.'

So I went under again. I was going to hold my breath to at least fifteen. *One banana, two banana.* I liked playing this game with Sarah and Jonathan. I could pretend, if I tried, that Jonathan was my uncle and they were taking me out for the evening. *Five banana, six banana.* And after the bonfire, they would take me in their car for a milkshake.

Nine banana, ten banana. If they really did get married, I would be a flower girl. I could wear a bright white dress that came to my ankles and swung around my legs like a bell when I walked down the aisle. And I would be allowed to wear lipstick. *Fourteen banana, fifteen banana.*

I burst through the top of the water.

'Did you see?' I yelled, my eyes still closed to squeeze out the chlorine.

Only they weren't at the ledge. I turned around in the water, but couldn't see them anywhere. One of Sarah's friends saw me and said, 'Beth, honey, they went that way,' pointing to the changing rooms.

I wouldn't leave them if they had asked me not to. I wouldn't leave anyone in the middle of a game. I took my towel from off the lounger and wrapped it around my shoulders. The terry cloth was rough, not soft, and the water stuck to my skin. I couldn't find my sandals, but I walked to the changing room anyway. I was crying, but not hard, and I hoped that my face wasn't red and just looked wet from the pool. I had stayed under for fifteen seconds, and they would never believe me if they didn't see.

And then I heard some shuffling and whispering from around the building. The sound of feet sliding over gravel, the sound of someone catching her breath, like she was coming out of water.

I peeked my head round the corner, and that's when I saw them. Jonathan had Sarah up with her back against the wall, her chin on his shoulder, and he pushed into her with his hips. He had one hand under her bum and the other on her back, and she squeezed her eyes shut, her face tight and red. He rocked against her, and her bikini strap fell loose off her shoulder.

I turned to run away because suddenly I knew I shouldn't be there. But the ground was slippery, and I fell hard against the palms of my hands and my knees. I cried out so that they'd stop and know I was there and remember where they were.

'Dammit,' I heard Jonathan say and then the sound of them scrambling away from the wall.

'She was spying,' he said. Sarah was beside me, all of a sudden. She held me close to her chest and rocked me on her lap.

'Leave her alone, Jon,' she said to him. 'She's just a little girl.'

I looked up at him while wrapped in the arms of my aunt. I thought, *that's what I look like when I'm in trouble* – big eyes, white skin, mouth partly open. Then Jonathan took off, and I watched his back as he disappeared.

Sarah's hair was down and messy around her face.

'Do you want to go home?' she asked. I did, but her asking made me cry harder.

'But what about the bonfire?' I managed, in between sobs.

She kissed my hand. 'You'll have plenty of bonfires,' she said.

We walked back home slowly. Halfway there, I told Sarah that my knees hurt, and she carried me on her back. We didn't talk at all about the pool. I looked up at the sky and counted the stars beginning to peek out.

When we got to the house, Sarah put me down to unlock the door.

'I won't tell,' I said, while she struggled with the key that always stuck a bit anyway. She took it out of the lock and sat on the steps, taking off her sandals.

'Thank you,' she said, looking at her feet. She moved some of her hair behind her ear. I was afraid she would start crying so I wrapped my arms around her waist and lay my head on her lap. A mosquito bit me, but I ignored it.

'But I'm quitting swimming,' I said.

She laughed a little and rested her chin on my head. 'I'll tell your parents he left to go back home,' she offered.

We sat like that for a while, and I danced my fingers over her knee. It was nice – just me and Sarah on the steps with our shoes off. I held my breath to see how long it would last.

9

Things got better for us, as they sometimes do. After my mother woke from her long sleep, she went back to helping my father in his store, but only part-time. Dad started a sandwich counter at the back of the pharmacy, and Mum was in charge. It meant she could be home in time to make my lunches, and I chatted to her about my friends and school over bowls of tomato rice soup. She listened more than before and asked questions about the games I played at recess. She even laughed when I imitated my teachers. Sometimes I made up stories just to hear her say, 'Oh Beth, you're such a card.'

When I was eleven, my father came home one day with a set of keys. He tied a scarf around my mother's eyes and then led her away. Carrie, Sarah and I followed, though I quickly figured out he didn't need to lead my mother along. She and I both knew this route with our eyes closed. When he took the scarf off, she drew in a breath and started to shake. My father put his hands on my mother's shoulders like a weight and said, 'This is it. It's ours now.'

My mother stood staring at the McAdam Avenue house, with its back porch and crabapple trees. She shook under my father's hold, and I watched her eyes jump from window to window, to the sloping roof and then the freshly painted front steps. Sarah and I ran in right away and claimed our rooms. She got the bigger one because she is older. I didn't mind. My room had a window that faced the oak tree at the side of the house. There was space on the ledge for me to sit on, and the room was big enough for a writing desk, which my father said we could now afford. It took my mother an hour before she came off the front porch, and then she walked slowly throughout the house, touching every wall. She ran her finger along the wallpaper in the hall that had rose vines reaching up to the ceiling. She opened every cupboard in the kitchen and checked the taps in the double sink. The only place she didn't explore was the summer room, which my father eventually had taken down and then rebuilt before the following spring.

While we explored the new house, Carrie stayed outside. She sat with Mum on the front porch, and then when Dad came to get her, Carrie patted her hand and said, 'You go. I'm going to stay here.'

She admired the front garden, which was lit up with tulips and tiger lilies. The grass needed cutting, but she could see where children had played soccer and hide-and-go-seek behind the front bushes. Then Carrie wandered to the backyard and counted the crabapple trees. There were three, plus four lilac bushes. In one of the bushes, she saw a robin's nest with two blue eggs.

'Why doesn't she come inside?' Sarah asked me. I shrugged my shoulders. From my new bedroom, I could see her circling the lawn. There was a room waiting for her, and she didn't even look up.

When we got back to Baba's house to prepare for the move, Carrie commented to my mother that she would have to learn a lot about gardening to keep the place beautiful.

'Well, that can be your job, Carrie,' Goldie said. 'You've always had such a green thumb.'

'No,' Carrie said. 'Thanks. But I think it's time for me to get my own place.'

'Don't be ridiculous, Carrie.' My mother was often telling Carrie to stop being ridiculous, and this just made Carrie sigh. 'There is plenty of room at the new house for you. Saul picked out a room just for you because there's enough space for a sewing machine.'

Carrie shook her head. Her eyes were wide, but her smile was kind of sad. 'But you didn't ask me,' she said. 'You never asked me if I wanted to come with you.'

'Why should I have asked you?' my mother said. 'You're part of this family.'

Carrie reached out for my mother's hand. 'I'll still be. Even if I'm on my own.'

We all moved on the same day in November, the day after President Kennedy was shot. The movers packed everything in their truck and unloaded our house first. Once Sarah's bed was moved into her room, she spent the rest of the day crying into her pillow. She cried more than when Baba died. My mother dabbed at her own eyes with a handkerchief, especially while she put away the dishes. The CBC ran interviews on the radio all day, and my mother listened to the commentators while she cleaned her new kitchen to make it her own.

'That poor woman,' she kept saying. 'That poor, poor woman.'

Once we had our television hooked up, I watched as the news showed the parade over and over again. While our new house got filled with our old furniture, I watched them show this man waving to the world and then in an instant dying next to his wife, who was devotion incarnate.

We then took what was left (Baba's bedroom furniture, which my mother still wouldn't touch, and just a few boxes) over to Carrie's place. My mother sent me to help

Carrie unpack so that I would be out of her way. She had found a one-bedroom apartment just north of where we lived, on Jefferson Avenue, which was on the other side of Main. Everything was beige, except for the kitchen which had dark wood cupboards and sea green tiles. Carrie couldn't help but love it. The whole time I helped her unpack her boxes (she took Baba's meat dishes and cutlery, and I helped her arrange the kitchen), she talked about how she had been eyeing this place for years.

'I used to take walks too, you know. Your mother wasn't the only one. Only I wasn't crazy enough to break in here.' She stood up from the floor and held a dinner plate to her chest. 'I used to watch people wandering in and out of this building, and I wondered about their lives and what it felt like to wake up and not have to worry that someone else was using the bathroom when you needed to. You know what I mean?'

I shrugged my shoulders while sorting her knives, forks and spoons. 'We all took turns. It was still private,' I said.

'Not the same. Not the same,' she answered. 'And besides, Sarah and I should never have had to share a room. What an odd couple of roommates we made!' She laughed to herself. I felt something catch in my throat when I realized she would not be there that evening to whisper a story to me as I fell asleep.

'Well, I'll miss you,' I said. I would. Right then she might as well have been moving to China. Her apartment felt that far away.

'Really?' she said. 'And I always thought you had grown tired of me.'

Once we finished unpacking everything, Mum called to say that Dad was coming over to pick me up. Carrie's place looked pretty lived-in already. She had the old couch from my parents' first apartment above the store, and she had already laid some of my grandmother's crocheted doilies on the armrests. She took three plants from Baba's place and put them by the large window. My mother also let her have all the artwork from the living room. In our new house, she was going to fill the walls with real art, not just prints (it took years before there was any real art on our walls, and somehow, my mother never found it empty).

When I came out of Carrie's bathroom, she was sitting on her bed, cradling a pillow.

'I'm going downstairs to wait for Dad,' I said.

'Okay,' she said back. She held the pillow like a baby, running her finger along it as if it had a face to trace. She rocked back and forth. The image of her like that made me feel cold from the inside.

'What are you doing?' I asked her.

'Nothing,' she said. 'Just pretending.'

I didn't realize until then how long she had dreamed of a place like this. How my mother wasn't the only one who used bedrooms and kitchens to fill her dreams at night. I didn't know until I was much older that in Carrie's mind, her dream apartment had a bedroom big enough for her bed, a deep oak dresser, a nightstand, and the bassinet I had used as a baby. She hummed to herself as she rocked, and I'm pretty sure she stayed like that for most of the evening, rocking this stuffed pillow, which was as close as she was going to come to realizing her fantasy life.

Carrie came over for coffee and cake on the first Sunday morning after we moved. Mum showed her everything – all the bedrooms, the bathrooms with the tiles to match the toilet and the sink, and the new dining-room set to match the wood panelling along the ceiling and the floor. It had been four years since my mother wandered into this house like a ghost and then floated out on Carrie's arm. But my aunt knew more than anyone that ghosts don't just leave you. They find you when you are facing corners, away from everyone, when your face is struggling to hold back tears. And they catch you just when you think you are truly and completely happy.

'Well?' Mum said.

Carrie settled into my mother's kitchen and sighed when she sat down.

'It's a lot nicer than I remember it,' Carrie answered.

Once we moved into the McAdam Avenue house, my mother could join the Monday Group. The women in the Monday Group lived only on Scotia and McAdam. They had large backyards, and in the summer, they took their children to Winnipeg Beach. They also ran teas and rummage sales for *Hadassah* and Pioneer Women. When my mother worked with my father at his pharmacy, she always had to turn those women down when they came into the shop and told her how important it was for her to join Hadassah and help raise money for the Jewish orphans in Israel.

'I wish I could,' she'd say, handing them their soap, shampoo, pink tablets. 'Maybe next year.'

It was after those women had visited the shop that she'd lean her whole body on the counter and hold her head in her hands.

'Oh,' she would sigh. My father would look over to her, maybe reach out and rub her shoulder.

'I'm so sorry,' he might say, as if he had said something wrong, though he often didn't speak at all when at work. 'Go sit back down for a while.'

She would wander to the back and perch on the small wooden chair amongst the mop and the spray cleaner, then she would pull out the book she was reading that week. She read Thomas Hardy and George Eliot. Sometimes she read Russian novels in Yiddish. It was a different book every week. If she found a line she liked in one of her books, she underlined it in pencil and bent the corner of the page. Some of her books had a hundred bent pages.

But that year, the year we moved to the house on McAdam Avenue, Dad hired Fredrick to help in the shop. Fredrick was Ukrainian, twenty years old, and rented the apartment above the pharmacy. My father expected him to speak English to the customers. Fredrick had white-blond hair and made my mother laugh when she came into the store.

'You see, Mrs Levy,' he said once, 'I you now.' He put his hair back in hairdresser clips, put on some lipstick and danced around in the white coat. His hair bounced off his head like chick feathers.

'Go home,' he told her. 'We no need you.'

So she did. She stayed home and read the old *Chatelaine* and *Good Housekeeping* magazines my father brought her. She gave the house a once-over every morning. She baked a lot, and I took butterscotch brownies and Rice Krispies squares to school to share with Cheryl, Norma and Marilyn. Their mothers made chocolate chip cookies and M&M's brownies, and there were days we sat in the schoolyard at recess, devouring sugar and picking leftover crumbs off of our skirts by licking our fingers, never missing a morsel. Soon after my mother began staying home, she joined Hadassah and then the Synagogue Sisterhood, and she was in charge of organizing used book sales for both. It was after her first used book sale (where she made $400 for the unfortunate orphans in Israel) when she was asked to become a Monday Group member.

The ladies in my mother's Monday Group did not have pale, invisible faces. They wore blush that carved their cheeks as though from stone, and they had wide, shouting eyes. I had been waiting for so long to have a face like that, all angles and curves, a maze and mystery the way the skin fell elegantly over the bone. None of these women looked cheap. They commanded respect.

I knew what my mother looked like without makeup. Even in the new house, she grew old and tired, her feet up on the couch, her body hidden beneath her deep green robe. My mother's face had deep curves by her eyes and smaller ones along the side of her mouth. When she was worried, or concerned, or confused, two deep lines formed between her eyebrows leading to her nose. My father called them her worry lines. 'The more you worry, the deeper they get,' he said. When my mother had the Monday Group, she smiled for so long those lines didn't even leave a shadow on her face.

Sometimes the Monday Group ladies invited their daughters to join them for a meeting. (Never sons. The mothers of sons in the group commiserated about basketball games and insect collections. They sipped their coffee in envy of the other women who were raising future Monday Group members.)

This was not so much an initiation – we were not expected to attend regularly – but more of a preparation so that we would know how to conduct our own group when we were married and raising their granddaughters in Winnipeg's South End, which was as far as any Monday Group member imagined her daughter moving. Only one daughter was brought in at a time, usually around her thirteenth birthday. She wore tights, a sweater set and a pencil-straight skirt. Her mother would spend the weeks leading up to the invitation listing her daughter's achievements – the piano exam results, report card marks, ballet recitals and other such accolades. The other mothers would nod with satisfaction, impressed.

'My,' they'd say, 'doesn't she have a bright future ahead of her.'

Behind their smiles, they'd pat themselves on the back,

thinking, 'Aren't we raising the daughters our mothers wanted us to be?'

One of my mother's struggles with the Monday Group was having a daughter with no obvious talents. When the other women talked about their daughters, she longed to jump in about her Beth, but without the awards or any obvious spotlight, it was difficult for her to do. So she listened carefully and asked engaging questions. The other women appreciated her interest, and when they asked about me, she would say, 'Oh Beth, she's only eleven. You know what that age is like.'

'Yes,' they'd all laugh. 'We remember.'

One woman, with a daughter in her teens, would put her hand on my mother's arm and say, 'Don't worry, Goldie. She'll come into her own.'

Sometime around then, before the weather turned cold, I started crawling out of my window at night and sitting on the wide, flat ledge of the roof beneath my window sill. I watched the stars and learned their patterns, drawing my own sketches with a marker and flashlight. I could find Andromeda and Cassiopeia, the teapot and the Milky Way. All of our world's finest stories were illustrated up in the sky. Sometimes I made up my own constellations. I even named one Romeo and another Juliet, and found they were reaching for each other. I wrote an essay for my English class about 'The Mythology of the Night Sky,' for which I got an A. When I brought it home, my mother's face lit up right through her eyes. She positively sparkled.

'Beth! This is wonderful!' and then, the words I hadn't realized I longed to hear: '*I am so proud of you.*' (She didn't actually read the essay. The mark was all that counted.)

She took the report and went immediately to call the women in the Monday Group, even before she called my father at the pharmacy. She called each and every one of them, almost breathless.

'Just listen to what Beth's teacher said on her report,' I heard her say over and over again. "*A very mature look at a complicated, impressive subject. Your writing is well beyond your years.*' Well beyond her years! She's so modest, we had no idea how talented she was!'

That night, after all the phone calls (including one to Auntie Carrie, who asked to speak to me and then said, 'You keep up this good work, Bethy. Nothing is more important than your education.'), my mother came into my bedroom and told me I had been invited to come and read at the next Monday Group meeting. At eleven years old, I was the youngest daughter ever to be asked to attend.

'We're going to look at *Romeo and Juliet*, but we want you to read Juliet's soliloquy "O Romeo, Romeo," my mother told me. She gave me a copy of the play so that I could practise before going to sleep.

I got into my pyjamas, and Mum sat with me and put my hair into two French braids.

'All the women are so impressed with your English marks,' she continued, as she brushed my hair and pulled it back tight. The next morning I would have waves, almost like a perm. 'Normally we wouldn't invite a daughter until she was much older. But the ladies really feel that you're ready.'

She finished the braids and knotted the bottoms in two elastics. When she let go I felt them fall against my back.

'This is a big honour, you understand,' she said. I nodded. I could feel the braids against my shoulder blades. 'I am very proud of you,' she told me, leaving the play in my hands.

I didn't read it that night, but I did sleep with it against my chest. I dreamt of being tied up by my braids and someone tearing up my mother's book in front of me. Every time I reached for it, the person jumped back, laughing. I woke up clutching the book and bending the front cover.

'Plays are not meant to be studied, they're meant to be seen!' Sarah said when I told her about my dream. By then, Sarah was a university student, and she was studying psychology and theatre. We were sitting in her room, which was across from mine, and she was reading her Behavioural Psychology textbook, while I practised my soliloquy. She pushed the book away from her and fell back against the pillows she had propped up against the wall. 'Those are the stuffiest, most know-it-all women I have ever met,' my Auntie Sarah continued. 'If you want to really understand Shakespeare, then you have to act it,' she told me. 'You can't just read it in some North End Jewish accent and expect it to come alive.'

'Mum says her books are like mini worlds.' I heard my mother say that to the women once and they all agreed.

Sarah took her book back. 'Yes, well. Your mother needs her own mini world.'

For my inaugural meeting, my mother made spinach cheese pie, tuna salad sandwich rolls (with relish), marinated bean salad on iceberg lettuce, and a pineapple upside-down cake for dessert. When it was a woman's turn to host the meeting, she had to provide lunch. Some of the women got help with their party sandwiches and cheese *kugels*. But my mother insisted on doing it all herself. I practised my soliloquy in the kitchen the night before the meeting, and my voice seemed to echo out of the oven, the sink and all of the cupboards.

> '. . . O, be some other name!
> What's in a name? That which we call a rose
> By any other name would smell as sweet'

I attacked the words at the exclamation marks, but said 'rose' and 'sweet' in breathy whispers to make them sound soft.

The whole time I performed, I was Juliet. I imagined I had long, golden hair and a nightgown that floated around me like angel's wings. I leaned on the kitchen table as she would have on her balcony.

'Remember not to exaggerate,' Mum said when I finished. 'The women appreciate subtlety.' She dried her hands and then held my cheek. Her palm was cool. 'They will be very impressed with you.'

I pictured them, their makeup painting *impressed* on their faces, their lips shaped like red Lifesavers, and their eyes not blinking, but framed by long, mascara lashes. And, of course, I pictured my mother, like a cartoon character, her heart beating out of her chest in neon colours, blinking the word '*Pride.*'

Sarah laughed at me as I performed my soliloquy for her. It wasn't a cruel laugh. She said I actually read it very well. So well, she would tell her friends at the drama society she was a part of, and if they were doing a play with a role for a child, maybe they would use me. She laughed because she said this reading was like an initiation.

'Don't you get it, Beth?' I was in my pyjamas holding my reader at my side. Sarah was dressing up to go on a date with someone my mother did not approve of because he was not Jewish and he was from Dauphin.

'They're making you become one of them. You and all their daughters. You guys are going to have to pledge to continue the Monday Group for eternity. You know, or you'll be written out of their wills, or something horrid like that,' she said.

Later, I would hear her arguing with my mother as her boyfriend honked for her from his car.

'Don't you care about your life?' my mother would say to her.

'This is my life, and I love it.'

'He is going to rip your heart out and eat it, Sarah. And he's not going to care if you lie there bleeding while he does.'

'It's going to feel fabulous,' Sarah responded. 'I would take having my heart broken over making tuna fish sandwiches for my lady friends any day.'

I heard the front door slam, a car door open and close, and music blasting as they drove off. Then I heard my mother sink into the couch, crying, as if it was her heart Sarah had torn out and thrown on the floor.

Inevitably, Sarah came home, maybe late at night, maybe early in the morning. She would throw herself onto her bed and sob into her pillow. She woke me up when she did this. She sounded like a puppy torn away from its mother. Once, I went across the hall into her room and sat on her bed, reached out to touch her hair, and then took my hand back. Sarah brushed me away and said, 'Don't look at me, Beth. Just leave me alone.'

I climbed off her bed and went into the hallway where I sat outside her room and listened to her cry until she had fallen asleep. In the morning, my mother found me on the floor in the hall and she woke me up by patting my face.

'Your aunt does not need you looking after her,' she told me. 'She's making her own choices, and you don't need to be any part of it.'

And then, as if nothing had happened, Sarah would emerge from her room, her hair brushed so that it shone, her lips freshly painted. She would eat an orange, peeling it with her fingers and wiping the juice from her chin. She would say nothing except, 'I'm probably going out with some friends after class today. Don't expect me home for supper.'

And while I wanted to hold her back and never let her go, my mother would just nod, not looking at her. Only after

Sarah left the house, would my mother turn around, shaking her head, and say, 'Stupid girl. That stupid, naive girl.'

The morning of the meeting, I watched my mother do her face. She sat in front of her three-way mirror. She wore green eye shadow, coated her lashes and used a lip pencil to outline her mouth before applying her lipstick. I really wanted to dress up that day, like a proper actress. I remembered Sarah had a fuchsia feather boa in her closet from some performance (my mother never went to see her, nor would she let me go, because Sarah wore fishnet stockings).

'You're too young,' Mum told me when I asked if I could dress up.

'But you said I was old enough to read!'

'You will be a much better reader if you don't look ridiculous.'

I walked out of her room and into Sarah's. Sarah had left already for class. I took out her lipstick and smelled it. It smelled like crayon, and I thought of the way she would laugh with a bright red mouth, the one my mother told her was too bold. I outlined my lips with the thick paint and watched them bloom. Then I draped the boa around my neck and shoulders and let the feathers caress my cheeks.

Downstairs, the women began to come through the door. It was winter, and each time the door opened, I could hear them coming up the walk slowly, the packed snow squeaking beneath their weight like old floorboards. I waited until all the women were in – Millie, Lil, Tess (that's Norma's mother) and Myrna – before I descended the stairs. My mother greeted each by singing, 'Hello! Welcome!'

'It is so bitter out,' they said.

'You poor dears,' my mother said, 'coming all this way in the cold!'

My mother took their coats and hung them in the closet. The women removed their boots and slipped on their shoes, which they had brought in cloth, drawstring bags. My mother's back was to me as I came down the stairs.

'Beth, Sweetheart,' Lil said, which made all the other women look up. 'Don't you look grown-up.'

The women smiled, each held back a quick laugh and a sigh that spread into a smile. I stayed halfway up the stairs like a movie star in perfect view of all her fans.

My mother turned around, and she stared at me. All I saw were those lines carved into her face.

'Beth, dear. You'll come with me.'

I could almost feel the stairs crumbling beneath me. I hadn't understood that the invitation had actually been a test that I had just failed. My mother came up the stairs, and I followed behind her as she passed me. She walked straight into the bathroom and ran the water in the sink. I could see the steam rising from the basin. My mother was talking into the mirror while I stood in the doorway.

'This is a privilege that our daughters only receive when we feel they are ready,' she said. 'Being grown up is about knowing your limitations.'

I let the boa fall to the floor while she lathered up a washcloth with soap.

'A young woman does not push her luck. Only children do.'

I stood in the doorway and tried to swallow the tears and the lump quickly forming at the back of my throat. My mother's disappointment was as close as she would come to not loving me.

She motioned for me to come to the sink and when I stood close enough to her, she took my chin in her hand. The soap seeped through my closed mouth and tasted sour and sharp. I couldn't help crying while she scrubbed all of the colour away. I could see its stains on the cloth once she was done. When I looked in the mirror, I could see red blotches by my mouth, where it had once been an elegant pink.

My mother handed me a towel and watched as I dried myself.

'My ladies are waiting for us,' she said. 'Do you think you're ready to join us properly now?'

There was nothing I could do but nod. It was the first time I realized I was being bred for a life that nobody ever asked me if I wanted. It was the first time I wished I could disappear. My mother still wanted me to read, but I knew I was going to choke through the words. All I could imagine were the Monday women, eating their cake in their crisp winter suits, waiting for a proper Juliet who would never appear. My mother put her hand over my head and then down along my cheek. It felt cool and soft against my hot face. I imagined it making an imprint on my cheek, knowing she would soon take it away.

'Bethy,' she whispered, 'just come downstairs and be yourself.'

She let me cry a bit against her chest. She wore a pearl necklace, and it left a chain of indents on my forehead. I left wet marks on her blue dress with the V-neckline. When I was ready, we went down together where the women were smiling, colourful, waiting. They had helped themselves to coffee; the steam from their cups rose in thin, dancing lines, like dangling threads. My mother led me down, her hand on my shoulder, me clutching my book in my damp palms.

10

Sarah got married the year I turned twelve. I grew very tall, my face broke out in red and white pimples, and I needed a bra. I had always thought that breasts would make me beautiful, but instead, they felt like ripples of fat folding out of my body. When I sat down, I could feel my pudgy stomach rising to meet the flat, triangle-shaped mounds that overtook my torso. They did not look anything like my Auntie Sarah's breasts, which were round, firm and came accompanied by her flat stomach, narrow waist and peachy skin. That spring, Auntie Sarah decided to get married, and still she made men turn their heads when she walked downtown. I wore baggy blouses and big sweaters and folded my shoulders inwards, trying to swallow all of my extra self and hide.

'You're never going to be a little girl again,' she said to me a month before the wedding.

I stared at my auntie and realized I didn't recognize her anymore. Sarah used to wear matching sweater sets with her auburn hair down over her shoulders. Now that she was engaged, she had taken to wearing tailored suits and matching hats, like former First Lady Jacqueline Kennedy. She sat with her legs crossed at her ankles and her hands folded on her lap. She looked out the window most of the time and only turned to speak to me when she had revelations like the one above. If I had something to say back to her, I had to say it fast or else I would lose her to her daydream. She was busy calling herself Mrs David Gold again and again. If she stopped for a moment, it might not happen.

'Well you're never going to be one again either,' I said. It was the best response I could think of.

'Never going to be one what?' she asked. I caught her in the middle of her chant.

'A little girl. You'll never be a little girl again.'

After a moment she laughed. This was the other thing about Auntie Sarah. Ever since she had gotten engaged, her laugh had changed. She used to laugh open and long, like she had nothing to be ashamed of and she didn't care who heard. Now she laughed short and through her nose, as if swallowing the real sound.

'Yes. I suppose you're right. But I haven't been a little girl for a long time.'

Up until Auntie Sarah got engaged, Cheryl wasn't allowed to come over if she was going to be looking after us. The problem started when Norma told her mother that Auntie Sarah wanted to be a singer who made men blush. And then Norma's mother called Cheryl's mother, who asked Cheryl if this was all true. Of course, Cheryl said yes, and that actually, she wanted to be just like Sarah because she wanted to wear fancy black dresses, the kind that show off your boobs. That's when Cheryl's mum called my mum and said that Cheryl couldn't come over to play with me when Auntie Sarah was around because Sarah was a bad influence. I sat on the stairs when that phone call came and watched my mother shake her head and then nod in agreement.

'Yes . . . well . . . you see with Sarah . . . You're right. You're right.' And then she sighed. 'I'll make sure it stops.'

The reason why I remember this so well is even then I

felt my heart sink away. And later, when Mum spoke with Sarah behind the bedroom door and used words like 'disgraceful,' 'inappropriate' and 'shameful,' I felt like a dream had been shattered and I stood there not knowing how to gather the pieces back together.

Auntie Sarah used to have incredible ambitions, and Cheryl, Norma, Marilyn and I would sit for a whole afternoon in her bedroom living them. Sarah wanted to be a famous actress and singer like Marilyn Monroe. She told us she wanted to make men blush when they heard her sing. Sometimes she would sing a deep, throaty jazz song that came out of her like purple velvet. She would wear the black silk dress with the plunging neckline, and she'd pin her hair to the top of her head. One of us would be the master of ceremonies, and the rest of us would play the audience. I always liked to play the audience because Sarah would sing the song as if she had made it up just for me. She pretended she was on a red stage and that we were sitting around a small table for two with a candle in the centre. Then she'd sing 'My Funny Valentine' and 'Summertime' with her eyes closed and her head tilted back, throwing her voice up to break through the ceiling with her song. When she opened her eyes and she looked at me really deeply, I did blush.

Marilyn had no shame asking Sarah questions. The rest of us fell into red hot giggles, but Marilyn would come right out and say things like, 'What's it like to French kiss someone?'

Even I wouldn't ask Sarah that, although we all wanted to know. Sometimes she would answer, cool like powder, 'Oh, you know, if it's the right guy, then it's fabulous. Otherwise, it's like kissing a goldfish.'

Sometimes, when Marilyn took it too far (like, 'How far have you gone, Sarah?'), Sarah would politely fold her hands and say, 'I think I choose dare over truth.'

That's the Sarah I loved – the mystery and honesty all wrapped up in this brightly coloured package with the ribbons, the sparkles, everything.

Carrie also got more colourful as time passed. She began to wear pantsuits (which she sewed herself) in eggplant and teal. She bought herself glass beaded necklaces and a green macramé rope to wear her glasses around her neck. The Carrie that always seemed to walk around like the heroine in a black-and-white silent movie now talked and laughed more. She went to the art gallery on Sundays. She planted flowers beneath her windowsill and stuck pink plastic birds in the mud with them. But while Carrie may have become more colourful, Sarah was still fluorescent.

Before she got married, Sarah used to go to nightclubs with Fredrick, my father's assistant. My mother told her it was inappropriate because Fredrick was Ukrainian. Sarah said he was harmless, but Mum replied, 'That's not the point.'

Sarah once sang on a dare when she was out with Fredrick at a café on Main Street near the train station. The pianist had started playing some jazz, and Fredrick, who was aching to hear Sarah's voice, said, 'I'll give you fifty cents if you sing.'

So Sarah stood up, went and put her arm around the pianist (a young, thin man, she told me, with thick, wavy hair and black-rimmed glasses), and she began to sing. The café went quiet and for three songs she held her audience with each note; they rose and fell with her. She sang to Fredrick, who sat in front of the stage, and she made him cry when she finished. He asked her to marry him, but she just kissed him on the cheek and laughed. At the end, she sat back down at their table and pocketed her fifty cents.

When she told me about it in the morning, she didn't say much about Fredrick, but she did say that the piano player did not stop looking at her the whole night. On her way out, he caught her by her wrist and begged her to sing with him forever.

'We need each other,' he said. Fredrick grabbed her arm before she could answer. She laughed about it the next day, but I could tell she was playing those words like a melody over and over again in her head.

Fredrick was in love with Sarah. That much was obvious. She worked some afternoons for my father, selling makeup and helping with the coffee counter. Women trusted her because she was beautiful, and they walked away from my father's pharmacy eager to try on their new purchases, wondering if they might look like her when they did, even just a bit. My father kept Fredrick on, even though he wrote poems for Sarah and left them in the shelves for her to find when she was cleaning up. They said things like,

> I am a gently fallen autumn leaf
> And you are my wind
> keeping me from touching the ground.

My mother found one once, when she was helping my father close up. Intensity like this frightened her now. My father had grown to love her in a gentle way, knowing she would always be with him. But the poem reminded her of his hands on her waist and the creak of their newlywed bed when they were young and making love. She put the poem in her pocket and felt it there the entire walk home. Before they entered the house, my mother took my father's hand and reached up to kiss him. He placed his hands at the small of her back, and it was as if the poem had been written by him for her. She meant to tell him about it, but somewhere between reaching for his hand and then taking him inside, she forgot.

I found one of Fredrick's poems the day Carrie took me to the Winnipeg Art Gallery to see a collection of Inuit soapstone carvings. We spent a long time looking at a carving of two seals, entangled, their mouths touching like a kiss.

'I think it's beautiful that all creatures can love,' Carrie said.

I shrugged my shoulders. That morning I had heard Sarah on the phone to David, her fiancé. She was giggling, and for some reason it made me cringe right through to my teeth.

'How come people act so fake when they're in love?' I asked.

'What do you mean?' she said.

'Sarah. It's like she changed overnight. And I don't see what's so great about David. She's so different now with him.'

'Oh, I don't think so.'

'But she's so fake now. And she never sings anymore.'

'Sure she does. Just different songs for different people.'

'Why do women have to fall in love? It just makes them silly.'

Carrie nodded, 'Yup. You summed that up nicely.'

We walked some more. There were soapstone carvings of whales intertwined. Polar bears kissing. Seals being pursued by hunters. I made a plan never to fall in love. Always to be in control. Then Carrie piped up, 'You know, I was in love once.'

'Really? You?'

'Don't sound so surprised. It can happen to anyone.'

I vowed to be the exception. 'Who was he?'

'Someone who was a wonderful dancer who eventually broke my heart. But I'll tell you something, I don't regret it. Falling in love. And it did change me, but I think for the better.'

'How?'

'I learned not to take advantage of the ones I love.'

Sometime before Sarah met David, she sneaked out to the café at night, without Fredrick. I heard her creep down the stairs in the dark. I heard the echo of the door closing behind her. And then, in my quiet panic, I listened for my mother pouncing from her bedroom to catch Sarah racing down the street in her skinny black capris and a matching top with a V-neckline. My mum never did, and so instead, I lay awake imagining Sarah and a mystery piano man lit up by soft candlelight, cigarette smoke, and jazz music, making other men jealous. I wondered why Sarah would bother coming home if she could have a life like that.

But the next morning, I woke to find Sarah curled up on my parents' bed; her head buried against my mother's chest. She was crying hard into my mother's nightgown and leaving traces of her black mascara on the fabric.

'I thought he loved me,' Sarah cried, muffled under my mother's arm. Goldie held her like a six-year-old. They rocked together. 'I thought I was going to sing with him forever.'

'I know, honey. I know. But men like that are never forever.' My mother was stroking Sarah's head. 'You deserve to be with someone who will treat you like a jewel. You see how Saul is with me. There is nothing wrong with being adored. I want to see you with someone who adores you.'

Sarah nodded into my mother's chest; she sobbed, trying to take a deep breath.

'Sarah,' Mum said, softly, 'we all know you are a gem. Why do you insist on being with men who treat you like dirt?'

'I'm tired,' Sarah whispered.

'Yes, dear. I know. We're all tired of seeing you hurt yourself like this.'

Sometime later, Sarah met David Gold. My mother introduced them to each other at someone's engagement party, her bright eyes luminous as David took Sarah's hand and said, 'This is such a pleasure.'

'You know my friend Simmy?' My mother was saying, tying all the ends together. 'David is her brother-in-law, her husband's youngest brother. He also comes from a family of four. All boys. Isn't that right, David? And they live in the South End.'

Sarah nodded her head. She wore her long hair back in a half-ponytail with a thin, green ribbon. I stood behind her while she met her intended and watched the green ribbon bob up and down to the beat of the introductions. David was going to run his own business, and when my parents left them to get to know each other, he told her she had a beautiful smile. She told him thank you and responded that he had lovely eyes. Then she turned around and said to me, 'Don't you have some friends to hang out with?'

I didn't. I spent the party on the wooden swing in the backyard, sipping a Coke, which my mother said would only give me more pimples. I sucked it slowly through the straw and watched my aunt fall in love. She and David spent the rest of the afternoon together. She listened to him telling her how he wants a chain of shoe stores, how he longs for a family and a dog, how he wants his home to be in the South End of the city, where the Jewish community is really growing. Sometime, during that afternoon, Auntie Sarah's jazz dream officially died away; all she wanted now was to be the perfect wife to Mr David Gold. By the end of the afternoon, she was telling him how much she too longs for children, how she can't wait to get married and how she thinks the family unit is so important in this modern day and age. Sarah stayed at the party later than we did. She did not move from her spot with

David on the back porch, in full view of the other guests via the kitchen window. Before we left, my mother insisted on taking one last peek at the two of them.

'They're not puppies,' I mumbled. Only my father heard me.

'Your mother is just proud of her matchmaking skills,' he said, his arm around my shoulder.

'This sucks,' I said, and he kissed my head.

'This is life,' he answered.

'David's it,' Sarah said when she finally came home. 'I can't explain it; I can just tell. I've never felt like this in my life!'

Sarah practically floated up to her room while my mother and I stayed in the kitchen. I picked at my crackers and cheese, and eventually, Mum took them away. She couldn't contain her smile.

'I'm just so glad she's finally come to her senses,' she said.

'Yeah, but she's lost her marbles on the way,' I said back. Mum ignored me. She was already on the phone to Simmy.

As soon as Sarah officially became David Gold's girl-friend, Cheryl was allowed back over to play. Cheryl told me that her mum said Auntie Sarah had finally made herself honest.

'My auntie's always been honest,' I said. 'She never lied.'

'Yeah, but, you know what I mean.' Cheryl said, in a way that I thought meant sex, and so I just left it because that was none of her business.

Soon after Sarah decided she would marry David Gold, Cheryl and I spent the afternoons in her room while she was out. I went into the back of her closet and found the black dress, and we took turns trying it on. When I put it on, I sang 'Summertime,' sitting on Cheryl's lap and twirling her hair with my fingers. She giggled a lot, but she didn't ask me to stop. The silk dress stroked my skin when I moved around. At the end of the song, I gave Cheryl a long kiss on the mouth, and then we fell onto the bed laughing.

'What do you think it feels like to do it?' Cheryl asked, lying on her stomach while I lay beside her on my back. I looked up at the ceiling and studied the light fixture, which was speckled with dead flies and dust.

'I dunno,' I said, although I felt like I should, wearing the black silk dress and all. 'We shouldn't talk about things like that. Your mum might not let you come back.'

'My mum's a dried-up old cow,' Cheryl answered. 'I miss your Auntie Sarah.'

She turned over so that her head was next to mine, and we both waited for Sarah, just like that.

But when Sarah finally got home from her Sunday afternoon date with David, Cheryl had left. David was coming back over later to take her to see Randy Bachman's band play at one of the community centres.

'Randy Bachman is one of David's favourites,' she gushed. 'He thinks he's going to be really big.' She was changing from her afternoon outfit into an evening sweater and matching cropped pants that hugged her bum.

'I think the Beatles are cool,' I offered, but she acted like she hadn't heard.

'David looks like Randy,' she said, and then she turned to look at herself in her mirror.

I took a breath. 'What's it like to sleep with a man?' I asked her.

That made her look at me.

'I beg your pardon?' she asked.

'What's it like to sleep with a man?'

Sarah folded her arms and looked off to the side. Then she said, 'Sometimes it's wonderful. And then sometimes it can hurt you a lot, and, if you're not careful, it can hurt for a long, long time.'

'Then why do you do it?'

She shrugged her shoulders and twirled a loose strand of hair between her fingers. 'You'll understand when you're older.'

She was fading away. I almost had to ask for the other Sarah back – the real one who always told me all the things I was too young to hear.

'Why can't I understand now?'

'Bethy.' She said my name in a whisper. She hadn't looked that sad since just before she met David.

The next night, Fredrick came by the house. He staggered to the front yard and sang 'I Wanna Hold Your Hand' up to Sarah's window. If a heart had a voice, that's what it sounded like – Fredrick crooning off-key and desperate for Sarah to fall into his arms. She hid by her window, crouched and crying, until my father had to go outside and walk Fredrick around the block to calm him down.

'Don't you love me?' Fredrick called out, as my father walked him away. His voice was so loud anyone could have answered. My father put that weighted hand of his on Fredrick's shoulder and called him 'son.' Somewhere near the end of the block, Fredrick broke away and said goodbye.

I'm not sure if anyone else thought about Fredrick at Sarah's wedding, but I did. I kept expecting him to come through the synagogue doors, to land on the dance floor on one knee and throw his heart out like he had that night, the last time any of us saw him. I waited for it while we were all dancing, waited for him to grab her arm, or pass her a poem, and for her to shake away her shell and follow him out the door.

Everyone danced, celebrating the match they had all been waiting for. I overheard my mother telling a family friend, 'I knew Sarah would come around. Everybody has their dreams, but in the end, I knew she would realize this is where she belongs.'

I looked around at the guests on the dance floor and wondered what their dreams had been. I thought of my dead uncle, and all of a sudden, I felt him sitting next to me, pointing to couples and saying things like, 'That one? He really wants to run a farm of horses. And see her? She always wanted to study maths, but you know, back then girls only studied home economics, if they were lucky enough to go to university.'

'What about my mother?' I asked.

'No,' he said back. 'This is actually where she wants to be.'

And what about me, I wondered as the music got louder, the dancing a bit frenzied and then tapering off into a soft waltz. What about me?

My father swept my mother onto the dance floor, and she blushed while they waltzed. He was practically carrying her across the dance floor. When he got me up, I laughed at the way his arms seemed to move out of control with the rest of his body. He spun me around like a jewellery-box dancer, and the lights and music kept spinning long after I stopped. Carrie danced by herself for most of the night, but she stayed on the dance floor longer than all the rest of us.

I watched Sarah and David while I ate my dessert. They danced looking only at each other. He watched her knowing he had won her over everyone else, but not knowing how. She looked at him as if trying to erase everyone else, not just in the room, but everywhere.

II

David and Sarah lived in a lovely bungalow in the South End in a neighbourhood called River Heights, where all the streets were named after trees. They lived on Ash and had friends who lived across the lane from them on Oak and then two streets over on Elm. The first thing I noticed about their neighbourhood was all the churches. There seemed to be one on every street corner. My favourite was the one at the end of Elm Street with the message board that changed every week. *Life is like a volleyball game. You only win if you serve.*

Sarah and David moved into their home and had a baby within their first year of marriage, but they rarely entertained the family. This was a bone of contention with my mother, who, around the holidays, would be found muttering about why she is always left to host both meals for Rosh Hashanah and Passover. When we did visit them, my mother would find a way to subtly comment on Sarah's long, L-shaped living/dining room. Once she even came right out and said, 'You could easily fit thirty or forty people in here for dinner.'

'I don't have a table that long,' Sarah answered.

It was obvious to all of us that she had no intention of ever acquiring one, or even borrowing my mother's. The thought of hosting thirty or forty family members quite simply terrified Sarah. Instead, she kept a small table in her dining room to seat six. And on it, she placed a doily with a cut-glass bowl and fake fruit. Never to her face, but often later when we were driving home, my mother would say something about Sarah putting on airs.

'Oh, leave her be,' my father would answer her. 'She's doing the best she can. And she's here, isn't she?'

But she wasn't really. It was never obvious to me until much later, when I looked back on that time, that my aunt, who had become quiet and dutiful, always had one foot out the door. Passover, 1968, when I was fifteen, was when she let her carefully wound-up self unravel. I was with her that morning, helping her peel potatoes for the cold potato soup she was bringing to our family *Seder* that evening. Martin Luther King Jr. had been shot only ten days before, and I had prepared a short speech to read at the Seder sometime after we read about ourselves being freed from Egyptian slavery. My speech made some reference to freedom and segregation and learning our lessons, and I read it to my aunt while she prepared her contribution to the evening.

There she stood at her kitchen sink, washing out a pot she was going to use to boil potatoes. We had peeled fifteen potatoes, and she would boil them until they were soft, and then she would add them to salt water. The salt water was for the tears of our ancestors when they lived in slavery in Egypt. Sarah dropped the potatoes she had cut into chunks into the water, and the rising steam mixed with the tears running down the sides of her face.

I sat at her kitchen table and finished my speech, quoting Dr King, 'I have a dream.' When she had no response, I looked up and saw her face.

'What's the matter?' I asked her.

'Nothing,' she said quickly. And then, 'It's beautiful. Your speech. Everyone will appreciate it, I'm sure.'

'Your eyes are red,' I said.

She took a deep breath. 'I was very moved by what you said. Come on, Beth. Help me by wiping up the table.'

Her table was covered in a cloudy potato juice puddle from the chopping and peeling. I wiped the surface until it shone. Sarah kept a small, ceramic sugar bowl and a cut-glass vase in the centre with two silk flowers. I placed them exactly how she liked it. She did not look at me, but instead stirred the potatoes in the pot, watching them chase each other in the water. I'm not sure when she first realized it, but sometime that day – sometime in the morning when she was preparing her part for the family gathering, maybe when she was stirring all those potatoes – some time around then I'm sure she knew she would leave us that evening, for good.

While she cried over her boiling potatoes, her daughter, my three-year-old cousin, Jade, played with paper dolls on the floor behind her. Jade sneaked into the kitchen in her socks so Sarah didn't hear her at all. I watched her play silently on the floor, dressing her dolls up in two-dimensional sleeveless gowns. She made them talk in whispers, and they said things like, 'You will be the most beautiful princess at the ball. My name is Princess Sarah, and I am going to marry the handsome prince. My name is Princess Jade, and I am going to wear a beautiful dress to the wedding.'

Jade, on the floor, looked up at Sarah's back. Her mother's hair was pinned to the top of her head because it was hot in the kitchen. Small auburn curls stuck to the back of her neck because of the steam. Jade couldn't see her crying because Sarah let her tears flow like smooth breaths. Sarah wore a freshwater pearl necklace, the same one Jade had asked to wear many times before.

Uncle David was the kind of man who lived for his dreams. He sold shoes on Selkirk Avenue, lots of ladies' heels, elegant slippers and pumps made of black patent or red leather. Jade always had good shoes to wear, as did Sarah, although they did not own a car and Sarah took up book-keeping for extra money. Jade wore my old clothes, and Sarah took hand-me-downs from some of her friends who had grown too broad to wear their tiny sweaters.

'Sarah, dear,' they'd say (somewhere, sometime, Sarah and her friends took to calling each other 'dear'), 'now you take this sweater and do something with it. You are so lucky your figure hasn't changed at all since you were a teenager!'

She took their sweaters and gave them to Carrie, asking her to redo the collars with a bit of lace or beading. Carrie would spend extra time on Sarah's clothes, and sometimes, Sarah sat with her at the back of the store, just in her bra and underwear, while Carrie took her needle and thread to the tops and made them look like new. After Sarah got married, I took over her position at the store, work-ing behind the lunch counter. From where I wiped down the counter, I could hear them in the back. They didn't talk much while Carrie worked, but Sarah still sat there, stretching out her long legs, every once in a while saying something like, 'You do such a good job on these, you know.'

'You're welcome,' Carrie would reply. She did not charge Sarah, and Sarah did not offer to pay her. Sometimes, when she came, she'd bring in a bag full of clothes in one hand and a box of shoes in the other.

'David asked me to bring you these,' she'd say to Carrie, handing her a pair of low pumps, or eggplant loafers, or flat sandals if it was summer.

And I could hear Carrie reply, 'These are lovely. Just what I needed.' She replied the same way every time, even though Carrie only ever wore one pair of shoes day after day, a plain brown lace-up pair in leather that she bought from David's store when he was in the back and not around to insist she take a discount.

Sarah also had Carrie take up her skirts, and sometimes, after she had brought the clothes back home, she'd put them on and take the hem up another inch. She made sure to wear short skirts to show off her legs and her shoes. Her friends told her that their clothes looked much better on her than they ever did on them. They'd say these things when they came over on a weekday morning for coffee, often unannounced, sometimes with their own children in tow, never noticing the typewriter in the corner of the living room, the pile of bookkeeping papers beginning to tip beside it. After they'd leave and Jade went down for a nap, my aunt cleared away the cups and dessert plates and dipped them in the soapy yellow tub in the sink.

I thought about this when Sarah turned around from the stove and nearly fell over Jade, who was still playing an epic saga without words.

'Jade!' she snapped, more sharply than she'd intended. She didn't realize her daughter, wrapped up in her own daydream, had forgotten she was there as well.

'You must be more careful,' Sarah said when she caught her breath. 'The kitchen is not a good place to play these kinds of games. I could have fallen, and we would have both gotten hurt.'

'Sorry, Mummy,' Jade said, her bottom lip beginning to quiver, her fists rising to hide her eyes. Sarah sat on the floor and pulled her daughter onto her lap. Jade cried like my aunt, no sobs, no sounds, just tears coming out from her body, soaking Sarah's shoulder. Sarah said, 'I'm sorry too,' but the words were so quiet and from some place in her so far away, I'm not sure Jade heard.

The seder was set to start at six, but Sarah, Jade and I were going over to my mother's place just after lunch to help set up. Carrie would be there, too, and I was supposed to look after Jade. The three sisters would set my mother's extended table. They expected twenty people for dinner, including a number of cousins and an elderly aunt who had recently been admitted to the Sharon Home. They planned to pull out Baba's china, which they used for Passover and Rosh Hashanah. Sarah had offered to polish the silverware before they laid it out. I helped Jade into her dinner outfit, and Sarah combed her hair back in a thick, soft roll off her face. I wonder if she thought of, if only briefly, who would polish the silver next year.

My father's first cousin, Harry, came over in our green Chevrolet to pick us up. David planned to meet us all at the Seder after he finished work. Harry was in town from Toronto helping David improve his business. Harry owned five shoe stores in Toronto, where women's feet were far more elegant.

Jade and I waited for him by the window, her nose pressed up against the glass. She had been in our car a few times and loved the feel of the vinyl back seats against the backs of her legs. In the winter the seats were cool, but in the summer the material stuck to her like toffee. That day was a hot day for April, and Jade turned to me and said, 'Is it hot enough for my legs to stick in the car?'

'Maybe,' I answered, and she bounced on the couch until Sarah told her to stop.

Harry came in without knocking and picked Jade up high off the ground.

'Hello, Tweety-bird!' he called her. She giggled, high above his head. She could touch the ceiling if she reached.

'Hello, Two-two bird,' she called him from up above for no other reason than that it sounded funny. Later she and I would sit in the back of the car when he drove us to our place in the North End, and she would call him names like, 'Two-two bird, do-do bird' or even, if she dared,

'Poo-poo bird.' She would giggle and giggle. Harry would smile. Maybe he forgot I was there. Maybe Jade's musical laugh made him daring. Somehow his hand found its way onto Sarah's knee, which was bare and exposed because of the hem she recently took up on her skirt. Sarah, looking out the window, would not hear Jade's language, but she would feel that hand, his fingers gently massaging her skin like a very tiny octopus.

When we got to the house, it already smelled like boiled chicken, matzo balls and fried onions. And fish. Lots and lots of boiled, minced fish. This smell must lay trapped in the wallpaper all year long and then come out specially on Passover to coat the house. I wonder if my mother spent the rest of Passover scrubbing the corners of the walls to try and get it all out, only to find her house was left smelling not only of fish, but also of Pine-Sol.

In the kitchen, the conversation revolved around simple tasks. Carrie wanted to take a trip to Clear Lake that summer, but she needed a new pair of sneakers. Could David get them for her, for a good price? She was going with a couple of girlfriends. They might need shoes too. Would he have a few pairs in stock? My mother wandered in and out, digging up crystal serving dishes and lace napkins she kept in her cupboards close to the ceiling. 'Clear Lake? We might like a trip to Clear Lake,' she said. 'On a weekend. Just to see what it's like. Would you like to come, Sarah? You and David?'

By five o'clock, Sarah had grown pale and my mother told her to go lie down in the spare room. (My mother told me later that she wondered if Sarah was expecting again. It would have been about the right time.) Sarah lay down in the bed that Harry had been using since he got to town two weeks before. In the room that used to be hers. She fell asleep, smelling his face and hair from somewhere deep within the pillow.

Sarah decided to stay up in the room and told me that she wasn't feeling well. She said the same thing to my mother when my mother came up just before the Seder started. Goldie didn't feel her forehead, and she didn't pull up the covers. She stood in the doorway and watched her youngest sister for a moment before saying, 'Harry says that David will be here within the hour.' Sarah nodded and fell back to sleep, dreaming of nothing.

I don't really know when she disappeared. In the middle of the meal, when I was sent to check on her, I think I knew she was gone before I got to her room. I could smell her perfume as I walked up the stairs, as if the scent was racing past me and out the door. I sat on her empty bed for a while and heard my family downstairs the way she would have. All of us laughing and eating and carrying on without her. I imagined her waking, our family below her, singing '*Dayenu*.' She could hear my father, his deep, commanding voice. She thought she heard Carrie, who had taken to singing loudly in the last couple of years, though she couldn't keep a tune. She couldn't hear my mother, but assumed she was stirring soup in the kitchen. She didn't hear David, but she heard Jade calling to him.

'Watch me, Daddy,' she said over all of the singing. 'Watch this.'

Over all of the noise, I imagined Sarah could pick out Harry, very much in tune, very much in time with everyone else.

And then somewhere between the point where we all ate the horseradish spread on matzo and I delivered my speech about Martin Luther King Jr. (my father commented that it was an appropriate, modern addition to our Seder), Sarah slipped out of the house by the front door, which no one could see from the dining room. She came down the stairs as if floating, as one might walk in a dream, not touching the ground. She closed the screen door gently behind her and waited a moment on the front step to see if she was actually alone. When the voices in the house continued around the table and when she heard my mother serving up the cold potato soup and saltwater tears, Sarah walked down McAdam to Main in her stocking feet, having left her shoes back at the house by Harry's bed.

12

We tried looking for Sarah. But how do you look for someone who found a way to make herself invisible? David flew all over Canada whenever someone told him they had seen her in Toronto or Montreal. He even once left for New York. When he did, Jade would come and stay with us. I let her sleep in my bed with me because when she slept alone she had nightmares and woke us all up with her screaming. But every time David got to where he was going, Sarah ran even farther. When I thought about her (and I tried not to), all I could think of was a marathon runner with no finish line, refusing to stop for a breath.

After a while, there was nothing else we could do. People said things like how dear Jade was and what would happen to the poor girl without a mother and all. My mother, in her kitchen, fixing Jade an after-school snack, mumbled to herself that as long as she could help it, nothing would happen to this child. Jade ate whatever my mother put in front of her, and eventually my mother wondered if maybe it was better off like this after all.

We all got busy then. I joined the physics club at school and was the only girl. They made me secretary. My father bought into a pharmaceutical chain, opened another store and brought on more staff. My mother, proving her charity expertise with her yearly book sales, opened a second-hand shop for Hadassah where she sold clothes, books and hand-me-down housewares. Sometimes she donated goods to Jewish Child and Family Services because there were so many needy families out there. Her body grew soft, rounded, and everyone forgot about when she was skinny and tired all the time from chasing ants out of a two-room apartment. Now, she was the one who recruited young women for Hadassah. She sent out letters to new brides, and she visited the university sorority to make a pledge every autumn. Young Jewish women saw her plump body, heard her stern voice, and many assumed they would be just like her when they grew up.

But I wouldn't have called her satisfied. Every year she wanted to raise even more money for Israel; whatever she managed to accumulate was never enough. She despaired when the Sisterhood membership started to decline. If a fundraising tea didn't go well, she comforted herself by promising next time it would be better.

I decided when I was sixteen that I wouldn't be like that. I would not feel guilty. I whizzed through math tests knowing I had made some mistakes but not wanting to waste my time worrying over little details. I raced my sewing project through the machine, creating jagged edges and asymmetrical sleeves. It felt liberating putting on the blouse and watching it fall lopsided on my body, telling myself it didn't matter. There would be no next time, and this is what I had to work with. I laughed at the mirror realizing this, knowing that I would get a C and that I didn't care. None of my marks changed my appearance, my emotions nor my mood. And when I handed that shirt in, I watched my sewing teacher (Miss Melnyk) turn the blouse around and around, wondering if it was really mine.

'Are you sure you want to hand this in now, Beth?' she asked. 'I think it could be improved.'

'No,' I said. Without thinking. 'It's done.'

*

People were beginning to tell me that I looked just like my mother. Her friends said it was uncanny how we had the same smile, how I used my hands just like she did to emphasize a point. How, with my hair the way it was, short and close to my face, didn't I look like she did when she was my age, being courted by my father and so much in love? They told her how lucky she was that her only child was a daughter. That, at least when she and my father got older, they would have me to take care of them. I saw my mother and my life all mixed up. I saw my face, my hands, my fingers becoming hers, looking after hers. Until then I never considered my parents getting older, nor myself growing into her place when she was no longer able to be the woman she was now. There were nights when I lay in bed, almost out of breath, for fear that I would grow up and have no say about the woman I would become.

One afternoon, I sat on my bed and spread out photos of my mother around my lap. Her hair was thick and long, bouncing in loose curls over her shoulders. She wore it partly back with barrettes, tacked behind her ears. In some of the photos, she stood by my father, who was looking proudly at the camera, and she was smiling at the camera because that's what she was meant to do. I couldn't see it. I couldn't see me at all. And I did look at those photos for a long time, trying.

I spent quite a bit of time at Carrie's. Sometimes, when I needed a break from home, she let me sleep on her couch. We watched the evening news together and talked politics. Carrie wrinkled her nose whenever there were clips of Pierre Elliott Trudeau riding in his sports car, with his ascot neatly tied around his neck.

'He'll never last as Prime Minister,' she declared. 'He's too much of a show-off.'

'He's fabulous,' I said. 'He's going to turn this country upside down.'

'Why? Because he knows how to drive a sports car and how to have a different woman beside him each time the camera is there? I don't think that makes a good leader.'

'He's not afraid of change,' I said. 'You just want things to stay as they are.'

'That's not true. I don't mind change. I just don't like his version.'

I was quiet after she said that and, for some reason, thought of Sarah. 'Maybe she wasn't happy,' I said suddenly. 'Maybe she just needs some time away, and then she'll come back.'

Carrie stopped watching the television and turned to me. 'Anyone who leaves their daughter like that is just sick. Sick in the head. Sarah has no idea what she has here. I know people who would kill for her life, and she just threw it away. You don't throw away children, Beth. Understand? Once you throw away a child like that, you can't ever get her back.'

Carrie stood up then and went to the bathroom. She closed the door, and I heard her running the water in the tub. I felt like I should apologize, but then I realized I wasn't abandoning anyone. I wasn't Sarah. She called to me from the bathroom, asking if I could pass her an Aspirin and that they were inside her nightstand. I opened the drawer, and beneath the bottle of Aspirin, there was a photo, one I had never seen and probably shouldn't have. In it, my Auntie Carrie stood with three children by her side. I didn't recognize them. One of them held her hand, one sat at her feet, and the third had her arms spread around Carrie's enormous pregnant belly. They were all looking at the camera, laughing. Someone had caught them in mid-joke. My aunt's mouth was open wide, her eyes crinkled up in a smile, her arm around the girl holding her belly.

'Did you find them?' she asked.

'Yes,' I said, bringing the bottle to the bathroom counter. Carrie was in her bathrobe, sitting on the closed toilet seat, cutting her nails.

'I'm sorry if I got a little excited before,' she said. 'It's just I'm so angry at your aunt right now. I don't know why David keeps trying to find her. She doesn't deserve to be found.'

'I understand,' I said. I pushed the Aspirin bottle across the counter so that she could take one.

'No one deserves to grow up motherless,' she said.

'I have to go,' I said back. And then I did. I left her room and her apartment. I left her sinking into her hot bathtub while her nightstand drawer lay open, her photo exposed for no one else to see.

The year Sarah left was also the year I met someone. Timothy Stuart was in my English class. We discovered during group work that we both loved Thomas Hardy, and he wooed me by saying that he thought I made a perfect modern-day Tess. Timothy was quiet and tall. He wore Buddy Holly glasses, but when he took them off, he looked a bit like Sean Connery. We started fooling around together one afternoon when we were supposed to be working on a character sketch of Heathcliff from *Wuthering Heights*. Timothy and I were in the habit of meeting around the corner of McAdam and Scotia Avenue on weekends. He had a car and I, with my newfound attitude, had fallen in love with the smell of his leatherette seats and the way we contorted our bodies to find each other around his steering wheel and stick shift.

That day, I had told my mother I was working late in the library. Instead, Tim took me back to his parents' place, while neither of them were home. They lived off of Inkster Avenue, just a ten-minute walk from my parents' house on McAdam, but the homes couldn't have been more different. The Stuarts were Presbyterians and had cross-stitched phrases about The Lord Saviour all over their walls.

Timothy poured us some Cokes and came back in while I was reading 'The Lord is My Shepherd.' Simon and Garfunkel played on the record player.

'My mum's really into that stuff,' he said, pointing to the cross-stitch.

'We don't cross-stitch stuff about God for our walls,' I said, taking the Coke from him. Before I could drink it, he leaned down and kissed me. He had soft lips, like little pillows.

'I think you're gorgeous,' he whispered.

That was all I needed. As we sank into the couch I thought, this is bliss.

When I got home, my mother announced she would be throwing me a sweet sixteen tea, even though I told her not to bother.

'For God's sake, Beth,' she said. 'Just let me do this for you. It helps me get my mind off things.'

'But I hate tea,' I said.

'So you and your friends will drink Coke,' she said. I asked her why she didn't just throw herself a party and leave me out of it.

'I want to celebrate my daughter's coming of age. And I never had a sweet sixteen. What's wrong with wanting you to have what I couldn't?'

Nothing, I thought. Nothing, bloody nothing. I agreed as long as I didn't have to wear gloves or a floral-print dress.

She agreed as long as I didn't wear my filthy embroidered jeans with knee patches.

In the end, I wore a denim mini skirt with black tights and a floral printed blouse. She approved of the blouse and didn't say anything about the skirt. She served matrimonial squares with dates and oatmeal, peanut butter cookies and blondies. She also used the silver tea set and china cups and saucers. She wore white gloves to serve everyone. I approved of the blondies and didn't say anything about the gloves.

Most of the guests were my mother's girlfriends, plus Carrie, Jade (in a party dress) and my girlfriends, Cheryl, Norma and Marilyn. We sat in the sunroom and Cheryl and Norma imitated their mothers by sitting with straight backs and lifting their pinkies when they drank their tea. I slouched, and Marilyn came to slouch beside me.

'This will help,' she whispered, pulling a small silver flask out of the straw purse her mother made her bring. She poured rum into my Coke, and it did help. The drink burned down my throat and warmed my insides like a deep breath. I drank just enough to hold onto that feeling for the afternoon.

It was Carrie who caught me by my arm as I was walking down the hallway and pulled me into the kitchen where no one was standing.

'What are you playing at? Are you trying to embarrass your mother? Because you are on the road to doing a fine job of just that.'

'Leave me alone, Carrie,' I said, my head fuzzy and my voice coming out like an echo. 'You don't know what you're talking about.'

'You're drunk,' she proclaimed.

'I'm just tipsy.'

'If you want your mother's attention, this isn't the way to do it.'

I laughed, maybe too loudly. 'I don't want her attention. I'd like her to leave me alone.'

'So respect what she does for you, and she'll come to respect you back.'

I turned away from her. 'That's rich coming from you. Just let me get back to my friends.'

'What are you talking about?' she asked. Her cheeks started to lose their colour. I watched them drain as I said, 'I saw your picture. In your nightstand. How can you lecture me about being respectful?'

'You don't know what you're talking about,' she whispered, sharp and fierce.

'That's because in all the stories you ever told me, you conveniently left out that one.' As pale as she was, I could feel my cheeks burning. I could feel my insides hot and my hands shaking.

'It was none of your business. And I have the right to tell you what I want, when I want,' she said.

We both saw my mother walking toward us, her gloved hands carrying empty trays of doilies and crumbs.

'You enjoying yourselves?' she asked us as she squeezed past.

I put on my most gracious smile for her. 'Absolutely. Mother, you throw a divine party.'

When the guests left and Mum and Dad went to bed, I snuck out of the house. Timothy was waiting for me at the end of the street.

'Can we drive somewhere else?' I asked him when I got into the car. I wasn't afraid of getting caught – we always parked somewhere different so that no one got suspicious.

He had his eyes on me, and I had deliberately left my top two buttons of my blouse open for him. He ran his finger along my collarbone.

'Where else would you want to go?' he murmured into my neck.

'Anywhere. Take me anywhere.'

In that moment, I remember imagining myself to be a Presbyterian, believing entirely in Jesus Christ and how just saying that I did could erase all of my sins. It was unbelievable to me that it was possible to give yourself entirely to a belief and that somehow guaranteed you eternal salvation. It seemed too easy. No yearly day of Atonement. No guilt eating shellfish. No begging God for forgiveness every time I did something wrong.

Timothy and I drove for an hour and ended up out in Gimli. We parked the car outside the cottage my parents rented one summer. The windows were boarded up for the winter, but I got one loose and crawled into the cottage through the kitchen. He followed after me and, giggling in the thick darkness, I led him to my old bedroom. I could see our breath when we kissed and we fumbled, trying to be passionate and stay warm at the same time.

We fell asleep beneath two blankets on the bottom bunk. I woke up an hour later and watched him breathe. It was late-September and there was frost already on the bedroom window. It looked like it was made entirely of crystal. I rubbed my hand over his stomach and told him I loved him, knowing he couldn't hear me. I then tried believing in anything that would forgive me of this sin.

The coffee shop and bakery in town opened at 6 a.m. By then my fingers were blue, and I had placed my hands under Tim's bum to keep them warm. My toes tingled and I wiggled them to stay awake. I nuzzled my nose into Tim's neck. His skin was cool, but he smelled like sleep. I thought about how intimate it was to wake up with someone, how you share a dream together, lying curled up, limbs tangled, almost as one person sleeping. I was desperate for coffee and for staying like this all at the same time.

Timothy stretched his neck and kissed my forehead. His lips were cool as well, and I could feel where he kissed me long after he pulled away.

'You cold?' he asked, tightening the blanket around us.

'I'm all right,' I said. 'Let's get coffee.'

We went to a local diner and sat at a wobbly table with a speckled, mint green top. The specks twinkled beneath the ceiling lights and looked like tiny blinking eyes. Timothy had sunny-side-up eggs and sausages, and I had toast with orange marmalade. We both drank our strong coffee in silence.

'What are you going to tell your parents?' he asked.

'That I stayed over at my aunt's. You?'

'That I drove out to Gimli with this Jewish girl, made love to her in someone else's cottage and then slept there.'

I laughed, but the truth of it made me blush. 'They won't believe you,' I said.

He took another sip from his stoneware mug. 'Let's stay here,' he said.

'Stay here?'

'Yeah. In Gimli. We could get married. You could work in the library or something. I could run a business, hardware, you know, nothing fancy but enough for us to get by. You could stop worrying about your mother, and we could be together for real.'

For real. The way he said it was like last night hadn't happened. And I could still smell his skin. My toast was cold now and the marmalade too bitter. Gimli had wide streets and everything was far apart. And quiet. I drank some more of my coffee, and after being quiet for too long, I just said, 'I don't worry about my mother.'

Timothy drove me home but dropped me off by St. John's Park. I told him I wanted to walk close to the river before heading home. The leaves were falling into the water in bundles, and I wanted to watch the colours rushing away.

'We shouldn't see each other anymore, should we,' he said. He had lovely eyelashes, dark and curled like a toddler's. He didn't look at me when he said this but out his front window. I watched his lashes in profile.

'No, we shouldn't,' I answered. I was standing beside his car as I said this. The wind was getting stronger, and I tightened my wool coat around my neck. I could feel the tip of my nose turning red. I made sure to walk away before he drove off.

This is what the Red River is like in the middle of September: it's like someone has tossed buckets of leaves on it and this blanket of brown, yellow and green rushes and floats away from the city. I used to like to throw things into the water to see how far they would go, or how strong my arm was. I often wondered what collection of rocks, bottles and sticks were stuck at the bottom of this river and how many of them had been carried away by the current and dumped somewhere else, for someone else to throw back in, float away and so on.

I walked all along the river, along Scotia, and then up to Main and Jefferson where, from a payphone, I called Carrie. She told me to come over, and when I did, she answered the door in her housecoat and her reading glasses. In one hand she held the photo from her nightstand, and as I leaned against the doorframe, she stepped aside to let me in.

'Are you trying to make the same mistake I made?' she asked me. I shook my head, and the thought of Timothy driving away made my throat tighten and my eyes well up. She sat me on the couch and passed me a cup of coffee with milk.

'First,' she said. 'Call your mum and tell her you stayed here.'

After I did that (my mother responded with, 'You could have told me last night, Beth. You frightened us half to death when we found your bed empty this morning. Do you really think that right now I need to find more empty beds in my house?'), Carrie sat beside me on the couch. She held the photograph on her lap.

'This picture represents both the best time, and the hardest time, of my life,' she began. 'These children were from a family I worked for in Montreal while I was pregnant. Their mother took in pregnant girls so that we had a place to go to when it got too obvious about our condition.'

She handed me the photo and let me look at it while she continued. Never mind the children I never knew, and would never meet, it was the image of my aunt's face so free and joyful that I could not stop staring at.

'Your mother was the only person who knew what was happening to me. She helped me find a place to go to. She made sure my mother and Sarah never found out. When I got back, and I couldn't get out of bed because I wanted to cry all day long, she was the one who came into my room, got me dressed and walked me back to your father's store where I could hide behind the piles of clothes people left for me. Then, at the end of the day, she walked me back to my mother, who, as you remember, was already starting to get sick. If it hadn't been for your mother, I'm not sure I would be here telling you this story today.'

'What happened to the baby?' I asked.

'They took him away. They had to. I couldn't look after a baby. What was I supposed to do? Bring him home to live under your grandmother's roof? It would have killed her. It was the most disgraceful thing to have a baby out of wedlock. I couldn't do that to her.'

I placed the photo on the coffee table. 'But you wanted to.'

She sighed. 'Oh, yes. More than anything. I took the train back from Montreal and the whole way home, for two days, my arms ached for him. They physically ached. And I never even had a chance to hold him. They took him from me as soon as he was born. I didn't see him, I didn't hold him, but I did hear him cry. They wheeled him out of the delivery room, and I heard him crying all the way down the hall.'

I reached out my hand and placed it over hers on the couch. She interlaced her fleshy fingers through mine. 'And I'll tell you one more thing. The ache has never gone away. I feel it every morning, before I'm fully awake. I lie in bed, and it's like a dull, throbbing pain. Sometimes it takes me a while to remember why it's there. Most of the time I know even before it begins.'

When I got back to the house, Mum was in the living room reading *Dr Zhivago*, the latest book for her Monday Group. She didn't look up when I came in.

'Good morning,' she said.

'Hi,' I answered back.

'You sleep okay at Carrie's last night?' she asked. I said, 'Yes,' and hung up my coat, smelling Timothy for the last time and tasting the lie on my breath.

She put her book down and went into the kitchen. I was nauseous from being so tired, but she poured me a cup of coffee, now my third that morning, and I sipped it slowly.

'This came yesterday as well,' she said, handing me a postcard. It said 'New York' on it, and there was a picture of the city skyline over Central Park, lit up like one huge theatre stage. 'I nearly forgot with everything else.'

It didn't say much. Just Sarah in her sporadic hand-writing insisting she was fine, and not to worry. She was singing, it said. Everyone loved her. She was living her dream. P.S., she put, *Happy Sweet Sixteen, Beth!*

'You can do what you like with it,' my mother said. 'I don't want to look at it anymore. Jade and David are coming over later so I don't want it lying around.'

I tore it up then. Right in front of her. She drank her coffee, and wordlessly I ripped the card until it was shredded all over the table and the floor. I piled bits of paper into what looked like a snow mound. My mother watched as I spread the pieces out again with the palms of my hands. Eventually she got a brush and dustpan and swept it all up herself.

'Thank you,' she said, tossing the last bits into the garbage. 'I couldn't have done that myself.'

13

Cheryl, at eighteen, ran off and married a Japanese man. They worked together in her uncle's jewellery store. The man was twenty-five. He called himself Simon, although we all knew that couldn't have been his Japanese name. When they got married, they had two ceremonies – one small one here in Winnipeg at City Hall (none of her family would come) and then a big one in Japan. She wore a traditional kimono for the Japanese ceremony, her hair all back in a bun, the two of them kneeling in front of a shrine. She sent us all a copy of that picture. That's when I realized she had gone off to live worlds away from the rest of us.

I went to the wedding at City Hall, with Norma and Marilyn. None of us told our parents we were going, mind you. They'd have locked us in our rooms. When word got out that Cheryl Moss was marrying someone from Japan, my parents forbade me flat out to see her anymore. I think they thought Simon had a whole crew of Japanese men stored away beneath his bed, ready to capture more lovely Jewish Canadian women. If they found out I had gone to the wedding, that would have been the end of me. If Simon's young friends were going to be anywhere, waiting for us, that's where they'd be – at the wedding with the Justice of the Peace right there ready to marry off the next runaway couple. We'd all get married off in one fell swoop, no chuppah to speak of and certainly no herring for the reception afterward. Just some quick, nothing ceremony and then hopping on the plane to catch another plane out of Vancouver. Never to be Canadian again.

That's not what happened, of course. Simon was the only Japanese man there. In fact, had Norma, Marilyn and I not been there, they'd have had no guests at all. We all brought flowers and pretended like we were brides-maids, even though Cheryl had said she didn't want any. I think any semblance of a normal wedding reminded her that it wasn't, and made her feel sad because her parents had basically thrown her out of the house when they found out who she was in love with. Her parents all but sat shiva – sitting in their living room, wringing their hands, crying on their friends' shoulders. They didn't go about ripping their clothes (Cheryl's parents weren't that reli-gious), but they cried and cried as if they had lost their daughter in some terrible accident.

My parents sat with them one evening after Cheryl and Simon announced their intentions. Then my parents came home, sat me down, and my mother – with (I swear to God) tears in her eyes – made me promise that I would never put them through what the Mosses were going through. I promised, only because what else was I supposed to do with my mother crying on my shoulder, as if she had lost me already?

The three of us stood behind Cheryl and Simon at that ceremony and tried to keep smiling. I think it's so impor-tant to have smiling people at your wedding. There are so many other occasions worth crying about, not weddings. I never understood people who cried at weddings. Funerals, yes, but weddings? Weddings are about futures, and start-ing out together, and new lives. And some people cry as if it's the end of everything they knew to be true. Norma and I did a good job of smiling; Marilyn looked like she needed some help. The one who really concerned me was Cheryl. She wore this lovely cream suit, with a pillbox hat with the tiniest net veil, and she had her makeup done all virginal with just the right amount of blush to make her look modest. But throughout the whole ceremony (which couldn't have lasted more than ten minutes), she stood there sniffling, her eyes welling up like cups about to overflow. She wouldn't let herself cry, though, and so instead, her nose turned all blotchy red, and her chin as well, which is what always happened when she was a kid and she started to cry. I tried to catch her eye to get her to smile because there was this photographer they had hired to take their pictures, and he was snapping away. The last thing she'd want ten years from now was to look at her wedding photos and see this terrified child of a bride looking like she didn't know which way was up. But I guess some things you can't hide.

Truth be told, we all liked Simon. He smiled a lot and his English was pretty good. After the wedding, we all went to Kelekis for a farewell meal. We sat at the booth near the back below the signed pictures of Monty Hall and Bachman and Cummings. They seemed to smile down on us, giving us their blessing. We ate foot-long hot dogs and french fries with vinegar. A far cry from the orange-almond salad and cold salmon they'd have had at a Jewish wedding, but then, who gets married for the food? Simon told us all we looked beautiful, but you could tell by the way he held Cheryl's hand that none of us were competition. He was decent, and that was enough for them to have my blessing. Although, to be honest, I don't know if I would have the guts to marry someone from Japan. Lose my family, move off somewhere totally foreign, different language, different customs. It sounded appealing enough, sometimes, but not in any real way. Besides, I knew how hard it was to patch a family back up once it had been torn apart.

Cheryl started to cry again as she and Simon climbed into the taxi to head off to the airport. She had so little on her – only what she could manage to take out of her room in a hurry before her father literally threw her out the back door (instead of the front, so as not to cause a scene). Simon promised that she needed nothing. He had everything waiting for her in Japan. They were going to live the life she had always dreamed of. He was going to stay in the jewellery business, and she was going to teach English. They would have a big family, and she would be a wonderful wife and mother. He had a house all ready for her, and his family couldn't wait to meet her. It's not so bad, I thought, holding her like I held my mother a few evenings before, as she cried on my shoulder. You lose one family, you gain another. They'd look after her. And how many of us get the chance at a new life, anyway? I tried to tell her these things as she left bits of her makeup smudged into my tangerine suit. I thought it was funny how Cheryl's tears were probably falling in the same place my mother's had. Only Cheryl felt much smaller in my arms, more like a kitten.

After we waved them off, we went back to Norma's to change. Norma and I talked on and on about how beautiful and brave Cheryl was, making her sound like a heroine. Like someone who did what she pleased. It was Marilyn who finally said that we all knew that wasn't really the way things were, and that Cheryl was just as trapped now as she had been in her own home.

'She's not going to have any more freedom where she's going than she had just down the street from here. Only now she won't be able to speak the language, she'll have a family who doesn't know her and a husband who's going to expect her to make babies for him for the next twenty years. You ask me? She's made the biggest mistake of her life.'

Marilyn was never much of a romantic.

That summer, whenever the three of us got together, the topic of conversation always turned back to Cheryl. What was she doing right this minute? What did her home look like? What was she eating? Wearing? Speaking? Sometime during the conversation, Marilyn always managed to pipe in with something like, 'Wonder if she's pregnant yet?' Marilyn had plans to go to law school, so I suppose it was a good thing that she always saw the other side of the story.

That was the other thing we talked about that summer, our own plans. Marilyn was going to do her BA in history, and then she was off to law school. Norma was going to be a teacher, and she wanted to marry Perry Goldberg, who had been her boyfriend since we were thirteen. I was going to do my BSc in physics and study the solar system. Maybe I'd even be the first woman on the moon. The Americans had already got there. I told the girls I wanted to move to Florida and work for NASA. They both smiled, and Marilyn said, 'Well, I guess someone has to.'

'Why shouldn't it be me?' I asked.

Marilyn shrugged. 'I don't know. I guess I never thought of you as someone so daring.'

Of course, I couldn't think of anything daring enough to say back.

'If you want a profession, be a teacher or a nurse,' my mother said when she found out. 'Studying Martians is not a profession.'

I tried to get ahead with my course reading by doing some over the summer. My mother would make a point of coming upstairs to my room while I was studying and saying something like, 'You know, I was talking to Sissy the other day, the one who has a daughter who's a teacher? And her daughter was telling her that the schools really need more women who can teach the sciences to these kids. Of course, I thought of you.'

'Of course.'

'All I'm saying is that you could consider it, Beth. You need to be realistic in your life plans.'

Some afternoons, I took my textbooks and escaped to Carrie's apartment and read at her dining table, while she worked at her sewing machine in the living room.

'Did you know,' I said, 'that planets, moons, asteroids and meteoroids shine with reflected light? That's why they don't twinkle the way stars do.'

Carrie was hemming a pair of pants for my mother. She didn't look up from the machine. 'I did know that,' she said. 'Your uncle said something about that to me once.'

'It's not fair that he knew so much and never had a chance to use his knowledge. It just seems like such a waste.'

'It is,' she said. She held up the pants in front of her so that the legs dangled evenly. 'The hardest part about losing him was knowing how much potential he had.'

I crossed my arms and lay my head on the table. 'I need to get away, Carrie. I need to get out of here, to get away from Mum, and become something.'

Carrie ripped out one of her stitches and placed the pants back under the sewing machine. She spoke with three pins sticking out of her mouth. 'I don't think staying here means you won't become something, Beth. What you do is up to you, not your mother, and that doesn't change whether you're here or halfway around the world.'

'But haven't you ever wanted to see the world, Carrie?' I asked. 'Aren't you curious?'

She took the pins out of her mouth and finished the hem, this time satisfied. 'Look, Beth, by all means spread your wings. All I'm saying is don't forget how to fly home.'

*

At the end of the summer, almost two months since Cheryl left for Japan, I came home to find my mother changing the bedroom sheets in Sarah's old room.

'Your aunt is coming home to stay with us for a while,' she said. 'I don't want to hear a word from you about it. She needs her peace.'

Auntie Sarah needed a lot more than peace. She needed a good knock over the head. It had been two years since she left Uncle David and Jade to run off around Canada and the United States, pretending to be an actress and a singer. Sarah always had crazy ideas, but no one ever thought she would do anything with them. My cousin Jade spent hundreds of nights calling out for her mum. After a couple of months, she stopped. In fact, she stopped saying much of anything. Jade and David: the silent father and daughter.

My mother not only made up the bed for my disappearing aunt, but she also dusted the room, Sarah's old dresser and her vanity table.

'You really think she deserves all this effort?' I stood in the doorway and surveyed the room, which now smelled like vinegar and lemon.

'Beth, I don't want you to be ridiculous,' my mother said. She wiped the top of the chest of drawers. It looked as if she'd just painted it. 'I would do this for any guest.'

After a pause, she continued. 'I don't know how long your aunt will need to be with us, but I think we need to encourage her to stay as long as she likes. She needs our help.'

'She needs a psych ward,' I mumbled. Mum didn't respond to that. I'm not sure if she didn't hear me or if she did and agreed, but didn't want to say.

My mother did a lot of baking for Sarah, and the house smelled of a new cake every afternoon for the week leading up to her arrival. I complained to Carrie that Mum was wasting her time, but Carrie said, 'In everything, we have to believe we've done the best we could.'

After Norma and I shopped for school supplies together later that day, we spent the rest of the afternoon sitting on her bedroom floor dividing our pencils and notebooks.

'I think she's adventurous, your Auntie Sarah,' Norma said. 'I could never do what she did, go and chase a dream, trying to make something of herself.'

'Yeah, leave her husband and daughter behind. She's a real hero.'

'But she's come back,' Norma said. 'She's trying to make it work.'

'Right,' I said, counting my pencils and Bic pens.

Norma had become what people described as 'pleasant.' She had really straight teeth and straight blond hair like gold thread, which curled out just above her shoulders in a perfect flip. Perry was totally in love with her and was forever sending her little notes and cards that said things like, 'To my little doll,' and 'For the love of my life.' She stuck them up on her wall around her bed so that she could read each and every one before falling asleep. By that summer, there were thirty-two.

Marilyn had become a proper feminist. She wore her hair really short, like a five-year-old boy, and she refused to wear a bra even though she was close to a double-D. One day, that summer, she managed to convince us all to spend the day braless.

'You will feel freer than you've ever felt before! The bra is just another way of men confining women,' she said.

So, not wanting to be confined, I walked around for a day braless. However, because I bounced everywhere (on the street, the bus, in the shops), I had more men staring at me, whistling and offering me evenings of passion than I ever had before.

I was neither pleasant nor a feminist. I couldn't become a hippie because my hair wouldn't grow long enough. I certainly believed that women should have the same pay and opportunities as men, but I was never convinced that men were to blame for all of our insecurities (which is what Marilyn always claimed). I could hold a decent conversation, and I knew how to make a nice lemon bundt cake. But I wasn't waiting to graduate so that I could get married and have babies. And I wasn't going to become a dental hygienist so that I could marry a dentist. Norma told me she worried about my future and how I would possibly be looked after. Marilyn called me a moderate, as if it were a curse. I spent a lot of that summer thinking about Cheryl and how lucky she was to have escaped all of this labelling.

Sarah moved in with us one week after my mother made up the spare bedroom. She came by Greyhound, and my father picked her up from the station. When they walked through the front door, I didn't recognize her. Sarah had always been glowing – her skin, her hair and especially her eyes, which used to be a deep coffee brown. Funny how two hard years could change the colour of her eyes. Now they were faded, dull and almost grey.

Also, she was skinny. She had no breasts left, and her arms were limp pipes at the sides of her body. She leaned against the wall in the front hall while she took off her shoes. She didn't look at any of us as she did this, slowly sliding the backs of the red pumps off of her heels and then letting them drop to the floor. And then once her shoes came off, Sarah started to cry. She stood in our hallway in her stocking feet, and her shoulders started to shake. She put her face in her hands, and I wondered if she wished she could disappear. My mother wrapped her up in her arms and held her so that Sarah's face was pressed against her breasts.

Over the following week, life was like this: Sarah walking around in bare feet, Mum trying to feed her things like vegetable soup, peanut butter sandwiches, weak tea. Sometimes Sarah stayed in her bed for most of the day, and Mum brought her meals on wooden trays. Sometimes she came into the kitchen and sat at the table, looking into her bowl, studying her reflection, holding her spoon as if it were a weight. She didn't speak at all during this time, except to answer some of Mum's simple questions. Yes, she is comfortable in the bed. No, it's not too warm in the house. Yes, a bowl of soup is all she needs.

But if Mum tried to broach the bigger subjects (Jade and David, Montreal, why did she come back? why did she go away?), Sarah's face turned empty. She would sit there drinking her tea or eating her soup as if nothing had been asked. As if she knew nothing about these questions. As if they were asked in another language.

I was starting university that week. Norma, Marilyn and I had all been accepted at the University of Manitoba. We spent our first week eating lunch together, but knew we wouldn't be able to keep it up. Marilyn was already involved in student politics ('We need to hear more women's voices on this campus!'), and Norma was getting anxious that she and Perry were never going to get to see each other with his busy pre-med schedule. Lunches might be the only time they had together. By the end of the week, I was eating on my own and thinking a lot about Cheryl. I would eat my tuna sandwich and watch the groups of students sitting around me in circles on the floor, their backs against the concrete walls. Lots of laughing. She'd have liked this, I thought, finding a group of students she could speak French with on her breaks (Cheryl had always been a good student, particularly with languages) and share dreams of going to France, studying abroad. Cheryl started sending us postcards at the end of the summer, and that's what made me think of her. We each had a card of the women with white faces, dressed in kimonos, on the front, and some two-line inscription of how beautiful everything was on the back. And how Simon was fine.

'She's miserable,' Marilyn said after getting hers. Norma thought she was fine; she had a good marriage, and she was making things work (Norma would often say things like this around Marilyn). Earlier in the summer, I might have agreed with Norma. But when I got my postcard, it gave me shivers. I can't really say why. All I know is I picked it up, read the back and felt cold. Like the words were poking me.

On Thursdays I only had class until 2 p.m., which meant I got home early. A couple of weeks after Sarah moved in, I came home, and Mum had gone out grocery shopping. Sarah was sitting in the living room, staring out the front window, curled under a blue and pink log cabin quilt. Since moving in with us, she had not left the house. She did not answer the phone when it rang, and if someone came to the door, she ran upstairs. David had not been by to see her, and she did not ask about Jade. She sat with her head supported by her upright arm, resting her elbow on the back of the couch. A couple of the neighbours' kids played on tricycles across the street.

I walked past the living room into the kitchen, but she called out to me. 'A letter came for you today,' she said.

She had it in her hand when I came back into the living room. She was wearing one of my father's old plaid shirts and a pair of blue, flannel pyjama bottoms. By her side was *Good Housekeeping* magazine with a picture on the front of a smiling, young mother and a glowing baby with plump, pink lips and long, adorable lashes.

'It looks interesting,' she continued. 'From Japan. How do you know someone in Japan?'

'Cheryl's there,' I said, taking it from her and opening

the flap carefully. The paper was really thin, which made it cheaper to mail. There were four pages, double-sided, and Cheryl wrote very small.

'Really? That's neat. Is she having a good time? Japan must be very exciting.'

Cheryl's pages were full of smudges where teardrops had fallen. I skimmed through the letter, and I could hear her crying about how she missed us and her family and how hard it was for her to fit in.

'She's miserable,' I said, folding the letter up and putting it in my pocket. 'She's made the biggest mistake of her life.'

'Oh,' Sarah said. She sunk back into the couch and started to look out the window again. 'What makes you say that?'

'She's left everyone who loves her to chase some ridiculous dream. And now she's realizing it's not real.' I just couldn't resist. I watched Sarah's lips tighten and relax and then tighten again. But she didn't say anything.

It was only when I was back in the kitchen, pouring myself a Coke, that she answered me. She had followed after me into the kitchen, but I didn't know until she spoke.

'It's not easy,' she said. I waited for her to say more, but after a pause she just repeated herself. 'It's just not easy.'

I felt cold and hot and full of lumps wanting to erupt out of my body.

'Like hell it's not!' I snapped. I turned around, and Sarah was still wrapped in the blanket standing small by the table. She put her hand on the back of the chair for support. Her hair was tied back loosely off her face, but a few strands fell out in frizzy wisps.

'You shouldn't speak like that,' she said to me in a whisper.

'And you shouldn't abandon the people who love you.'

She turned to go upstairs, but then stopped and faced me again.

'Don't you judge me, Beth. And don't think it's going to be any easier for you to leave. Your dreams are no different than mine. And if you do go, I've got news for you: it won't be any easier for you to come back.'

We stared at each other for a long time, and then she left to go upstairs. I turned around and knocked my glass over by accident. My Coke spilled all over the counter and fizzled as it dripped onto the floor. As I wiped it up, I cried for missing Cheryl and for hating Simon for making her miserable. I cried for my aunt I knew I would never be able to trust, and I missed the time when I thought I could. And then I wondered if things can change, why don't they ever change back to the way they were?

That night, really late, Sarah packed her bags and left her room. I heard her on the stairs, and I watched her from my bedroom window as she climbed into a cab. I think she saw me, but I don't know for sure. She certainly didn't wave.

I told the girls about Cheryl's letter. Marilyn said I told you so, and Norma didn't believe me.

'Everything is hard at the beginning,' she said, as if she was an expert on trying new things. 'She just needs to be patient.'

The three of us had decided to eat lunch together once a week on Wednesday in the student lounge. Marilyn said that would work all right until elections, and then she would be busy, but she expected us both to help her out. And Norma said she thought she could manage once a week, but she would have to monitor Perry's schedule.

It took me a while, but I decided to write Cheryl back.

Dear Cheryl, I wrote, *We all miss you like crazy. But don't even think about coming back right now. We won't let you until you know enough to teach us all Japanese . . .*

14

When my mother was my age, she had already found my father. They had their first date when she was eighteen and he was twenty at a bonfire at Winnipeg Beach, where they sat beside each other roasting marshmallows and hotdogs on sticks. If you ask my father he will tell you that my mother wore a red sweater, the colour of valentines, and that she had her hair clipped up to the side of her head. She had the tiniest ears he had ever seen, and he spent the evening trying so hard not to touch them. My father will also tell you that although there must have been twenty other people at the bonfire, he does not remember anyone else. From the minute he saw my mother, it was as if everyone else disappeared with the wind.

My mother remembers things differently. She liked my father's laugh, and he told funny jokes. When she came to sit down, he laid out his jacket so that she didn't have to sit on the ground and dirty her skirt. She said he was skinnier than she imagined her husband would be. And a little awkward. She wanted to kiss him to stop him from being so nervous, and that kept her from looking right at him for the whole night. She worried that if she looked up at his eyes, nothing would stop her from leaning over and covering his lips with hers.

'You should go to some mixed events,' my mother said to me once when I was home on a Saturday night.

'I see a lot of boys at school,' I said to her.

'I mean Jewish events. You're not going to meet someone in your classes. Don't people have get-togethers any
more? For kids your age?'

'Sure, Mum. We play pin-the-tail-on-the-donkey and
we swing at piñatas.'

That was usually all it took to get her to throw up her
hands and leave the room, saying, 'I just want you to be
happy, Beth. That's all I'm thinking about.'

Other than my mother's new obsession with marriage,
life had become pretty predictable since Sarah left again.
Norma and Perry announced their intentions to get married the summer before Perry went into medical school
(we all knew he'd get in. His father and uncle were both
doctors). Marilyn won the elections at the university and
was so involved in school politics that she flew to New
York and Toronto to hear incredible speakers like Gloria
Steinem.

While Marilyn was pursuing politics and Norma was
pursuing the perfect bridal gown, I started to play baseball
and joined the university's recreational team. I was the
only Jew on the baseball team, and often the only one at
the games we played against other girls' teams, like the
St. Mary's Girls' School faculty or the YWCA Masters'
team. Afterward, when we would go out for something to
eat, often at a Salisbury House, I ordered french fries,
while the girls had cheeseburgers and milkshakes. And if
the other team joined us (because our games were only
ever friendly and non-competitive), and one of the other
girls asked me my name, I only ever said, 'Beth,' never
'Beth Levy.' It's not that anything dangerous would have
happened, and all of my teammates knew I was Jewish, I
just hated the insinuating questions that I knew would
follow.

'So you must live around Scotia, then?'

'My father knows a Jewish family on Wellington Crescent. They have this huge house. Where is your house?
What does your father do?'

And once, one of the Catholic girls took me aside and
said, 'I just want you to know that my family forgives the
Jews for what you did to Christ. You all seem so civilized
now.'

The girls wanted to have T-shirts made for our team,
personalized with each of our last names on the back. We
could be our team of Smith, Johnston, Gislason, Harris . . .
and Levy. I said I would only pay for my shirt if I had my
first name, and first name only, on the back. They all
thought that was ridiculous, until I made something up
about having a boyfriend and expecting to get married
and would have to change my name eventually. Then they
understood. In the end, we couldn't come up with the
money for the shirts anyway. But at least when I got up to
bat, the girls only chanted 'Beth.' Sometimes, when I hit
the ball, the crack echoed through their chants, and I
imagined it tearing my name apart while I ran from base
to base with the freedom of being nameless before the roar
of their appreciation. I hadn't felt that free since being
with Timothy.

That same year, Timothy and I ended up in a Canadian
history class together. We didn't sit beside each other. In
fact, he sat next to a girl I came to understand was his
girlfriend. They always walked in together, and sometimes
he would stir her coffee for her while she organized her
books before sitting down. She was petite with shoulder-
length blond hair and lashes made long by thick mascara.
Once I caught sight of her left wrist, and I noticed the
watch, a silver bangle with a delicate face and roman
numerals. He was like that, very traditional and appropriate. A watch was like a promise ring, something for her
to show her parents so that they wouldn't be concerned

that he was wasting her time. In class, while our professor spoke of French explorers, she would play with her watch, twisting it around and around her wrist, feeling the silver on every inch of her skin. Once I caught him lightly stroking the back of her neck. Her cheeks flushed at the feel of his fingers. I remembered that feeling, and wondered, if later, if before he dropped her off at home, if he would move his fingers to her delicate thighs, her hand resting on his hand, not sure whether to stop him or move him forward.

While my life became routine, it was my mother's turn to shine. That year she learned she was being honoured by the community at a fundraising dinner for her tireless charitable efforts. She would receive a plaque with her name on it, and we were all invited to sit at the VIP table (including Carrie, David and Jade) to listen to her speech about community viability, encouraging young people and building resources to ensure that our children and grandchildren could live proudly as Jews. She had finally made it.

The night before the awards dinner she was laying out outfits on her bed. She had three suits – one in olive green tweed, a brown wool she had bought for High Holidays, and an aquamarine polyester blend. She was trying each one on with their matching hats and wanted my opinion. For the aquamarine, she needed her girdle, which helped to fill out the cleavage she needed up top for the jacket's fit and brought her waist in by three inches. I sat on her bed while she changed, marvelling at her body with all its lumps and bumps. She had beautifully shaped calves, but her thighs reminded me of bread dough. Same with her breasts, which hung forward like deflated bagpipe sacks as she bent down to fit them into her one-piece girdle/bra contraption. Since I had recently taken up baseball, I was in pretty good shape. But I couldn't help wondering, as I watched her, when my body would go from being tanned and smooth, to this terrain like a lakeside beach – full of mounds and valleys.

The phone rang while she had her skirt done up, but not before she got her blouse on. I reached for it while she went to get her robe, as if whoever was calling could see her.

'Beth,' Sarah said on the other end, a bit crackly, 'can I speak with your mum?'

'Who is it?' my mother was mouthing to me. Sarah did not ask me how I was, how school was going, or whether I missed her (not that I would have expected her to on the last one). But there she was on the other end of the phone, calling us for the first time since she up and left us again, and she spoke to me like I was nothing more than my mother's secretary. So I passed the phone over to my now modestly robed executive mother and told her it was her youngest sister. And then I sat on the edge of the bed and sunk back into the pillows.

'Sarah?' my mother said, breathless. 'Sweetheart? Where are you? We miss you. Please come back. We can fix whatever's frightened you. Oh dear, it's so good to hear your voice.'

Mum waved me away, then. She sat on the bed with her back to me and leaned into her lap, covering her exposed ear to lock herself into this precious conversation. She waved me to the door and didn't watch as I went to my room to study. My father, never a regular synagogue-goer, was downstairs listening to one of his cantorial records, sitting on the light blue brocade sofa, his feet up on the matching ottoman. He was sipping his Scotch, closing his eyes and letting this man with his commanding, God-fearing voice, take him to a spiritual plane he could reach in no other way. I sat at the top of the stairs, half-listening to the Day of Atonement melodies and half-listening to my mother's voice behind me, rhythmically answering my aunt as she once and for all explained herself, but never actually asked for forgiveness.

After my mother got off the phone with Sarah, she walked past my room and down the stairs to my father, floating onto his spiritual plane. I heard her sitting, sinking into the couch, and her voice, high-pitched and wavering, which is how it sounds when she is trying hard not to cry.

'She's lost to us now,' I heard her say. 'And I don't think we can ever get her back.'

'She'll come back,' my father said. 'She knows we're here.'

'I feel like I've lost a daughter.'

'You haven't. She's a grown woman who is making her own choices. She always has. And you did everything you could for her as her sister.'

The cantor sang 'Adon Olam' with a fifty-person choir while my father moved to my mother's side. Someone in the choir had a voice like a piccolo, chiming above everyone else. My mother rested her head on my father's shoulder.

'She doesn't belong here anymore,' my father said, stroking her hair and her arm. 'She never really did.'

'Why do people have to move away to belong?' my mother asked. 'I would have taken her any way she wanted to be.'

My mother and I never finished our fashion consultation that evening. The next night, she chose her brown suit without asking me and decided against a hat after she had had her hair done in big set curls. She looked like a president's wife. I wore a camel tweed pantsuit and only cared to put on lipstick when she said I looked washed out. Carrie came over to ride with us to the Fort Garry Hotel. My mother's gala dinner was being served in one of the smaller ballrooms on the seventh floor. She and Dad had been there last year when Rita Hornstein was being honoured. She had talked all the next day about the high ceilings, the gold accented pillars and the waiters who served everything with white gloves. I had to remind myself that my mother never thought that white gloves would exist in her world, at least, not worn by someone serving her stuffed Cornish game hens. That is what she told Carrie when they spoke that afternoon before Carrie arrived at our house.

'Did you ever think,' she laughed, her voice spinning with excitement, 'that we would be a part of all of this?'

I don't know exactly what Carrie said to her rhetorical question, but Mum continued to laugh off her answer. 'Don't be ridiculous, Carrie. You are just as much a part of this as the rest of us.'

Carrie arrived in a purple palazzo pantsuit she had made herself. Lately, she had taken to using extra fabric from her homemade clothes to make scarves and other accents. This time, she wore a paisley scarf with thick fringes she had tied herself. Carrie had grown wider as she grew older and told me once that she was tired of old women's clothes. It was not uncommon to see Carrie walking to the store in orange-panelled trousers with a light denim jacket, which she had accented with lace and ribbon. She bought herself new glasses, with lenses that no longer looked permanently clouded-over pink from sun exposure and dust. She collected necklaces and had friends who travelled and brought her back freshwater pearls from Florida, or stones strung on black satin rope from their Indian safaris. Carrie talked a lot now about making trips like these, her face almost always animated with a bit of blush. Her cheeks flushed even more when she thumbed through the travel guides she took out of the library on Europe, Mexico and Israel.

She came up the stairs to see me while I brushed my hair and stared at myself, wondering if I looked presentable.

'You're looking very nice,' she said to me from the doorway.

I was. Even if I hadn't put on lipstick, my pantsuit showed off my waist and hips. I was stockier than Sarah had been at my age, but I preferred to think of myself as athletic. I didn't wear makeup because I preferred to look in the mirror and see my naked face. I wanted people to see me for who I was.

Ever since Carrie put on weight, her knees had started to bother her, and she was using a cane to get up and down stairs or to walk long distances. She called it her *shtecken*, or sometimes 'Herbie' when she was in a silly mood. That evening, she leaned on Herbie while coming into my room to sit on the bed. The weather had been unseasonably damp for November, and Carrie had been complaining that if she wanted an Atlantic climate, she'd have moved to Boston a long time ago.

'You're looking nice,' I said back. 'Very regal.'

'I figured it was about time.'

She watched me scowl at myself in the mirror.

'How long do you think this evening will last?' I asked her.

'Oh, I don't know. You know how these things are. We like to make our own feel honoured and special. It's your mother's time. I guess it will go on for as long as that takes.'

'I have a lot of studying to do. Do you think I'll be able to come home early?'

'Beth,' she said, 'your mother really needs you right now. Don't do anything that would make her regret this evening in any way. She has worked a long time for this.'

Everything about me seemed to sink when she said that. I kept seeing myself at this table of glowing, colourful people, in a room full of idle chatter and self-congratu-latory conversation, and I'm sitting there, translucent. And everyone around us is wondering, *Is that really Goldie's daughter? Is she it?*

In the car ride there, I picked at the lint on my pant leg. Carrie sat beside me in the back and looked out the window. Once we got into downtown and drove by the legislature building, she sighed and said, 'Aren't those flowers just beautiful? We really do such a nice job of keeping our city pretty.'

My mother answered her that she was right. My father watched for parking, and I shook my head.

My Uncle David and cousin Jade were waiting for us on the steps as we drove up. Dad dropped us off before going to park the car, and Jade waved wildly from where they stood. At six years old she was now nothing short of stunning: long, dark hair tied half back in a ribbon; matching bittersweet chocolate eyes with baby doll lashes. She smiled much more now as the memory of her mother began to fade. Life as she had almost always known it consisted of her, her father and sometimes all of us. We all loved her ferociously, each of us with our own nicknames for her and special activities she did only with us. David had begun to date again, and often I took Jade Sundays so that he could be out for lunch with a sensible woman, someone maybe only a little bit older than me who had likely been engaged once before, but never married. There was one woman he saw quite a bit of now, and Jade sometimes spoke of her as 'The Margaret Who Brings Me Barbie Dolls.'

Jade gave us each a hug, and she let me swing her with her arms around my neck.

'Careful, Beth,' my mother warned. 'You don't want to make her dizzy before she eats.'

'I'm fine, Auntie Goldie!' she said before David took her from me.

'Yes, but we promised Auntie Goldie that we would behave all grown up this evening, didn't we,' he said to her.

As I let her go, I realized that Jade knew nothing better than how to act all grown up. We had all gotten so used to her silence. Now, at six years old, she was starting to shed it. It was as if we were worried that her words were linked to memories that we had all been trying to keep tucked away from her until she got older.

Jade smoothed out her skirt and took my mother's hand. 'I am all grown up. See? Margaret bought me these nice new shoes.'

The ballroom was everything my mother described it to be. Women wore their hair up in stiff beehives (a few even had flowers stuck in for accents). The men wore thick, black-rimmed glasses and smoked cigarettes, laughing loudly, their hands on the backs of their beehived wives. There was a piano player in the background on a baby grand, gently coaxing us with Gershwin and Rodgers and Hammerstein. My father hummed along with 'Summertime,' until my mother needed to introduce him to women from Hadassah he hadn't met, or a community council member. My father shook all their hands, keeping his other hand always on my mother's back. It was not to steady her; she didn't need him there. She could have worked that room with all the charm in her little finger. People flocked to her. He kept his hand there as if to connect himself to this incredible source of energy and so that his quiet self wouldn't get lost in this sea of well-wishers.

The rest of us took our places at my mother's table. We were seated at the front (though there was no head table) with easy access to the podium. There were, I figured, 150 people in this room, all sitting around elegant white tables with sparkling water goblets and small silver trays of pickled cucumbers and miniature onions. Carrie had already started eating from the tray. Jade reached for a bun from the bread basket, but David caught her arm.

'Not until Auntie Goldie sits back down,' he said.

'But Auntie Carrie's already started,' she pointed out.

'We wait for Auntie Goldie,' he said to Jade.

My mother finally took her seat, and still we had visitors coming to our table all throughout the salad course. All of the women from the Monday Group were there with their husbands, and each came in her own time to place her hand on my mother's own carefully manicured hand and wish her mazel tov on such an auspicious occasion.

'You remember Beth,' she would say to them, opening her arm toward me, across the table.

'Of course! How are you, Beth-dear? What is it you are studying now? Astrology?'

'Astronomy,' I'd correct them.

'Yes. Something to do with the stars. Very unusual for a girl, isn't it.'

'Beth is very talented at science,' my father would say.

'She'll make an excellent teacher,' my mother would add. 'She's been told that many times.'

That's not true. I was never told that. But it was pointless trying to correct her.

'Well,' someone would pipe up, 'young women today are really trying to spread their wings all over the place.'

'Yes,' said my mother. 'But we don't have to worry about Beth. She'll always be here to look after us in our old age.'

And then everyone would laugh and talk about their retirement plans, minor health concerns, etc., while I picked at my salad and wondered what would get stuck in my teeth first – a piece of lettuce or a poppy seed from the dressing?

The waiters circled around us like penguins in their long

white coats and black pants. I waited for Dick Van Dyke to come out from the kitchen and join them all in a tap dancing, cartoon routine. Then, after my plate was cleared and we were waiting for our hot leek and garlic soup, I saw Timothy serving up tables at the back.

He wore the white gloves with the buttons by the wrist. He also had his blond hair slicked back (all of the waiters had to grease back their hair) and was wearing new glasses, wire-rimmed, which you could barely tell were there, all delicate on his face. Timothy was serving his table wine, red or white (I had, at this point, already had two glasses of red), and looked each of his guests in the eye when he asked them what they would like. Something about this stuffy evening combined with the dry red wine made my heart race. I kept looking at him, remembering what it was like to have my skin burning from the inside.

'Ladies and gentlemen, good evening,' the host speaker began. 'I want to welcome you to this most special event where our community has the opportunity to honour its own. In this busy world of politics and world events, we forget sometimes about our local heroes, those that make the heart of this community tick. Those without whom we could not be as successful a people as we are. It pleases me today that you have all chosen to be here to honour our community members, and I would like to applaud you for your dedication.'

Everyone applauded along with him. What would happen, I wondered, if one day we all received a little plaque with our names on it? A little something to say congratulations for sticking it out this far. Winnipeg would be nowhere without you. Then we wouldn't need awards evenings like this. Everyone would be looked after, and we could spend our evenings watching *The Brady Bunch*, which is what we all would rather have been doing, anyway.

'Our community awards this evening cover the young,

the old, and some in-between for whom age is not really an issue.' (Light laughter here.) 'And it is my extreme pleasure to introduce them all to you. I'd ask each of our recipients to stand. You will hear from each of them later in the evening when they give their own addresses of appreciation.'

Timothy was busy handing out soup while all this was going on. I had mine already, but didn't like the smell, nor the colour of it. Neither did Jade, apparently, who had already filled her small stomach with bread rolls once my mother sat down and gave her permission. Jade now sat a bit slouched in her chair, laying her head on Carrie's shoulder and playing with the tassels of her purple scarf.

'Mrs Goldie Levy has been a pillar in this community for more years than she would like us to count,' continued the host.

My mother stood smiling (but not too straight, so as not to appear immodest). Many of her friends nodded in agreement with each of the speaker's praises. He made it sound like she had created the Winnipeg Jewish women's movement. Dignified in her brown suit, I tried to picture her at my age marrying my father in my grandparents' tiny living room, nobody noticing her as she walked to the grocery store to do her shopping in those early days. She never knew what a suit felt like until she was into her mid-thirties. Never knew, until then, about good pantyhose and proper, polished shoes.

I looked around again when the speaker moved onto the next, and last, recipient, and there was Timothy, looking straight at me from the back of the room. I nearly turned away, but he smiled and nodded before I could. We hadn't acknowledged each other all year, and yet it felt so natural and right that here, away from school, away from his girlfriend and her watch, we could at least be pleasant from a distance. I waved, and he went into the kitchen.

*

Sometime after the waiters were clearing our dinner plates away (dinner had turned out to be roast beef, whipped potatoes and green peas – all my father's favourites; he ate some of Jade's as well), I excused myself to get some fresh air. From the seventh floor, you could have access to a balcony that overlooked Main Street and the train station. When I went out, there was a passenger train backing away, but I couldn't tell if it was headed for Toronto or Regina. I leaned on the railing and tried to imagine being inside, being carried away over the rails, the rhythmic clipping of the wheels against the tracks, falling asleep while the city receded farther and farther behind me, the lights twinkling and becoming dimmer.

'Do you want a cigarette?' a voice asked me.

I turned around slowly. Tim was standing there, holding a cigarette out to me. He was sweaty from the heat in the kitchen and the unforgiving work. I took the cigarette from him. I knew he would light it for me, and I could lean in toward him while he did. He smelled like fresh laundry and sour skin.

'I didn't know you were a waiter,' I told him. We both shivered, and I could see our breath in the cold night air.

'It's a good part-time job. I need the money for tuition. Just until I get my teaching degree.'

'You'll be a good teacher.' I flicked the ashes over the balcony and blew the smoke out of the side of my mouth. Marilyn had taught me how to smoke one afternoon in her backyard while we were in high school. Her parents were out looking at buying an above-ground swimming pool. She laughed at me when I coughed and turned a little green, but then she got me to relax by imagining myself somewhere like Monte Carlo, lounging on a deck chair, a femme fatale with red toenails and dark sunglasses, surveying my potential suitors around the pool, deciding which one of them would be next.

'My mother thinks I should be a teacher,' I said. He laughed, and the smoke came out of his mouth in a small cloud.

'But what do you think?' he asked. His eyes were sea blue, and they locked into mine so that I couldn't look away.

'Oh, you know. I don't know. Right now I just want to fly to the moon.'

'So you should, Mrs Armstrong. So you should.'

I leaned my back against the railing and studied Tim while he watched the tracks. He took another puff and this time let the smoke out in a thin trail from the side of his mouth.

'Isn't it amazing how this country was built by the railway?' he said. 'And to think that this city was once considered the Gateway to the West. We were some people's Jerusalem. Can you imagine?'

'You've been paying too much attention in our history class,' I said.

'It takes my mind off of you,' he answered back, not looking at me, but knowing full well I was now staring straight at him.

He smiled slightly and shifted slowly to face me while I drew circles in the imaginary dust of the balcony floor.

'You're looking good,' he said. 'Who are you with now?'

'No one,' I answered. 'I'm busy. School, studying. You know. Your girlfriend is pretty.'

He nodded, but didn't say anything. This was like a train, I thought, my heart moving faster, the conversation carrying me farther away from my mother's accolades and the constant reminder of everything I was not doing. I shifted closer to him, and he reached over to run his hand along the outside of my thigh and then over to the inside of my pant leg.

'I would have taken you to the moon,' he whispered,

near the top of my ear. His words tickled. 'I would have taken you anywhere.'

'Beth!'

My mother was standing in the doorway framed by the light from dozens of crystal chandeliers. Tim and I jumped away from each other, and he dropped his cigarette before brushing past her to get back to the kitchen. This was not like a train, I thought, standing there abandoned and facing my mother who looked as though she were being backlit on a stage. I watched Tim run away, and I thought of being left by the trackside, not knowing where to go from here.

'The speeches are beginning,' she said. 'I need you in here with me. Now.'

I dropped my cigarette and crushed it with the toe of my shoe. She stopped me before letting me pass and said, 'This is not finished.'

Then I followed her back inside where she faced 150 captive faces and spoke of the importance of being role models for our children.

'If we don't show them the value in community, then who will? Who will be our legacy if we don't teach them?'

She held onto her applause, along with her plaque, the whole ride home while I let myself get dizzy by staring into the passing street lights.

'Do you have oatmeal for brains?' my mother asked me when we got home. She shut my bedroom door, while my father fell asleep in their bed, mercifully many feet away. 'What if I had been your father? Or one of the women we know in the community? What were you thinking?'

Nothing. I didn't answer her, but I thought, isn't it nice sometimes not to think at all?

'Did you even know that boy?'

'He's a friend from school.'

She laughed. 'Last time I checked there were more appropriate ways to interact with friends.'

'Nothing was going to happen with Timothy. Don't worry.'

'Oh, good. I'm so glad to know that my daughter thinks having an acquaintance stroke her inner thigh in public is nothing.'

'Give it a rest, Mum. You caught me, okay? I can guarantee you that it won't happen again.'

I sat on my bed and pulled back the covers, but she placed her hand on my wrist, firmly.

'Don't you sass me. As long as you live under my roof, you will live by my expectations and act accordingly. Is that understood?'

'That's rich!' I snapped. 'You have a sister who's abandoned her family, is sleeping around with God-knows-who and you're begging her to come back. You have another sister who got pregnant and had a baby that nobody ever talks about. I get caught with one guy's hand on my leg and all of a sudden I'm the big disappointment?'

She sat down next to me, slowly, the bed creaking as she settled, and looked straight ahead as though her thoughts were lined up in front of her and she was filing them, in order. She clasped and unclasped her hands while she thought and then smoothed her dressing gown before she turned to me to speak.

'You need to understand something,' she said, now much quieter and very controlled. 'In this family, we do not give up on people because they have made mistakes. You have a lot to learn. Your Auntie Sarah had been punished plenty. She didn't come home for more. As for Carrie, you don't have the right to judge something you don't know the half of.'

'I know plenty.'

She laughed and then sighed.

'Bethy,' she whispered, 'I see you watching us and I know the stories you create in your head. You've got to remember that you can't ever know it all. That's why we have to accept the ones we love just because we love them.'

She reached over and pushed my hair back. She still had her eye makeup on, green shadow now faded against her eyelids, as though her skin were tinted.

'And I just want you to always act in a way that will let you love yourself.'

'You mean a way that will let you love me,' I said. She didn't respond, so after a moment I added, 'You can't expect me to live here forever.'

'I don't. But I do expect you to know your responsibilities. And always live like you haven't forgotten them.'

'Mum, I am tired of you always being the one who tells me what my responsibilities are. If it means that I have to leave here, so that I can live my own life, then I will.'

She laughed. 'I have never doubted that you will lead your life as you want. And it doesn't matter where you live.'

'I don't believe you. I don't think you mean that.'

'And I don't think you give me enough credit.'

That night, I sat staring at the wallpaper that was beginning to peel at the edge of the ceiling and thought about Sarah. I wondered when she had stopped loving herself and if, by being away, she was learning how to again. I pictured her in her silk dress, and the way the material would stroke her skin when she swayed slightly while singing. I remembered being twelve and wearing that dress, my body warm from the inside when I pretended to be her. That's what it felt like to have Tim touch me, like my bones were melting and, if I touched him back, maybe his would too. My mother thought only she knew what it meant to love oneself, but I knew then that every night, Sarah was on a stage somewhere, loving herself in a way she never could have been loved here. I envied her for knowing what she needed and then leaving when nobody would have told her she should.

15

I don't know about love. I am not afraid to admit that. I know about loving my aunts and my parents, but not that true love someone feels, or that deep attachment to a child or that all-encompassing fire for a lover, I know I haven't experienced those yet. Timothy was not love. Passion, maybe, but nothing more. Growing up, I waited for those experiences like I waited for a lot of things. I romanticized what my life would be like when I found them. As a child, I imagined my life with my faceless husband and my faceless children like a fuzzy television show. This, I knew from my parents, is where I would end up. This is what Successful Jewish Women did. Maybe they also worked, but first and foremost, they had families. My mother had become a Successful Jewish Woman. While young, my Auntie Sarah showed all the potential to get there as well, but chose not to. My Auntie Carrie did not, and no one was disappointed when she never did.

Carrie still had her loyal customers. She had one or two women who even brought in their bridal gowns for their daughters. On her lunch break, Carrie would sit at the lunch counter and eat a tuna fish sandwich I had made for her. She would pass on stories to me about these women, in a low voice so that no one else heard. One of the bridal gowns she worked on had to be let out around the waist rather urgently because the daughter was expecting a baby seven months after her wedding date.

'The mother and the girl come in,' Carrie said, 'and they just hand me the gown saying, 'It doesn't fit around her stomach.' Like I mismeasured it in the first place. So the daughter puts it on, and she can't do it up in the back. Her breasts have grown too big, and her tummy has that rounded shape already. So I say, 'Oh, yes, I see. Sorry for the mistake.''

I nodded, quietly listening and remembering the stories Carrie would tell me when I was a little girl.

'"Just fix it," the mother says to me.' Carrie used her hands now to tell stories. When imitating the mother, she pointed her finger in my face, slightly crooked as if arthritic. She shook her head, laughing at her own memory. 'I didn't know if she meant for me to fix the dress or her daughter's condition! I almost said back, "Sorry, I don't offer that kind of service here."'

'Carrie! You didn't!'

'No, of course I didn't! But can you imagine her face if I had?' She laughed again, and then took a bite of the sandwich. 'Anyway,' she continued, her mouth full, 'her daughter looked pretty pleased with herself. I get the feeling it wasn't an accident.'

'Gawd,' I said back, wiping off the crumbs from the counter. 'When did you become such a gossip?'

'Oh, Beth, come on. I'm only having a little fun. Life is too short.'

I watched her customers coming in and out of the back room. She still had the knack of making them walk taller in their well-fit clothes. Many gave her tips, which she kept in an envelope in her sewing kit. She was saving for a trip to Mexico. She said that if she made enough, she would see about taking me along. I told her to save her money for something else that she wanted, and not to waste it on me. She told me my company was never a waste, and for the first time, I realized that I had something to offer her in exchange for the stories she had been giving me all my life.

Near the end of the day, I was cleaning the back counter when a woman walked into the store. She was about my mother's age, very petite with a round face and a pageboy haircut. She came up to the lunch counter and asked me where to go for alterations. I pointed to the back door and then watched as she knocked and let herself in the back. She carried two garment bags, hanging limp over her arm. I remember that her cheeks were very pink and her eyes were aquamarine green, which I had never seen before. I wondered if she was Icelandic.

My father had asked me to close up the store so that he could go get a badly needed haircut. When the Icelander left, I called back to Carrie, asking if she was done for the day. She didn't answer me, so I went around to check on her.

'Carrie?' I asked. She was behind the changing screen, running her fingers along a suit dress the woman had brought in.

'Are you done for today?' I asked again.

'Yes,' she answered. She didn't look at me. She was staring at the dress, but blankly, as if seeing something completely different.

'What's wrong?' I asked, as she stroked the fabric. The dress was brown polyester, with brown ribbon panels down the front on either side of the buttons and button holes. It had a straight skirt and was the kind of dress you would wear to a first interview, or a first day on the job. Neither Carrie nor I could ever fit into the dress. The woman was about the size of a ten-year-old pre-pubescent girl. Looking at the dress, I thought, I'm not sure I was ever that small.

'It's a nice dress,' I said.

'I think she wore it when I was in the hospital,' Carrie answered. She looked over at me and then sat down on a chair behind her.

'When were you in the hospital?' I asked. She looked frightened and elated all at once. Her lips were dry from her mouth hanging half open.

'When she took the baby from me,' she said.

'Carrie, are you all right? Do you need water?' I thought about calling my mother, but Carrie closed her mouth and shook her head.

'That woman used to be a social worker,' she said. 'She doesn't remember me, but she helped me a long time ago when I was in Montreal. She was the last one to see my son. She doesn't remember me, but now she's come here to get me to fix this dress. I think it's a sign, Beth.'

I knelt down in front of her on the floor. She wore a faraway grin like she used to when we played pretend, so I held onto her hands, firmly. 'Carrie, that's impossible. This is Winnipeg, not Montreal. That woman is not from your past.'

'You weren't there,' she said sharply. 'Do you think I could forget her face? It was actually her hands I recognized first. When she came to see me after he was gone, I held onto them because they were the closest I could come to touching him myself. Do you really think I would forget that?'

'It's been a long time,' I said.

'I've been waiting a long time,' she said. 'She doesn't remember me, but she came here for a reason. Everything happens for a reason, right? I've always needed to know what happened to him, and, of all people to walk in here, she's the only one who will know. How incredible is that, Beth?'

'Incredible,' I said.

'She's coming back in a week. I could have all my answers in a week.' She stood up and went back to the dress, pinning and then repinning the shoulders. She held the sleeves out, and it looked like the dress could take her into a hug.

'I'm going to close up now,' I said to her.

'I've been waiting all my life for this,' she said back to me.

'Come on, Carrie. We have to close up.'

I didn't see Carrie for the rest of that week. She cancelled all of her appointments and told my father she was taking some time off to reorganize her apartment. When I tried calling her, she didn't pick up the phone. When my mother tried to go over to talk to her, she came out of the apartment door with her grocery cart and said that she needed to go shopping. She was all out of fruit and vegetables.

'Come eat with us, then,' my mother said.

'No, thank you,' she answered, heading down the hall. 'I may be having company soon. I need to make some soup.'

'I have plenty of soup in my freezer,' Mum called out to her as Carrie headed down the stairs. 'You can have some of mine.'

'I need to do this myself,' Carrie called back. 'Really, I don't need your help. I'm fine.'

'She's going to get herself so hurt, and there's nothing I can to do stop it,' my mother said to me later on when we were eating supper, just the three of us.

'Maybe she just needs to go through this,' my father said. We were eating pea soup, but I just swirled it around with my spoon. My mother did the same with hers, and eventually Dad ate both of our bowls. 'You can't protect her from everything.'

'I would like to make sure she doesn't go off the deep end.'

'I think she's already there,' I said.

'No,' my mother said, shaking her head. 'It can get a lot worse than this.'

That's when she told me about Carrie coming home from Montreal and refusing to get off the train because she wanted to go back so badly. My mother had to get special permission to board the train and then coax her out of her seat. Carrie made that train two hours late for Saskatoon while she sat in silent protest. She held onto the handle of her handbag so tight her knuckles were white. She told my mother she was going to go back to Montreal and get her son, who should have never been taken from her.

'I tried to tell her that he wasn't hers to have. She looked at me with such venom, I felt like I had been spat on. "What the hell do you know?" she said. And she never swore. I don't know what made me feel more taken aback. Her swearing or what she said next. She said to me, "You never wanted me to be happy anyway."

'"Of course I want you to be happy," I said to her.

'And then she asked me, "Then why won't you help me?" She started to cry, and all I could do was hold her until she stopped, and she was so tired she had to walk off with me because she didn't have the energy to argue any more. Do you remember that?' my mother asked my father, who nodded.

'Very well,' he said. 'You moved into your mother's house for two weeks to make sure she didn't try to run away.'

'And she would have,' my mother continued. 'If I hadn't been there to walk with her to the store the next morning, she would have run right back to the train station.'

'With what money?' I asked.

'Beth, she was so adamant. She would have done whatever it took to get back on that train.'

I helped my mother clear the dishes while my father excused himself to retire to the living room. Before leaving us, he kissed my mother's forehead and said, 'She'll be all right, you know. She knows she has us to fall back on.'

'But Sarah did too, and it didn't work then,' Mum said.

'Carrie isn't Sarah,' I added. I took the dirty bowls from her hands and went to wash them up in the sink on my own.

How do you reach out to someone who is reaching in the other direction? When Carrie didn't answer her phone, I walked over to her building and stood across the street at a convenience store, where I could see her moving about in front of her window. I called her then from the store, letting the phone ring and ring so that she knew I knew she was there. She moved around like she didn't hear it (maybe she went so far as to unplug her phones), and still I let it go on as she pulled her curtains back, as she watered her plants on her sun porch. It was March, and her phone continued to ring while the city melted winter away, while cars drove slowly down the street bumping in and out of potholes, throwing slushy puddles that splashed into the shrinking grey snowbanks on the side of the road. Once she sat out on her porch, on a folding chair, in a T-shirt and a pair of trousers, when it was not nearly warm enough to be without a jacket. I watched her pull out a piece of paper from her pocket, unfold it, and read it aloud to herself. It was only one sheet, and she read it over and over again, although I couldn't hear what she was saying. When I finally decided to cross the street and yell up to her, she stood up from her chair, stretched and walked back inside. I yelled up anyway, but she had closed her sliding door, and so my voice was like her phone, calling silently.

*

The night before the Icelandic woman was due back in the store, Carrie came in while I was closing up. She carried the clothes in their original garment bags. I could see the brown skirt of the dress peeking out from the bottom.

'Hi,' she said, hardly looking up as she unlocked the door to the back.

'We've been trying to reach you all week,' I said. 'You're really frightening us.'

'I'm fine. I've just been busy.' I followed her to the back where she turned on all the lights I had switched off and hung the clothes from the rack up against the wall.

'Carrie, I don't know what you've got planned, but none of us want to see you get hurt.'

She straightened out the suit dress and brushed her hand over it to wipe away any stray threads. 'Beth, what did I always tell you about reaching for the stars?' She didn't look up at me, and I didn't answer her. 'I've always told you to go for your dreams. I've always supported you in what you want to do. Don't you understand that this is my dream? This is my star?'

I hated watching her like this, so sure of something that could never be true. It was as if she were telling me that she had invented a way for the clothes she made to walk themselves out of the store.

'But Carrie, what you want can never happen. Whatever happened to your son, he's probably living a very full life, with a family of his own. Whoever this woman is, she can't bring him back to you.'

'I just want to talk to her.'

'I don't think it's a good idea. It's too risky.'

'You've never taken a risk, Beth. You don't know anything about being risky.'

She had never before spoken to me that way – as though she disapproved of me. I took a step back out of the room and felt that anything I had wanted to say was stuck in my mouth. I couldn't let it out, and I couldn't swallow it either.

'Now, if you don't mind, I have some questions I need to rehearse before tomorrow,' she said, sitting down at her sewing machine, her piece of paper laid out in front of her. I left her alone in the store and could hear her talking to herself in the room. She was asking all sorts of questions she could never answer.

When the Icelandic woman came back to pick up her clothes, she spent a few minutes wandering around the store looking at hair products and then face cleanser. She picked up a container of Noxzema skin cream and read the product information on the side. I thought that she would make a perfect model for any facial cream: her skin looked like it came out fresh from a bottle, painted on her face flawlessly. When she was handling Carrie's baby boy, I thought, did she nuzzle him with her button nose? Did she hold his newborn hand, wrapped around her finger, and bring it up to stroke her cheek as she carried him away?

'Can I leave this here while I go pick up my clothes?' she asked. She put the facial cream on the counter, to the side and out of the way.

'Of course,' I said. The store was empty. It was mid-morning, and we wouldn't have any kind of crowd for another couple of hours until lunch.

'Take your time,' I said, and she smiled. She had dimples and round apple cheeks. My aunt must have loved and hated her face all at once, I thought as the Icelandic woman thanked me. She looked like a pixie from out of a fairy tale, and for that reason alone, she could make you believe that everything would turn out happily ever after. She headed toward the back, and I felt an impulse to stop her. All I could think to say was, 'Excuse me, but did you ever live in Montreal?'

'Montreal? No,' she said, 'I've lived in Winnipeg all my life.'

It took her no more than five minutes to pick up her suits and thank Carrie for her good work. She paid for the skin cream on her way out and said to me, 'You know, my husband and I just moved into the neighbourhood. I'm so pleased to know that there is a drugstore within walking distance from our home. I'll be sure to be back.'

And then she left.

As the bell above the door rang out her departure, I watched her stand outside the shop, open her umbrella and tighten her silk scarf around her neck. It was drizzling out, earlier it had been wet snow, and I could see her shiver as she walked away. For someone who had lived in Winnipeg all her life, she was not wearing proper shoes for this kind of weather. She wore black leather pumps, and they splashed through the icy puddles, making her feet wet, as she walked farther and farther away.

'I'm sorry,' I said to Carrie as soon as I saw her in the back, hunched over her sewing machine. She ran stitches through a scrap piece of fabric, pushing it under the needle that raced up and down to the pressure of her knee against the side pedal.

'It was an understandable mistake,' I continued when she didn't say anything. 'She looked a lot like someone you used to know.'

'Yes,' Carrie answered, without looking up. 'She did.'

The fabric was a scrap from the brown dress she had taken in. The edge of the fabric had been cut using a pair of jagged scissors. It looked like a cartoon shark had taken a bite, leaving perfectly spaced triangle mounds.

She continued to run the fabric under the needle until she nearly caught her thumb underneath it.

'Carrie, I think you need to stop.'

'I was very close,' she said. Everything seemed to stop

when her machine did. The store was still, and no one came through the door. The only noise was our breathing and the drizzle outside thrown against the window with the wind.

'I feel like I've lost him all over again,' she continued.

It seemed like there was nothing I could do but rub my hand up and down her back, as rhythmically as she had run the material under the needle. 'You didn't have him to lose.'

'Oh, but I did,' she said, pulling away and looking up at me. All week, when I saw her, her eyes had seemed desperate. Now she just looked wistful. 'I was all prepared to meet him, and now it's not going to happen. Beth, you know when you're asleep and you have a really good dream, and then you wake up right in the middle of it? Right when you've decided you'd rather stay where you are than ever get out of bed? That's what this feels like.'

I nodded my head, and we sat together, silently, until she said, 'You know, when he was born, I gave him a name. I called him Phil. I never told anyone that because we weren't supposed to name our babies, but I did anyway. I've been calling him that ever since.'

'You've kept him with you through your stories,' I said, suddenly understanding that there were two Philips taken from Carrie's life who had been feeding her imagination all this time.

'You're right,' she said. 'It was as close as I could ever come to either of them.'

My father told us to go get some lunch, and he said we didn't need to hurry back. Carrie and I walked down Main Street, over to Selkirk Avenue and past Oretzki's, where, for the first time, I thought that the mannequins and clothing in the windows looked old. We walked into Gunn's Bakery where we both bought pizza bagels, which never had any cheese but always had baked tomato sauce, spicy, with chopped onions and soft bread. The drizzle had finally stopped and the sun came out, reflecting off the puddles and drying up the sidewalks. The Palace Theatre down the street had closed a few years before. Nothing had been done with the building, and so it stayed empty, faded movie posters still locked in their display cases. Soft drink cans and potato chip bags littered the entrance, as if the building had now become a giant garbage bin. Across the street there was a farmers' market, and someone was lifting a tarp with a broomstick to let the water drain. It fell over the side like a waterfall. Carrie and I sat on a bus bench to eat, and we both watched the water splash onto the sidewalk and then find its way down a street drain.

'That market has been there since I was a girl,' Carrie said. 'I bet some of the farmers are the same ones from when I was little.'

'I think Mum used to buy us fruit and vegetables from them.'

'Now everyone shops at Safeway,' she said.

'It's easier.'

'Not for those farmers it isn't.'

I finished my bagel before Carrie did. Bits of sautéed onions and tomato sauce were scattered around the bench. Carrie was eating very slowly. She tore bits of her bagel off to put in her mouth, rather than biting it whole.

'You not hungry?' I asked.

'Not particularly.'

'Everything's going to be okay,' I told her. 'You know that we all love you.'

'Thank you,' she said. 'I do know that, but it's nice to hear it all the same.'

I waited for her to eat some more before stretching to get up. Only elderly people were stopping to buy produce across the street. There were large containers of honey out on a table. I felt in my pocket to see if I had enough to buy some, but I only found fifteen cents. The sun was hot enough for me to undo my jacket, so I sat back down, feeling the heat on my neck, vowing to come back tomorrow with more money so that I could buy something at the stand. I had never shopped there before.

'Let's not hurry,' she said. 'I don't have anyone scheduled for the rest of today. And it's nice now, with the sun out. You can really smell spring in the air.'

'I'm not in a rush,' I said. Carrie's face was softening. She closed her eyes and leaned her head back to let the sun shine on her face. The light caught the rim of her glasses, and I could see little rainbows where it sparkled. I leaned my head back also and imagined us surrounded by little rainbows.

'Do you know what the smell of spring always reminds me of?' Carrie asked.

'No. You've never told me.'

'I know. It reminds me of falling in love. The one time I've been in love was during a spring evening. I was wearing your mother's leather coat that tied up at the side. When these first few days of spring come, I always expect to smell leather mixed in with the flowers and wet grass.'

'Who was he?'

'A young man. From Regina. Very nice.' She thought for a moment before continuing. 'You know, I was very ill-prepared for dating and love and those sorts of things. So when this man came in to town and said he wanted to take me out, I didn't know what that meant or what to expect. And we had such a lovely time talking. He made me laugh. He was the first man I ever met who really reminded me of my brother. I didn't want the night to end. And, you know, things got a bit carried away, but I didn't know any better. When he dropped me off at the house, he told me he would write to me from Regina. The only time I got a letter from him was after I came back from Montreal. He wrote to tell me he had got engaged. I didn't get out of bed for weeks. In such a short period of time, my heart had been broken in so many ways.'

'Did you ever tell him? About the baby?'

She shook her head. The sun caught strands of her hair and made them glow golden. I had never noticed those highlights before.

'What would be the point?' she asked. 'He wasn't going to come and marry me. And I'm not sure I wanted him to. Telling him wouldn't have brought the baby back, or him. I just left it.'

'I was just thinking that maybe he could have helped you.'

'No, he couldn't have. I had to learn to do that on my own.'

We sat for a little bit longer, and then Carrie gave me some money to go and buy her a container of honey. The plastic tubs had a picture of a cartoon bee smiling, giving a thumbs-up sign. I picked up two different sizes and held them up for her to see. Carrie wasn't looking at me. She was staring off down the street, very far away, probably at nothing. A bus drove up, stopped in front of her and then drove past. For a split second, I wondered if she would disappear behind that bus, if it would drive away, leaving an empty bench. But once it left, she was still sitting there with her legs crossed and her hands folded on her lap. She looked like someone waiting to be picked up, carried away, and dropped off somewhere new.

16

I have now seen a house grow old. Our McAdam Avenue home, which once swelled with the potential of large family gatherings and cousins hiding in corners, under stairs, of children running in from the front door, down the hall, and out the back to roll in the grass, now seemed to sag with emptiness. There was only my mum, my dad and me to fill the long dining room, the four bedrooms upstairs, the damp basement and the empty pantry because my mother had few people to bake for. The rose wallpaper in the hall had started to peel up near the ceiling, and in the dining room, the ceiling bubbled where there was water damage from an old pipe bursting. When one of us walked along the hardwood floors in the front hall, we could hear the echo of the footsteps in all corners of the house. The stairs creaked when we climbed them. It sounded like someone moaning, softly. Sometimes when my mother walked up to bed, I wasn't sure if it was only the stairs I heard, or if she was sighing along with them, climbing higher and higher into a house with a foundation like elderly bones.

I caught my father outside surveying the garage. The ground had shifted during the winter, and for the first time, we noticed the garage leaning slightly to one side. It looked like it needed a shoulder to lean on, someone to kiss its forehead and then set it upright again.

'This needs a lot of work,' he said. He walked inside where he kept his big tools and gardening supplies, none of which he had ever used. The saw hanging on the wall had rusted to the same brown colour as the paint peeling off the inside walls. White paint was peeling off the outside walls as well, flaking off like dry skin.

'What do you want to do about it?' I asked him.

'Honestly? Nothing. Everything. I'd prefer to just close my eyes and pretend it wasn't here.'

'So, do that. What's the big deal about a garage?'

He peeled off a strip of paint, crumbled it in his hand and then dropped the flakes to the floor. 'I promised your mother a long time ago that we wouldn't let the house get like this.'

There was a bird's nest in the rafters. Two sparrows flew into the garage through a broken window. They flew right up to their nest with a prize of cotton or paper and then sat in their home, watching us.

'Is Mum bugging you about it?' I asked.

'No, not really. But we haven't done any work on this place since we moved in. It's been almost ten years, and it's beginning to show.'

'I don't think it looks that bad, Dad. It's not like we're trying to be in *Better Homes and Gardens*.'

He laughed, but I could tell he didn't believe me. He walked out of the garage and the birds started to chirp. I think a few more came in to join them, and it occurred to me that it was more crowded in our empty garage than it was in our house.

'Your mother and I had a vision of this house when we were younger, and one day I woke up, and it didn't look like that anymore,' he said.

'Everything gets older, Dad.'

'You're right, you're right,' he said. 'I guess I'm just in denial.'

*

Marilyn, Norma and I still got letters from Cheryl. She was feeling much more at home and was expecting their first child. She would send us pictures of herself in a kimono and she wrote her letters on delicate paper, tinted green like the tea we imagined she drank every morning. She begged each of us to come and visit and wrote on and on about the English classes she was teaching and how eager her students were to learn. Simon's family was lovely, she wrote, very accepting. She travelled with them all over the country and had seen landscape we could only imagine. In my letters, she said that I should consider coming to teach with her for a while. It was, she promised, the experience of a lifetime. She sounded very happy. And though she always said that she missed us, I got the feeling that was less and less the case as time went on.

Norma obsessed about floral arrangements and honeymoon spots. Perry wanted to visit the new Disney World Magic Kingdom in Florida. She wanted to go somewhere with a beach where she could wear a bikini and Perry would be proud to be lying beside her. She wanted somewhere with sunsets and barefoot walks through the sand. He was more interested in rollercoasters. I tried to assure her that Florida had both, but Norma was the kind of person who let herself get very stressed about these things. And she was not very good with confrontation. In the end, the best I, as her maid of honour, could say was that they still had time to decide these things. It was a while yet before the wedding. She would calm down once I had said that, hearing, 'I still have time to convince him.'

That summer, I began to look after Jade during the week. Every Tuesday we would go to the Planetarium and watch the show of Apollo's Fiery Chariot. She never tired of climbing into the plush, folding auditorium seats and swinging her legs as she looked up at the overhead screen, concave like the sky, displaying stars that would magically come together to make Greek mythological characters. During the show, Apollo drove his magic chariot across the sky, leaving a trail of flames behind him.

'Does that really happen?' she would ask me. 'Can you really see Apollo dragging the sun away at night?'

'No, honey. You know it's just a story. People would tell these stories to explain how the world worked in a way that other people could understand.'

'Then how does the sun move?'

'It doesn't,' I told her. I held her hand as we walked out of the theatre. 'The earth moves around the sun. So do the other planets. While the earth turns, it looks to us like the sun is moving.'

'The earth is moving?' she said, stopping. 'Right now.'

'Sure,' I said. 'The earth is always moving. It's always moving around the sun and it's always spinning.'

She stood in one spot and closed her eyes. Jade had Sarah's lashes and the same shaped lips, full and strawberry pink as if always beginning a kiss. Standing still, she kept her lips parted and seemed to be holding her breath.

'I think I can feel it,' she said, squeezing her eyes shut tight.

'Really? That's very difficult.'

'Really, Beth. Try it. You'll see.'

So I held her hand and closed my eyes. 'Whoa,' she said, letting out her breath. 'I just felt a big turn. We must be going somewhere fast.' I tried not to laugh, but I didn't feel anything. 'If you hold your breath, you feel it better,' she said.

I did as I was told, and soon my head began to spin a little. If it's possible for darkness to swirl, then it did behind my closed eyes. I knew I was only losing balance, but that didn't matter. Jade tugged on my hand, 'See? See?'

I let out my breath. 'You're right, honey. I never noticed that before.'

I also continued working for my father in his North End store, helping to manage things while he ran back and forth from there to his South End branch. When I took my shifts at the store, I mainly worked behind the lunch counter, mixing tuna salad and grating hard-boiled eggs for sandwiches. Cheryl's father came in to eat his lunch with us twice a week – on Tuesdays and on Fridays before he would head out to Gimli for the weekend to join the rest of his family. By this point, his other children were all married with children of their own. The family owned a large cottage two blocks away from the beach with five bedrooms, two bathrooms and a kitchen with a long break-fast counter that could seat twelve. From our lunch coun-ter, Dr Moss would call out to my father, 'It's like living in a zoo! With all these pishers crawling in between my legs. My wife loves it, but I tell her, "This ain't a vacation." We need a real vacation!'

Dr Moss had the same lunch whenever he came, a tuna sandwich on toasted rye, a black coffee and a soup bowl of ripple potato chips.

'You were always a real good girl,' he said to me once. 'I liked that Cheryl played with you.'

'She's doing well,' I told him, ignoring the look my father shot me. 'I hear from her sometimes. She sounds really happy.'

'Hmmm,' he answered, looking at his plate.

'Beth, I need your help,' my father called.

'I could give you her address,' I went on. 'I'm sure she'd love to hear from you. I catch her up on everything I can . . .'

'Beth!'

'. . . but I'm sure there's lots more you'd like to tell her.'

Dr Moss still didn't look up. He had lost most of his hair on the top of his head, except for a few greasy stands which he combed over. He had a wide nose and droopy cheeks, and he reminded me of a hound dog about to howl.

'Beth, I need you. Now.'

My father took me into the back of the store and handed me an inventory sheet.

'I can do this later,' I said.

'You can leave that poor man alone,' he told me. 'I'll look after the counter for the rest of the afternoon.'

'But Dad, it would be so good for Cheryl to hear from them. She loves her parents. C'mon. If it were me, wouldn't you want to know how I was doing?'

'The Mosses will come around in their own time. They don't need your help. You know better than to judge people. Everyone deals with their family in their own way.'

We heard the bell chime from over the front door. My father pointed to the inventory list and the shelves of prescription drugs in front of us. 'Do this for me this afternoon, please. It will keep you busy for the rest of the day.'

'You didn't answer my question,' I told him.

He peeked out the door to the store. It was empty now. Dr Moss had left two dollars and fifty cents on the counter, along with half an uneaten sandwich.

'Yes, dear,' he said. 'I would always want to know how you are.'

Later that evening, I was sweeping behind the coffee counter when he came over and sat on one of the stools. Dad gave me pharmaceutical magazines and journals to read through, and he was always sure to share the latest drug findings with me.

'You know, Beth, this place could be yours one day,' he said. 'You're extremely capable. You'd make a good pharmacist. I want you to know that.'

His eyes were red and sagging from the end of a long

day. He took his glasses off and rubbed his eyes, the skin on his cheeks dry and flaking from his hands.

'You need to get your prescription checked, Dad.'

I had been telling him this for a while. He had been answering me the same way, as he did now. 'I suppose you're right, Sweetheart.'

He sat with his eyes closed while I finished up the floor. I thought he had fallen asleep with his head propped up against his hand. He was breathing very deeply, and I almost thought to leave him there, resting. As I went to put the broom and pan away, he said, 'So you'll think about it? Right?'

I felt like my life was becoming a series of one-act plays where I played myself but as different characters. There was Beth, the Dutiful Daughter (*sweeping the store, silently washing dishes while Mother drones on in background about friends' eligible sons*). There was Beth, the Confidante (*listening intently to Norma pulling her hair out over fabric swatches*). And then there was Beth the Insomniac. I would wake up in the middle of the night, listening to my heart beat while I buried my head into my pillow, covering my ears. It probably wasn't my heart I was hearing, but some artery close to my ear. Still, I thought of it as my heart ticking like a second hand, only everything was standing still. I think that's what kept me up – pondering how I could feel both like a clock mechanically working, but never moving time forward.

My mother also suffered from insomnia. She got tired earlier and earlier. At the end of the day, she lay in bed and watched the news with an electric heating pad on her shoulders, which ached from arthritis. She asked me more often to reach for things in high cupboards, or to lift her groceries from out of the car. She began to drink hot water and lemon in the evenings, rather than coffee, because her doctor told her to lay off the caffeine to help her sleep better. But it didn't help. At night, while I lay awake, struggling to fall asleep, I'd hear her pacing the hall and then walking down the stairs to the kitchen where she'd sit at the table, reading.

One night I followed her downstairs and told her to go back up to bed if she was so tired all the time.

'There's no use,' she said.

'Mum, you have to let yourself fall asleep.'

She shook her head. 'The same thing happened to your Baba when she got older. When she'd complain to me, I'd tell her to go back to sleep. Just like you. She said it was no use. And you know what? She was right.'

So while she sat up counting the creaks in her aching bones, I stayed upstairs wondering when the process of our roles changing began without my knowing, or my permission.

After getting caught at the awards dinner, my love life became decidedly uneventful. Timothy ignored me in class (as he had before), and after the exam, I didn't see him at all. Marilyn had a boyfriend, an American who had one Canadian parent and had moved to Winnipeg to avoid the draft. He was a huge anti-war protester and handed out lots of peace buttons in his spare time. I wore one and went to a few of the rallies he organized on campus. I went to the after-parties too and made out with some other anti-war protester at one of them. But the truth? It was all boring. The guy kissed like a fish and felt me up with the gentle touch of someone tuning their car. He also smoked, and I was tired already of the taste of cigarettes. When I came home at the end of that party, I took off my peace pin and stuck it onto my bulletin board, where it stayed.

As the weather warmed up, I tried sleeping outside in the backyard. We had a couple of weeks early that July where it was comfortable to sleep outside in a T-shirt.

Except that I woke up in the morning with mosquito bites up and down my arms and along my back. I was learning not to care, though. If you ignore the bites, they don't itch as much. I could chalk that up as the one lesson I learned that summer, but that wouldn't be fair. There were plenty of others.

I would lie out back, do my stargazing and just wonder. God or no God, every star had its place in the universe. Many were likely suns for other solar systems. I thought about the universe spreading infinitely into space and wondered, if it stopped, what did that look like? Where was the black void we could theoretically fall into if we travelled long enough? It had been a long time since I imagined my uncle's ghost, but during those nights in the backyard, I had no doubt that he lay there beside me, knowing some of the answers but not willing to give them up to me so easily.

I discovered his journal in the basement, in the box of photos I had hidden away from my mother when I was younger. I took it outside with me, and sitting underneath the canopy of stars, I devoured those journal entries, his desire for adventure, his passion and his fear. I could taste it as sweetly as my own.

Every day, it feels, another friend is signing up to fight in this war. Our high school holds dances and orchestra concerts to raise money for bombs and food for the soldiers. But outside of class, I suppose when we should be studying, we count down the days to our eighteenth birthdays. Jerome and I will be pilots. He has family in Poland, and they have not been in touch since the war began. We hear rumours of Jews being taken away in the middle of the night. Entire communities disappear by the trainful. Jerry says he's going because we're needed more over there than here. I couldn't agree more.

My father begs me to stay and work.

'This is also the war effort,' he says.

'It's not the same, Pop,' I have to tell him. We all see our older friends walking the Winnipeg streets in their uniforms while they get ready to leave. There are days when I think we are like dogs, our tongues wet with desire and panting, just to be like one of those guys. Every one of us wants to be the one who drops the bomb on the Nazi headquarters. Or the one who shoots Hitler or Mussolini in the head, right between the eyes. I have long grown out of collecting War Savings Stamps. My booklets are filled with tanks, planes and soldiers. I have stamped out the enemy more times than any army can count. That's why I told my dad, now it's my real turn. Now I have to make a difference.

The amazing thing about war is that all of a sudden, everyone has a role. This summer, while I enlist, my sisters will be working at a local bakery making Christmas cakes to send overseas in coffee tins. My mother helps collect baby clothes for children in England who have nothing. We hear that as bad as our rationing may be, it is nothing compared to what is going on over there. There they have no fruit in their stores, only cut out cardboard pictures. Our local grocery store has a sign that says, 'Loyal citizens do not hoard.' Our mother repeats that almost every night when she serves us our supper with very little meat, or when she tells my father he must limit the amount of coffee he drinks.

In their spare time, Carrie and Goldie knit child-sized winter sweaters to send over to England with the clothes my mother has gathered. Goldie thinks I'm lucky that I get to go and see Europe. Carrie says she's worried about the fighting. I promise to send pictures and to stay safe.

I am training in Brandon, Manitoba. I don't know anyone here. This bunk, lined up with bunk beds for what feels like miles on either side, smells like a barn, and many of these boys are like the animals. The one below me, says he's from Dauphin, belches in harmony with someone lying beside us. The lights are out, but they are laughing, and a few others join in. They sound like cats, or maybe horses. Definitely horses getting round up before a big race.

I have never been with so many men of so many different sizes. Some are so skinny, you can count their ribs when they are lying down. Others are definitely not eighteen, and I cannot imagine what lies they told to be here. I think some of them may be as young as fifteen. They have no muscle and no chest hair. All of us have had our hair cut short, so when we stand in line, our heads are mirror images in different colours. The belching boy below me is a red head. Figures.

I think back to last night with Carrie and Goldie in our backyard. Carrie wore one of my old sweaters, and I said she could keep it while I'm away. Goldie shivered because she never dresses warmly enough for stargazing. Carrie wanted to know if the night sky would look the same in Europe, or Africa, or wherever I end up flying. I said I doubted it. She said, 'Well, at least we all share the same sun and moon.' And I said, 'You're right.'

Today, some idiot broke the lenses of my binoculars. These were the ones I saved for, very strong lenses, exceptionally clear view of some stars not seen by the naked eye. During a drill, he rolled over on them. The ass must weigh 250 pounds. Now, one of the lenses is cracked. I nearly punched him, and then someone else held me back and said we're not here to fight each other.

I naively considered my binoculars lucky. Some people have a rabbit's foot. I had these. I'm not superstitious and I am not any more afraid now of going to war. Just disappointed. I envisioned spying on the enemy grounds *through these, and then later, coming home to make other great discoveries. Now I've tossed them away, and I am embarking on this adventure, blind.*

I will leave tomorrow. In a moment, some of the boys and I will go into town for a farewell celebration. I have just spoken with my father and I have told my mother I love her. The baby was crying in the background. We didn't speak for long.

Before I go tonight, I stare up at the sky and get my bearings. I find Cassiopeia. I find the Big Dipper. I stand below them and I stare above until my neck hurts, and the stars are spinning from my eyes, which are watering. Tomorrow I will become a pilot. Tonight I savour the ground beneath my feet.

He could never have known what his absence would mean to our family, how his death could create one dreamy sister, one in denial and another who couldn't stop running. As I lay there thinking about my uncle, about my family, about the universe and our place in it, I saw two shooting stars. One of them was actually a satellite, or a small airplane, but as late as it was, the two seemed to crisscross in the sky. I held my breath, watching them, and while they faded into the navy sky, it occurred to me that I had spent most of my life like this, holding my breath, waiting for things to happen. Staying in Winnipeg meant I was waiting to see which of my mother or her sisters I was destined to turn into. I didn't want any of it – Sarah's unhappiness, Carrie's loneliness, or my mother's pride. As hard as I tried, my mother seemed to find her way into my body language. There were days when I caught myself making her gestures, and I would have to sit on my hands to make her disappear. When I complained about this to Norma, she told me not to be ridiculous.

'Of course you're your own person. Everyone is. But anyway, who wouldn't want to be like your mother? She's such a success story.'

This, of course, came from the woman who didn't go shopping for a sweater without taking her mother along for her opinion. Norma loved every part of her destiny. She read it like a guidebook, following each chapter page by page.

'So stop bitching and start a revolution,' Marilyn said when she lay outside with me one night (she would only stay until the tenth bug bite, she told me, and then she was going inside).

'I'm not bitching,' I said back. 'And besides, everyone is starting a revolution.'

'And the world is becoming a much better place for it!' she said, only to be bitten by mosquito number ten, and so she went inside. I lay out for a bit longer thinking that the thought of a revolution just made me tired when all I really wanted to do was let my breath out.

'Philip,' I said, the words hanging above me in the heavy night sky. 'Where would you be now if you hadn't fallen?'

The rest of my summer might not have been remarkable, had it not been for my mother. She was quietly retreating, sleeping less, sitting alone more, somewhere where she could tuck her legs beneath her and just stare ahead. Once or twice I caught her in the living room in the dark. Turning on the light, I asked her what she was doing.

'Just thinking. It's cooler in the dark. Better for my head. I'm fine, Beth.'

But she was pale. As her other friends turned golden from weekend trips to Gimli and other Lake Winnipeg beaches, Mum turned down their invitations to join them. She sat in the sunroom during the day and drank iced tea.

I'd find her there in the morning when I'd leave for my shift at the drugstore, and she'd be there again when I got home. After supper she'd retreat to the sunroom again while my father fell asleep in the living room in front of Wayne and Shuster or Bob Hope.

One night I came home late, close to midnight, after a night of stargazing at the university (some volunteer research I was doing for one of my professors; I was tracking Mars's movements across the summer sky). I would not have noticed her there had it not been for the cigarette she raised and lowered slowly from her mouth. The entire room was dark except for the red glow as she sucked inwards, and then the light, grey smoke dancing gracefully up to the ceiling.

'Mum?' I whispered. There were two other butts in the ashtray on the wicker coffee table in front of her. Once or twice I saw her smoke socially, occasionally when my parents hosted something like a holiday party for all their friends. But never on her own like this.

'What's going on?' I asked her. She glanced at me when I walked in and then turned her head again to look out the window. The porch overlooked our backyard where we had three crabapple trees. Most summers she would have started picking crabapples by now for jelly. This year, the branches hung heavy with fruit. Some pieces had already fallen to the ground, and in the nightly breeze, you smelled a hint of rotting fruit.

'I can't sleep,' she said. 'That's all. So I thought I'd sit here. I didn't realize how late it was.'

'I've never seen you smoke.' I pushed her.

'Oh, I sometimes do. When I'm thinking.' She smiled then. 'Gives me something to do with my hands.'

This time when she blew out the smoke, it outlined her face and floated up by the window. Outside a dog barked and then another one answered.

'What are you thinking about?' I asked her. She put her cigarette down in the ashtray and stretched her arms above her head. In her short-sleeved nightgown I could see the flesh on her soft, untoned arms. She stretched her neck as well, and the skin under her chin went taut.

'Nothing,' she finally said, standing up. 'Nothing you need to worry about.'

She kissed the top of my head before leaving the room. 'Don't stay up too late,' she said, hugging her arms and holding her elbows as she walked away. I picked up her cigarette and finished it, the smoke warm in my mouth and against my lips as I blew it out. How much did I look like her, sitting there, as she did, moving my hands toward my face and then away as I led her cigarette to and from my mouth? How long would I have to sit like that before no one would be able to tell the difference between us two, either in the dark or lit up?

Later that week, Norma and I ended up at the Salisbury House for coffee. I was helping her choose bridesmaid dress patterns (they were all hideous, various shades of sky blue with puffy skirts and puffed sleeves; no matter how she dressed us, we were all going to look like under-ripe blueberries). Norma had chosen nine bridesmaids and Perry only had six groomsmen, so they were arguing. Again.

'I can't believe he can't find three more men to help us out. I mean, he has cousins! He's being totally unreasonable.'

Across the restaurant, I spied my parents, tucked in the corner, sharing a plate of french fries. They leaned in over the plate and spoke in low voices, my father saying something witty, my mother smiling and looking over to him, coyly. At one point, he dipped a french fry into the mound of ketchup at the side of the plate and held it out for her to eat. She bit the fry and then kissed his fingers, chewing slowly and dabbing the side of her mouth where a bit of ketchup was left.

Norma followed my gaze and saw them. They noticed no one.

'See, look at that. Your parents are amazing, Beth. My parents would never do that, go out on a date. Gawd, you can't get my father to lift his behind from off the couch most evenings to get into bed! When I get older, I want Perry and me to be just like your mum and dad.'

It didn't feel like I was watching them. When my dad reached out for her hand and rubbed it beneath his fingers, I felt like I had caught him out with another woman. When my mother looked up, met his gaze, and sighed, I felt like I was watching a couple falling in love for the first time. My father leaned back into his booth, still holding my mother's hand, and neither of them said anything for a while.

'I guess,' I said back to Norma, who had turned around in her seat and focused her attention back onto the assortment of Vogue and Simplicity patterns laid out in front of us.

'You want to say hi?' she asked me, not looking up.

'No,' I said. They finished their food and coffee and got up to leave. 'Let's get fries.'

Later that night, with my father again asleep on the couch and my mother on her porch (this time not smoking), I noticed the dishes piled in the sink. Usually my mother rinsed and washed them right after dinner. Sometimes I helped, but rarely did she leave her kitchen untidy. In fact, I only remembered it being a mess when she spent her month in bed. Then, Sarah and I put away dinner plates and cutlery, wordlessly. I stood on a chair to reach the top of the cupboards. Carrie wiped down counters. In the end, we produced a nearly spotless kitchen, but every night, something else seemed to go out of place – a tea jar, a toaster, a napkin holder. By the time my mother woke up, she spent her first day downstairs rearranging everything, probably wondering how long she had slept for everything to get out of place.

While I washed the dishes, I saw my mother through the kitchen window, walking outside in the backyard. Her feet were bare, and she stood beneath one of the crabapple trees, picking fruit from its branches and dropping them into a plastic ice cream pail. She wore one of my father's old, long cardigans over her nightgown. Her hair, which she hadn't yet put in curlers for the night, was frizzy and wild above her shoulders. Once her pail was full, she laid it on the ground and sat down beside it, looking up at the sky, her legs stretched out in front of her with her feet pointing up.

'If you don't come in, the neighbours will start talking,' I said to her from the back doorway. She didn't move, except to turn her head to look at me.

'It's not their business when I decide to sit out in my backyard.' Even though it was summer, the evening was cool, and I was still shivering in jeans and a long-sleeved shirt. She leaned back on her elbows and let her head fall backward.

'Mum, c'mon. It's cold. Come inside.'

'For goodness sake, Beth. You spend whole nights out here, and your father and I don't say boo. When did you become such a worrywart?'

'When did you stop?' I mumbled, coming outside to join her.

I sat down next to her and held my knees close to my chest. It was a clear night. I should have been out at the university with my log book and binoculars. You could see the Summer Triangle, Deneb, Vega and Altair blinking like neon. I made out the Northern Cross and then further south, the Teapot. With my binoculars, so much more could have been made clear.

'I never understood the fascination,' my mother started, 'with stars. To me, they're just a light show. And most of the time we can't see them anyway because we're asleep.'

'Stars are like looking into the past,' I told her. 'When you're looking at a star, you're looking at something that took place thousands of years ago. It's the closest we come to having a time machine.'

'It's all science fiction,' she said. 'We need to spend our energy focusing on life on earth.'

'People can do both,' I said. 'Studying space helps us know how we got here, which helps us understand where we're going.'

She nodded silently. I felt the wind brush my shoulder like a hand. I closed my eyes and imagined Phil sitting between us, putting his arm around my mother's shoulder. *That one is your mother,* he said, pointing up. *And there's Dad.* The stars twinkled, like eyes blinking. *And that bright one, the really strong one, that one is me.*

'I need your help,' my mother said, after a while. 'Tomorrow I have a doctor's appointment. Your father can't come with me because he needs to be at the store. But I'm having some tests done and I'd like you there.'

'Tests for what?'

'Bumps,' she said, still not looking at me.

'What do you mean bumps?'

'In my breasts,' she whispered.

'Oh.'

The star I picked out for Philip pulsated and then fell behind a small cloud.

'I just need someone to come with me to drive me home afterward. I might not be feeling well.'

'Okay.'

'Your dad didn't want me to tell you, but I didn't see any other way.'

'It's okay, Mum. I'll come.'

She put her knees underneath her and rocked to get up on her feet.

'It's cold out,' she said. 'Help me get up and come inside.'

My mother and I didn't speak in the car on the way to the doctor's. That morning I went into her bedroom to make sure she was awake. She was lying in bed, with one arm above her head, her other hand feeling around her breast, over top of her nightgown.

'It's still there,' she said to me, her lips pale blue without her lipstick. 'Every morning I check to see if it's gone.'

'I'm sure it's nothing, Mum. Lots of these bumps turn out to be false alarms.' She rolled her fingers around the breast tissue, and it looked like she was rocking a small ball against her chest.

'It's so tiny,' she said. 'Compared to the rest of my body, it feels like nothing at all.'

'Exactly,' I told her. 'Let's get going.'

'I'll be downstairs in a minute.'

When I closed the door, she was still lying there, looking up at the ceiling while she felt around, as though if she lay there long enough a map or an X-ray might appear.

We sat in the waiting room, and I looked at all the women's faces, each one pale, each one trying to cover their concern with foundation and green eye shadow. My own mother had chosen her makeup to match her outfit, a lilac polyester pantsuit with a white blouse and large collar. She painted purple shadow across her eyelids and a carefully drawn black line by her lashes. Her real skin was so well hidden beneath her makeup, you could barely see the indentation of her wrinkles because they were filled in with powder. She sat straight and stared at the walls, which were covered in cheerful daffodil yellow and had a banner of yellow ribbons running along the ceiling. It was only when the nurse called her into the office, and she turned to her name, that I saw her face shift, the powder resettle, and her wrinkles revealed, all along her cheekbones, under her eyes, and by her lips.

'Do you want me to come with you?' I asked her.

'Yes,' she said. 'Please.'

The nurse gave my mother a gown to change into before the doctor came in.

'Make sure to do it up at the front,' she said. 'And take off your bra. You can keep your bottoms on.'

My mother unbuttoned her blouse, turning to the wall. Her shoulders hunched over while she unhooked her bra from behind. When she did up the gown, she folded her blouse and hid her bra beneath it.

'Do you think it's my colour?' she asked me. After she turned around I could see the dip of her breast through the slit of the gown. Her skin looked sea green under the harsh lights and against the fabric.

'No,' I said. 'Not this colour green. You need something richer.'

She settled into the chair beside me. We left the one on wheels by the desk empty. 'I don't suppose anyone would look good in this colour. Not even Mary Tyler Moore' (her favourite actress and favourite show).

'Not even.' I agreed. We both imagined, then, the cameras around us, and a director offset calling out stage directions. This scene finished with a good-hearted joke before we could walk away, and some other scene gets rehearsed, performed, filmed and then canned. The actor playing the doctor would be good-looking. Mary Tyler Moore would have a wide smile and a pocket full of one-liners.

I think I'd rather have a bump on my head, she'd tell him. *How's about we trade. You can take this one and in exchange give me a good, old-fashioned bump on the head.*

The audience rolled in their stage seats. Mum and I left

the set, dressed normally again, to sign autographs. We would leave the gown thrown on the chair for someone else to pick up and put away.

'Goldie, how are you?' Dr Bernstein asked as he entered the office. Dr Bernstein was a friend of my father's who fit my mother into his very busy schedule of seeing women with strange bumps.

'Fine, Hart. Very well. And you? And Shirley? What's new?'

He looked at her chart, 'Oh, you know. Nothing much, nothing much. Shirley's busy with Rebecca's wedding in the fall. I just pay the bills, you know.' He went over to wash his hands and then motioned for my mother to sit on the examination table. 'And Robin is applying to medical school this year. He wants to do radiology. I keep telling him not to rush things. Medicine has so many possibilities, and he has to keep his options open.' My mother lay down on the table, and he undid the gown. He felt my mother's breast with his hand, keeping his eyes on the wall; my mother kept her eyes on the ceiling. 'Shirley's having some trouble with her hips.'

'Really. That's too bad.' He found the bump. I could tell by how he rolled it under his finger. He dug his finger into the skin slightly to feel around all sides of the lump, to draw a mental picture of it in his mind. It could never match my mother's, which I knew by now was intricate and detailed with every curve.

'Hmmm,' he said, clicking his tongue on the roof of his mouth.

'Goldie, dear, we're going to need to check this with surgery, with a biopsy. I'll book you right away.'

'Of course,' my mother said faintly, closing her eyes.

'If we find anything, we'll deal with it right there. The beauty of the surgery is that there's no waiting time between your diagnosis and your treatment,' he said.

Doctor, if you're calling this beautiful, then I think you need to get out more! said Mary Tyler Moore. The audience laughs. My Mary Tyler Moore mother rolls onto her side. *Really, Doctor. I'm sure you and I could have a fun time.*

The Doctor laughs good naturedly. *I don't think we'll have anything to worry about here.* And there isn't. The gown gets left on the plastic chair. Mary Tyler Moore goes home and gets up to work the next day, the next episode, and never mentions the good doctor again.

'I'll give you a call as soon as the date is booked,' Dr Bernstein said. 'Then you and Saul can come in to see me if there's anything to worry about.'

Then he turned to me. 'It's good to see you, Beth. You'll help your mother home, I take it.' She lay on the table still with her gown undone, her right breast exposed. Somehow, lying down she didn't seem as naked as she would be should she sit up and get dressed with him still there.

'Please give Shirley my best,' she said to him, before he left. 'Tell her to call me when she knows what baking she needs. I can help.'

'I'm sure she'll call you,' he said, waving to us both before closing the door.

For all of the ride home, my mother lay her head against the car window frame. The car was new, my father had purchased it only three weeks before. A brown Cadillac with a tan roof and matching tan plush bench seats. The wide front window made me think I was pulling into the oncoming traffic, so instead, I bumped the curb two or three times on the drive. Each time, my mother's head was jolted and she had to resettle herself. I'd apologize, but she'd wave her hand and then close her eyes. Our doctor's office was no more than a ten-minute drive from our home, but she was asleep by the time I pulled into the driveway. It was a hot day, and although the windows were rolled down, we were both sweating. When I shut off the car, I watched how she slept with her lips slightly parted and the sweat dripping twice from the tip of her nose into her mouth.

It was as if all this time her body had been denying her sleep, storing it, and now allowing her access. She seemed to drink her sleep and would crawl into bed by 7 p.m., right after supper, and stay there until nine or ten the next morning. Carrie came to stay with her during the day when I was at the store. At night, my father followed her upstairs and lay beside her on the bed as she was falling asleep. Sometimes he fell asleep, too, in his clothes with his bedside lamp on. Sometimes he turned their small, black and white TV on and pretended to watch while watching her breathe instead. There were nights when I think he laid his hand upon her shoulder while she slept on her side just to feel the rhythmic rise and fall of her body. One night I heard him talking to her in a low voice, 'Sleep well, dear,' he said. 'You deserve it.'

By this time I was heavily into my research at the university for Dr Erikson, one of my professors in the department of physics. Each night, either from our backyard, or sometimes on campus with the other student researchers, I charted Mars's movements in relation to the moon. One night it was six degrees to the moon's upper left, the next night it moved seven or eight degrees below. Within the week, Mars had formed an isosceles triangle with the Gemini Twin stars, Pollux and Castor. I spotted the triangle while out with the group one night at the university. The stars were four and a half degrees apart with Mars ten and a half degrees below them. The triangle was perfect, something you'd only see in a trigonometry textbook. I stood for half an hour staring at this pattern in the sky. Every once in a while, we are privy to something perfect in nature, where everything lines up straight. Where nothing looks random. The next night this triangle wouldn't exist. I didn't know when I would catch it again. In my logbook, I sketched the constellation and noted the positions of the stars and planets. Then I put the footnote, 'A perfect isosceles triangle is formed 142 million miles away. A math equation from the past.'

Later, Dr Erikson invited us to his lab for coffee and store-bought chocolate chip cookies. There were five of us on his team, including two masters students researching black holes. We each presented our findings, and though it was close to midnight, I spent far longer than my allotted five minutes recounting Mars's journey over the last week. Dr Erikson shut the lights and put up some coloured slides while I spoke. I stood beneath the glow of the red planet, its craters and valleys.

'This is mankind's next destination,' he said. There was a poster of Neil Armstrong planting the flag on the moon on the wall behind him. It said, 'One giant leap.'

'The science community has long debated the possibility of life on Mars. When the technology is right, we'll get there to see for ourselves. Well done, Beth.' I took my seat and sipped my coffee. 'With any luck, you'll be right in the thick of it.'

Dr Erikson walked me to my car that night. He was my father's age and had been researching space for over twenty-five years. The University of Manitoba brought him on board because he had published papers in NASA's journals and was a member of the International Council of Scientific Unions when they called for the launching of artificial satellites to map the earth's surface in 1954. Dr Erikson was one of the first scientists to see the photos of earth from up above. In class he described it as a 'view from the Heavens.'

'I have some funding for a project you might be interested in,' he said to me. 'The University of Chicago wants me to research the effects of light pollution on the night sky.'

'Growing cities,' I said.

'Suburbs, actually,' he answered. 'The more congested and sprawling our cities, the more light we produce, and the less we can see. The more we sprawl, the less space there is for viewing and research. We are effectively killing our opportunities to study space, but no one has written about this yet. There is a conference coming up in a year's time, and I want to present a paper. I want you to be my research assistant.'

'But how can I? From here?'

'You can't. You'll have to come with me. I can arrange your credit transfer. But you need to think about this and make a decision in the next couple of weeks. You are a bright young woman, Beth. I only take on the brightest.'

In my head, Mars's triangle continued to shine bright.

'Think about it,' he said. 'It's a big move, but one I am sure you would not regret.'

It was as if someone had offered to fly me to the moon without any promise they could get me back. For a while I became a kid again, dreaming of stars and planets and bouncing from one to the next. I oscillated between bringing my mother cups of tea in bed and running her bath to poring over physics journals and library material by the light of my desk lamp while my parents slept. If my mother succumbed to her exhaustion, I rose over mine. I never felt tired. I slept maybe four hours a night. I craved the night-time when my father finally crawled into bed with her and I could cradle a cup of coffee and this astral physics fantasy, rather than facing his worried eyes and pressing comments about me and the store.

'Before you choose your courses for next year, let me see your list,' he said once, while restocking the shelves. It was just the two of us in the store. Carrie had cut her hours down to just three days a week, and she did a lot of her sewing at home. 'I can help make sure you're on the right path.'

'Okay, Dad.'

Then, without looking up, he added, 'Don't tell your mother, though. About what we talked about? She still thinks I'm going to convince you to become a teacher.'

I laughed. 'Tell her I hate children.'

'I tried that. She said teachers don't have to like children, they just have to discipline them.'

We both laughed then, imagining my mother in front of a class of terrified eight-year-olds, taming them with a spatula. My father said something about how she would make them all sit with books on their heads, one of her pet peeves being poor posture.

'Your back,' she'd tell me, 'is like the stem of a flower. No matter how beautiful the bud, no one notices when it's all doubled over.' I doubled over then, laughing, imagining her class, a bouquet of still, pale children, like white tulips, my mother pinching their necks to make them sit straighter.

My father took breaths, but kept chuckling, making small hiccups long after I had quieted down. When I looked over to him, I saw his shoulders trembling, his chest shaking as he breathed in and out. He let the tears fall down his cheeks freely. For five minutes, mercifully, no one entered the store. I didn't know whether to touch him, to hold him or to leave, so instead I stood and watched while my dad closed his eyes, clenched his fists and let his face turn red before he breathed slower again and the colour began to drain.

'It's the waiting,' he whispered. 'And the unknown. And not knowing how to help.'

'You help her all the time,' I said. 'You've been her biggest help her entire life.'

'And she has been mine,' he added.

He took his handkerchief from his pant pocket and blew his nose. This is the one and only time I ever saw my father cry. Even after the following week's surgery, where they took both her breasts while she was sleeping. Even after Dr Bernstein outlined her treatment, reassuring them that she had the 'garden variety' of tumours, but that she would need radiation once her scars had healed. Even after dinner that evening, when they had told me everything, and my father took me aside to put his hand on my shoulder and say, 'We're so glad that you're here.' Even during all of that, he kept the driest of eyes. Whereas in the freedom of the only space he created himself and could truly call his own, without any fear of my mother catching him, he let himself think the worst.

'She will be fine,' I said to him when he put his handkerchief back in his pocket. 'Whatever happens next week.'

'It's not her I'm worried about,' he answered, turning back to his stock. 'It's me.'

17

My mother treated her cancer like any of her other carefully planned events. After her diagnosis, she made lists of errands she needed to complete before her daily zapping of radiation began. She sat at the kitchen table with a small notepad, like a reporter, writing lists of groceries, cleaning supplies, gardening goals, baking for the freezer. Although Jewish New Year was still two months away, she made lists for that, too: guest lists for the meals, menus, and separate grocery lists she would need in preparation. I would find these lists torn out of her notepad and scattered around the house where she would work on them, adding items.

FIRST NIGHT, ROSH HASHANAH, MENU
Gefilte fish
Turkey soup, kneidlelach
Brisket
Roast chicken
Tzimmes
Farfel
Potato kugel
Salad

And then, sitting in the bathroom, she added in red pen:
Dessert: lemon meringue freeze – make next week.

She booked herself manicure and hair appointments and marked them on the Royal Family calendar she had hanging in the kitchen. She also marked in her treatment sessions, which were scheduled every morning at 8:30 a.m. The treatments she marked in red pen. Everything else got added in blue.

I never told my parents about Dr Erikson. After my mother's diagnosis, his offer seemed distant and almost ridiculous. I turned him down with a simple note, which I penned on one of my mother's notepad pages.

Dr Erikson, I'm sorry. I can't come with you. I have commitments that are keeping me here in the city. Best of luck with your research.

I couldn't even bring myself to deliver it to him in person. Instead, I waited until I knew he was out of his office, teaching a summer course, and I dropped the note on his desk. Then I drove away from the university campus and ended up next to one of the fields we used for stargazing. I lay my head against the steering wheel and cried, a screaming, angry, heaving cry that sounded as much like hate as I could imagine. The screaming and tears left my mouth pasty and tasting like salt. I cried so hard, I began to gag. After throwing up by the side of the car, I drove home tasting nothing but bile.

My mother had an operation that took away both of her breasts – the infected one and the one at risk. Afterward, she wore stuffed bras so that her clothes fit as they did before. But at home, when she was just in her nightgown, she wore nothing underneath, and her body, which before had been so round and voluptuous, now seemed lopsided. A smaller woman would just look like an adolescent boy. But my mother still had her hips and her rounded rear end. Missing her cleavage, she looked like a child's drawing of a woman, flat-chested in a triangle dress.

Sometimes I went with her for her treatments. Sometimes she took Carrie. She did not want my dad to come with her. The radiation made her progressively more exhausted. She never wanted him to see her at the clinic, in her hospital gown, the sags under her eyes illuminated by the unflattering lighting. Although my father never did cry in front of her, she knew his weakness. At night, when he whispered to her, she wasn't asleep. She learned how to breathe deeply, to stay still. Part of her would have wanted to roll over and tell him to be quiet, that she knew all of this love already. But the better part of her knew to lie there and let him recite his meditations. She could handle that better than him crying. My mother had a carefully crafted shell that she hid behind. The key that no one knew was that my father was the glue holding her shell together. Without him, she had far too many cracks and she would have crumbled years before.

She began to carry around a day diary to keep track of her busy schedule. Sometimes, at the hospital, we would arrive to find out that her treatment had been delayed for misscheduling or some other reason. The receptionist was a heavy-set woman in a too-tight, white uniform. The buttons across her bosom pulled, and as awful as that made her look, I was more insulted by the cruel irony she inflicted on her patients just by being the first person they met when they came in each day. My mother once described her as the octopus: 'I plan my week and keep everything together, but no matter how hard I try, one of her eight arms is always ready to reach out and choke me. In my head, I have a giant pair of scissors to cut off each of her arms. But they just keep growing back.'

Once when the woman tried to reschedule my mother for the afternoon, my mother took out her calendar and said, 'No, I can't make it. I have a Sisterhood meeting then, and I can't miss that. You'll just have to fit me in now.'

'I'm sorry, ma'am, but we can't. We're overbooked, and the doctor is away on an emergency. I've been strictly instructed to find you a time in the afternoon.'

'I'm simply not available,' my mother said, standing with a straight back. 'I plan my schedule around these appointments, and this is when you said I would be occupied with my treatment. I don't write these in pencil, you know. They are written in pen.'

'Mrs Levy, nothing is ever set in stone. I suggest you learn to make your schedule more flexible.'

Right then my mother dug into her purse and pulled out a pair of scissors. She lunged forward, quickly, and snipped the sleeve of the nurse's white coat. The nurse was so shocked she didn't seem to know where to look, and she darted her eyes back and forth between my mother, me and the small tear now in her shirt sleeve.

'Please,' my mother said softly, but firmly, 'keep me to my original appointment today.'

We were squeezed in fifteen minutes later, although the doctor did ask to confiscate my mother's scissors.

When she was ready to lash out, she did so at me. Little things, like how I did the laundry, could set her mood for the rest of the day. One day, I managed to wash a red sock with a load of white towels. Everything came out pink in uneven patches.

'Beth, I don't have the money to spend on new towels. These are ruined.'

'They still work, Mum. If you use one after a bath, it will still dry you.'

'When are you going to learn how to do something as simple as laundry without messing up?'

I threw my hands up. 'You know, I am trying.'

'You're almost nineteen years old, Beth. You need to know how to keep a house.'

'You know, Mum, someone out there may still want to marry me even if I did turn your towels pink.'

'I'll believe it when I see it, my dear.'

Later that evening, she complained about the state of her dishes.

'You're not using hot enough water to clean them. They're still very greasy.'

During her treatment, she lost her taste for food, so while she spoke she pushed her tuna noodle casserole around on her plate, leaving a trail of cream and peas.

'I take great pride in my dishes. These were passed down from my mother and I haven't lost one yet.'

'I'll look after it, dear,' my father said. 'The dishes are my job.'

'No,' she answered. 'Forget it, I'll look after it myself. I'm going to have to wash them again anyway.'

'You're being ridiculous,' I told her.

'I know how I want things done, and I intend for them to be that way,' she answered back.

'Maybe we should bring in some help,' my father suggested.

'No, we don't need it! I can do it myself.'

'For God's sake, Mum! There are days you can't even sit up straight! If Dad wants to bring in some help, let him!'

She picked up her plate then and banged it on the table. Noodles, tuna and peas flew up and onto the floor. The plate wobbled in its spot and all of us saw the hairline crack that started to form from the rim into the centre.

'I am NOT an invalid! And I am not going to let someone else come in and control this house. It's bad enough that I have lost control of the rest of my life. At least give me this.'

We all sat still for a moment. No one ate any more. My father gently put his hand on my mother's forearm. I saw her relax her shoulders, and as she breathed through her nose, she began to relax her face.

'This won't be for ever,' he said to her. 'You'll be yourself in no time. In the meantime, let us get some help so that you can at least enjoy your house the way you like to.'

I started to clear the table, making sure to run the water extra hot while I filled the sink with dirty dishes. She didn't answer my father out loud, but somewhere between me taking her plate in and coming back for the casserole dish, she nodded her head, ever so slightly.

That is how Ursula came to us. A Portuguese woman who worked diligently to keep everything as dust-free and lemon-scented as possible, Ursula made sure the house was cleaner and tidier than it ever was when Mum was well. Ursula made her stay on the couch and she brought her hot water and lemon while she vacuumed. She spoke a quick, accented English, and she commented on all my mother's knick-knacks and heirlooms. When there was nothing left for her to clean, she took out the silver and polished it even though there were no holidays for at least a month. But while she polished in the dining room, my mother stayed on the living-room couch and told her the stories behind the candlesticks brought over from Russia at the turn of the century, the tray presented to my grandfather as a founder of the now-defunct Propoisker Society and the *Kiddush* cup, which had been my mother's grandfather's, the one gift he received when he had his bar mitzvah, something that, as she spoke, seemed to have taken place eons ago in another world.

'Oh, I love stories,' Ursula said. 'Family and stories are the most important.'

With Ursula, my mother could talk in a way she never did with me. Lying on the couch, sometimes too dizzy to lift her head up, she told stories about my grandmother travelling into the United States to visit cousins in New

York and how she fooled customs officers by speaking Yiddish. She talked about my grandfather trying to learn baseball when he first moved here, but how he always ran in the wrong direction when he hit the ball. She talked about how her parents always wanted to take a trip back to Russia, but, of course, there was never any money then.

'You should go,' said Ursula (who had been back to Portugal three times since moving to Canada). 'Save your money. See your family.'

'I wouldn't know where to start,' my mother told her. 'Our family is really scattered all over the place.'

Sometimes, if I was home, I sat upstairs where she couldn't see me and listened. If I were to go into the living room, she would stop talking and expect me to carry on about my plans for next year, Norma's wedding, etc. I could not remember ever hearing my mother tell stories before. She had a way of building up a tale. She gave ample background to describe the setting. Then, she built on the setting with details, like staging a play, making sure Ursula knew what would play a part in the upcoming storyline. She played back conversations with a slight variation in her voice for each character. When she imitated my grandmother, I could have sworn Baba had come back from the dead just to illustrate that story. Ursula laughed at her punchlines. She sighed when my mother told something sad. She said *yes, yes* when something reminded her of her own life. As much as Ursula could talk, when my mother was telling stories, she stayed silent, sometimes even massaging my mother's legs while she spoke.

'You have a very good memory,' she told her.

'Yes,' my mother said, misunderstanding. 'Some of my memories are very good.'

We all took shifts with my mother, even when Ursula was there. Carrie's shifts were baking shifts. She took Ursula on a tour of the kitchen and taught her all of my mother's favourite recipes. They made roly poly together, and Mum couldn't tell the difference between Ursula's batch and Carrie's. When she felt up to it, she sat with them and measured out ingredients, pouring each into separate bowls and lining them up on the table in order of use. Carrie always told her she looked good, and there were days that she did. Some days she wore blush and lipstick, and she brushed her hair out into a flip. If she was careful not to exert herself, then those days she managed to last and not look overly tired. It was the days when the medication had her wiped out, or she tried to do too much, or she didn't bother to do her hair and instead wore it under a scarf. Those days she looked not only tired, but how I imagined her twenty years from now. Even then, Carrie would look at her and say, 'You look good today, Goldie.' And although my mother knew she was lying, she smiled anyway and said, 'I try.'

If Carrie was the baker, then I was the librarian. Mum's eyes hurt too much to read most days, but she could listen. She insisted on keeping up with the Monday Group, which had disbanded over the summer but was meeting again in the fall to study *Great Expectations*. Over the summer, I read her two to three chapters a day while she kept a cold washcloth over her eyes. There were times when I thought she almost fell asleep, and my voice commanded her dreams with Charles Dickens's words.

'I read this once when I was younger,' she mumbled once, turning onto her side away from me. 'It's so much better now, like this.'

Sometimes I read her magazine or newspaper articles. Sometimes we just talked about the weather. Once or twice she opened her eyes to tell me she was worried about my father.

'I never noticed until now how hard he works. The store is making him grow old quicker.'

This time it was me who said, 'It's all right, Mum. He's fine. He loves what he's doing.'

'I'm so glad you're helping him, Beth.' Both times she said this as she was falling asleep for her afternoon nap. I stayed by her bed watching her breathe, like one watches a baby, the rhythmic rise and fall of her chest and shoulders as she stayed curled and settled deep under the covers. Sometimes I would count thirty of these ascension/descensions before leaving the room.

Near the end of that summer my mother completed her treatments. By Labour Day, she had been told that everything looked clean. By the following week, her cheeks were looking pink again. We celebrated by my father taking the day off and the three of us, plus Carrie, going out to Winnipeg Beach for the day. I had already started my second-year courses, and everyone had an opinion on my schedule.

'It seems awfully packed,' my mother said when I told her that all of my science credits included three-hour lab sessions. 'I don't know when you'll have time to socialize.'

'She can socialize in class,' my aunt said. 'The main thing is that she learns what she's interested in.'

'Make sure you have a good chemistry teacher,' my father said, and then to me quietly, 'That will be key in your pharmaceutical exams.'

'It will be a good year,' I promised all of them, feeling the weight of that promise resting squarely on me.

Later when we came home, Ursula had left the mail on the kitchen table. My father handed me a letter addressed from the University of Chicago.

'What's this about?' he asked.

'It's probably just a brochure,' I said, seeing Dr Erikson's handwriting on the envelope. 'You can throw it out.'

My father opened it anyway. 'It's too thin to be a brochure,' he muttered. 'And you should never throw out unopened mail, Sweetheart.'

There in his hands was Dr Erikson's plea for me to reconsider my decision not to come to Chicago. One of his team members had not worked out. He wanted me because he rarely met a student with as keen an interest and desire for astral physics. My work was clear, methodical, and I showed all the promise to become a successful scientist. Then he added, *You owe it to yourself to take this chance and build a career that you will not be able to have if you stay in Winnipeg.*

My father and mother stayed quiet long after they had finished reading the letter. Finally Carrie said, 'That's definitely not a brochure.'

'You never said anything about this,' my father said.

'It wasn't important. I made up my mind on my own.'

'And what exactly did you decide?' he asked.

They all looked at me then. I had never before felt as if the sun had broken through our roof and was beaming down on me as the largest spotlight ever. It was as if I was on stage and had forgotten to memorize my lines. I looked at my feet and found myself finally saying, 'I told him I needed to stay here.'

My mother, who had been holding her breath the whole time, let it out, and that was the only sound in the still room. 'Well, that sounds like a very sensible decision to me,' she said, and she took the letter from my father's hand. 'Can I throw this out, then?'

'Sure.' The spotlight faded, but my heart did not stop racing. I watched her tear the letter in half and throw it in the garbage. 'Who wants tea, then?' she asked.

'It's not what you want,' Carrie said to me, 'is it?'

'It's fine,' I told her. I told all of them. 'I think it's better for me to stay here for now.'

'We agree,' my mother said, filling the kettle. 'There's plenty for you to do here.'

My father cleared his throat. 'Yes, I guess you will become the next in the short line of Levy pharmacists?' He said this without much conviction. Like waking one day to find the house had grown old, my father looked at me now as if realizing I had changed while he was sleeping.

'I don't know.' I was ready to take a cup of tea if it meant they would all stop looking at me.

'Yes, you do,' Carrie said, and my mother swung around from the stove.

'Carrie, leave her alone. Don't make her confused when she's made up her mind.'

'You've made up your mind, Goldie. You've never let her make up her mind in her life.'

'Carrie,' I said quietly, 'it's fine. Leave it.'

She picked up the pieces of the letter from the garbage and handed them to me. Then she held my wrists, and, ignoring the glares from my mother, she said, 'You are too bright, and this is too good an opportunity for you to pass up. My brother would have killed for this opportunity. You owe it to him, never mind to yourself, not to let this go.'

Then she turned to my mother, who was frozen by Carrie's stubbornness. None of us had ever seen Carrie like this. Her eyes were aflame, her cheeks blushing. 'Aren't I right, Goldie?' she asked.

My mother took a moment before speaking. When she did, her voice came out in a whisper. 'This isn't about Philip, Carrie.'

'You're right. And it's not about you. It's about Beth. I'm not going to watch you keep her back. Do you want her to be suffocated by you so much that one morning you find her bed empty and she doesn't call you for months?'

'Carrie, don't,' my mother pleaded.

'Don't let her make a mistake, then.'

My mother's water boiled, and she turned away from us to fill her teapot. Her hands shook, and the steaming water spilled over top of the pot and onto the counter. Carrie stood still for a moment and then walked over to help her wipe it up. I held onto my letter with both hands until my father touched my shoulder and said, 'I think you need to go upstairs and think about this some more.'

That night, my mother came into my room and sat on the edge of my bed while I slept. She waited there, her back straight, her eyes fixed on my window and the clear night sky, while I lay curled with my hand over my nose and my face toward the wall. I don't know how long she sat there before I woke up, but all of a sudden, I was aware of her sitting there, breathing quietly, patient.

'Mum?' I said, rolling over onto my back. My feet touched her side as I tried to stretch. 'You all right?'

'I've been wondering,' she answered. 'Maybe if I had let her go earlier, maybe we wouldn't have lost her.'

'Mum, what are you talking about?'

'Your aunt,' she said. 'Sarah. She wanted to travel when she was around your age, and I wouldn't let her. You know that your father and I were her legal guardians after your grandmother died.'

I didn't know. I sat up and leaned against the wall while she spoke.

'I never wondered before now. But now I'm thinking, if I had let her go travel Europe, or whatever it was she had it in her head to do – would she have come back to us and stayed?'

'Mum, there wasn't anything you or anyone else could do to pin Sarah down.'

The light from outside coated the room in a ghostly blue, and the white of my mother's eyes looked like pearls.

'She was a gorgeous child,' Mum continued. 'And with Phil gone, and your Auntie Carrie the way she is, I always looked forward to the two of us raising our families together.'

'It's not what she wanted,' I said.

'Is it what you want?' she asked me, turning to look at me for the first time.

I was startled by her frankness. In the middle of the night, in the blue light, without makeup, she looked almost vulnerable. Suddenly, I recognized myself in her features – her plain brown eyes, her wide nose, her thin lips and the way she parted them, out of fear.

'I don't know,' I answered her. She waited for me to say more. 'I don't know if being a wife and mother and living in Winnipeg is really for me.'

Her face crumpled and her voice turned into a whisper.

'I don't want to lose you too,' she said.

I hugged her while she cried and I rubbed her back.

'I'm not Sarah,' I whispered to her, but I don't know if she heard.

18

I knew I was going. I woke up early the next morning and pulled all of my notes and research out of my desk drawer. During the time my mother was sick, I hardly looked at them. But laying them out on my bed, I ached to be immersed in it again. I had a craving for it always to be night time, for me never to be sleeping, so that I could live among my stars and planets. I crawled back under my blanket and my papers, my heart pounding, not falling back to sleep, but with my eyes closed, picturing stars and comets swirling around me, me landing on one and being carried away on its random path.

My mother immersed herself in High Holiday preparations. She was hosting both dinners, as usual. The first night there would only be seven of us (me, my parents, Carrie, David, Margaret and Jade). But the second night we had family coming in from rural Manitoba, and they would bump up our numbers to thirteen. My mother leafed through cookbooks and magazines for new recipes, only to settle on the ones she used every year. She brought home groceries and filled the pantry while I emptied out my room and sorted my clothes. My father came home each day with new pieces of travelling advice until, finally, I handed him a notepad and asked that he write me a list. He did and it said things like:

- Arrange your travel insurance
- Take decongestants in your carry-on
- Take your shoes off on the plane so your feet don't swell

He kept the notepad open on the front hall table so he could add to it as necessary, and I could review it in between running up and down the stairs while I packed.

Carrie came over to sit with me while I organized. She ran her finger over the furniture, smoothing her hand over the wood of my bed frame. The bed had been hers when she was younger, along with the comforter, which she had made with my grandmother. The comforter, a quilt made of blue pieces of satin and cotton, had jagged stitching, and Carrie shook her head looking at it.

'This was one of the first things I ever made. Goodness, this stitching is awful. I can't believe my mother didn't make me rip it out and start over again.'

'It's all about the learning experience, Carrie.'

'Yes, but, Gawd. I can't believe you've kept it all these years.'

She looked around the room and sighed. 'Your mother has asked me if I'd like to move in with them after you leave.'

'Really? But you love your place.'

'I do. I don't want to leave it. But I know she's going to be very lonely with you gone. It's a big house for just the two of them.'

'Carrie, don't move in here just because Mum's pressuring you. You worked really hard to have your own place. Don't just give that up.'

'I won't, I won't. I want to help her, though. She'll drive me crazy, but she is my sister.'

'So come and bake with her.'

'Beth,' she said, 'once you leave, who does she have left to bake for?'

As well as my mother was, she would not get rid of Ursula. She seemed to find things for her to do. So the day of the first Rosh Hashanah dinner, while my mother was making cinnamon chicken with dried fruit and apple juice, Ursula was in the kitchen cleaning out her top cupboards and wiping down her dusty glass serving bowls. Ursula stood on the red folding stool, on her tiptoes to reach the back of the shelves. She used a spray cleaner, so everything in the kitchen smelled like candied lemon.

'So who is coming?' she asked my mother. She would be coming back later to help serve in the kitchen. My mother did not ask her, I should point out. Ursula insisted. She still wanted my mother sitting as much as possible for 'the healing.' That morning, Ursula and I had set the table, eight places.

Mum listed the guests, referring to Margaret as David's 'lady friend.' While she spoke, Ursula counted in her head.

'Mrs Levy, that's only seven. We set for eight.'

'We always set an extra place for my late brother on Rosh Hashanah and Passover. It's our tradition.'

Ursula nodded. I peeled and chopped carrots for the *tzimmes*. My mother passed me a handful of prunes to add in later. I watched for her reaction when Ursula said, 'What was his name?'

'Philip. Phil. He died during the war.'

'A soldier?'

'He was a pilot.'

'The wars take away the best,' Ursula said. 'My country is fighting right now. And my husband's nephew? Like that. Boom! Blown apart. And the army they give you these medals when they die. The boys for bravery. But who needs them? You just want your children back.'

Mum nodded. Her eyes were tearing but she kept working, rubbing the chicken with cinnamon. Her hands turned red from the spice, especially under her nails.

'Philip never actually made it to his destination,' she said. 'He was so excited to go to war and fight for our country. And he was supposed to fly to North Africa. But the night before they all left the base, he and a couple of friends were in a car accident. The truck flipped on the highway, and he had been sitting in the back. He just went flying.'

'A waste,' Ursula muttered, and I didn't know whether she was referring to Phil or her nephew. Or whether it mattered.

'Mum, I thought he died in a plane crash in North Africa,' I said.

'No, Beth. He never made it there. Where did you hear that?'

How do you trace back the origins of a story when you have been building on a family mythology for years? Maybe Carrie had said something. Maybe I mistook one of her stories from when I was little and filed it away under truth.

'I don't know. I always thought he was a war hero.'

'Well, he was,' my mum said. 'In his own way. I guess to us.'

'A waste,' Ursula said again, this time louder. 'Children do not need to be war heroes.'

That night, at dinner, my mother ran the meal with the elegance of an orchestra conductor. Blessing the *yontif* candles, bringing the red wine (room temperature) to the table for my father's kiddush, passing him the challah beneath her mother's embroidered challah cover – Goldie performed everything with precision and pointed ritual. When she brought the soup, she did not need to ask who wanted only broth, broth with matzo ball or broth, matzo ball and a chicken foot (Carrie was the only one who ate chicken feet; she would finish her soup and then suck on the tiny bones from the foot, rolling them in her mouth with her tongue, just like I remembered when I was young). She knew how long to let people sit with an empty bowl in front of them before offering more. 'There's plenty,' she promised. And there was.

She had purchased foil containers and some Tupperware so that she could package single serving leftovers of the meal for me to take to Chicago. Even keeping that in mind, she made enough food that the fridge would be full for a week after the holiday, and she and my father would be eating cold brisket sandwiches for dinner. Once she had served everyone, and sat down beside my dad, I watched her watching her guests as they ate and talked and praised her food. I did not remember a time when she did not know how to host, although she must not have at some point. Surely when she and my father lived in that tiny apartment above the store she could not have had the skills to entertain like this: crisp, ironed, embroidered tablecloth, matching cloth napkins, candles in the centre, sterling silver serving pieces. While she leaned back in her chair and surveyed her table, my father reached over and rubbed her neck. She closed her eyes and felt his fingers there, massaging her skin gently, smoothing out her tight, knotted muscles.

My sometimes-silent Aunt Carrie talked very openly about her plans to travel. She found a singles' trip to Mexico with three other women she knew. She spoke mainly to Margaret, who sat to her right, a thin woman with a long nose and large glasses, who spent much of the meal just nodding her head. She was most excited about seeing the Mayan Ruins and maybe trying snorkelling. And then after Mexico, who knew? There were so many places she wanted to see, like Africa. She would just love, she said, to see the jungle, the mountain shaped like a table and the place where the Indian and Atlantic oceans meet.

'Carrie,' I said, suddenly, 'why didn't you tell me that Phil never made it to North Africa?'

'Didn't I?' she turned away from Margaret to me. 'I must have, Beth. What else would I have told you?'

'That he died in a plane crash. Somewhere in the desert.'

She thought for a moment, staring at the table, and then said, 'No. No, you must be getting mixed up. I never would have said that.' Then she turned back to Margaret, 'Philip was our older brother. He was supposed to go to North Africa with the air force . . .'

I could have thrown away my Philip myth, I supposed, but I didn't. With everyone talking and eating around the table, I spied his empty chair at the end and pictured him sitting there, dressed in uniform, piling the food on his plate. Between the chatter and the cutlery chiming, I heard him laughing at something David might have said. Philip had a long laugh, and for me, it hung about the table for the rest of the evening, like the faint hum of an appliance in the background.

My Uncle David, who over the years had become much more comfortable in our family, especially since Sarah left, spent most of the dinner holding Margaret's hand and turning every so often to ask Jade if she would stop fidgeting. I could tell that as Jade was getting older, she made him nervous. My cousin had Sarah's spirit and was taking dance classes (Margaret's suggestion) to burn off her energy. After the meal, she would ask her father if she could do a recital for all of us, and he would defer to my parents for permission. David didn't let Jade get away with everything – the way you might expect a single father would. For example, if she wanted extra ice cream, he would judge her energy level and then gently explain that no, tonight wasn't a good night for her to have two bowls of chocolate ice cream. She should eat her first one slowly so that it lasted like two bowls. David had a way of saying these things to Jade so that she would turn to him and answer, 'Good idea, Daddy!'

We all wondered when that would change, when Jade would stop looking to her father for answers and believing all of his reasoning. She never seemed to throw tantrums, never used the words, 'It's not fair!' (although we all thought that in her short life, she had reason to). That night she ate everything on her plate and, when David suggested, she helped my mother clear the table by taking in her dinner plate and cutlery, neatly placed on the china.

Then, during dessert, David let go of Margaret's hand, cleared his throat and announced what we had all been expecting. Margaret blushed a little and put her hand on Jade's head, who was bouncing in her seat.

'See, Daddy!' Jade said. 'I can keep a secret! I didn't tell anyone, did I? Wasn't I good, Daddy? Aren't I good at keeping secrets?'

When David made the announcement, Margaret held her hand up for the first time that evening and showed us all the engagement ring, a simple yellow gold band with one small diamond. We all smiled, squealed, clapped and tried not to think of her hand as Sarah's how many years ago when we were all so much younger. I couldn't remember Sarah's ring, but it was something similar, something non-profound and understated, something, I remembered thinking, that was not like her at all. Margaret's ring looked like it had been there all along, and I wondered if she had only slipped it on that instant to show us, or had it been there all evening and none of us noticed? David had his arm around her, she had her arm around Jade, and they all made this lovely family unit, a photo my father insisted on taking to capture the event.

My mother was the one who got out of her chair, had Margaret stand up so that she could take her into a big hug, and then said, so that we all heard and understood, 'We're going to be sisters-in-law!'

Margaret blushed again (she blushed a lot) and asked whether she and David could have their wedding in Mum and Dad's backyard.

'It would mean so much to us to have it here. With family,' she said.

Once the announcement was made, and everyone fantasized about the wedding, which would likely take place the following summer, Jade danced for us in the living room to one of my father's Bing Crosby and Danny Kaye records. She looked at her feet when she danced, and I got the feeling she would forget that we were all there watching her. Jade had a repertoire of four dance steps that she used in different sequences: spins, lunges, kicks and jumps. Sometimes she closed her eyes and spun around and around with her arms out for balance. I remembered what it felt like to be seven – to want everyone to watch you and ignore you at the same time. After the song finished, and we all clapped, Jade bowed and then sat on the floor, rocking herself, as we let the rest of the record play.

Later, while David and Margaret got ready to leave, Jade came upstairs to my room to look through my closet.

'I want a really pretty pair of shoes for the wedding, Beth,' she told me. 'Not from Daddy's store. From somewhere else. Like these ones,' she picked up a pair of black slingbacks that had been her mother's and that I had inherited a long time ago and had never managed to leave my closet.

'Those will be a bit big on you,' I told her. Of course, she had already slipped them on and was shuffling around my room, the heels slapping against the floor as she walked. She stood sideways to look at herself in my full length mirror.

'Do these look pretty on me?' she asked, pulling her hair up and making her neck look long. 'How would my hair look like this for the wedding?'

'You'll be beautiful,' I told her. I lifted her up and out of the shoes, which fell to the floor while I cuddled her on my bed, her hair down and around her face now, her arms around my neck.

'You're going to be just gorgeous,' I said, while she laughed with her head tossed right back.

I woke up while it was still dark. My heart was pounding and my blood was rushing to my feet, making my skin tingle. I would be leaving in two days' time, and all around my room were open boxes and suitcases, everything half-packed. Why is it, on the cusp of something so exciting, so right, all I wanted to do was hide under my bed? I tried to close my eyes, but they wouldn't stay shut. I couldn't lie still. My feet were sweating. In the end, although it was three o'clock, I put on my housecoat and went downstairs.

Maybe it was her shuffling that woke me in the first place. Downstairs, in the living room, I found my mother sitting on the floor with a box of photos in front of her and a cup of hot tea on the coffee table. She looked up at me on the stairs, and then went back to the piles of photos she had laid out in front of her, in her lap and by her feet.

'Come help me with this,' she said, sorting black and white and faded colour prints.

'Mum, it's 3 a.m. Shouldn't you be asleep?'

'If you can be up, so can I. What's the point of lying in bed with my eyes open? I could be doing something useful instead.'

I sat down beside her, crossing my legs. The photos were from the basement; the lid from the shoebox was dusty and faded.

'This is silly,' she said, holding three photos in her hand like a fan.

'What is?'

'All of these photos, lying in the basement, getting creased. I want to get some of them up on the wall, in frames. Your cousin Jade needs to know her family. And if we can't share it with her, no one can.'

I helped her sort through the photos like puzzle pieces. We talked about the kinds of frames she wanted for the photos and where exactly we would put them. She made piles and placed one in front of me, saying, 'You can take these with you.' She had arranged photos of Uncle Phil as a baby, child and teenager. In a couple he looked really cocky, sticking his tongue out at the camera, laughing to show off his missing teeth. In one, he had his arm around my mother, who was no more than eleven, and they were holding up a frog, both of their faces a bit muddy, but their eyes sparkling. 'It always amazed me how much he meant to you, even though you never knew him.'

'I always felt like I did,' I said. 'Carrie gave me his journal, you know. You should read it.'

'I read that a long time ago,' she said. 'Carrie told me to, but it was all science stuff, which didn't mean anything to me. I would just rather remember him like I want to remember him.'

'You read it?' I repeated.

'Yes, and I didn't crack up. So maybe I'm not as fragile as you think I am.' She stared at me a while, and then said, 'Take it with you. He would have wanted you to have it.'

She leaned back against the couch and surveyed the room. 'I'm going to have an awful lot to sort through.'

'Why? What do you mean?'

'I think your dad and I will probably sell this house after the wedding. There doesn't seem to be much point in us living here if there's only the two of us.'

I considered that maybe she was trying to punish me for leaving. But then I looked at the worn carpet, the faded walls. I saw all the knick-knacks she was mentally disposing of. I realized this had nothing to do with me at all.

'I think that makes sense, Mum.'

'Some of our friends are looking at condos on Wellington Crescent. I imagine we'll look there too.'

'You need to go where you two will be comfortable.'

'Your father's been pushing me to sell for a while now. I guess I haven't been ready to.'

'It is an awfully big house for just the two of you,' I said.

She nodded. 'To be honest, it was probably more than we ever needed.'

We went back to sorting through pictures. There were photos of my grandparents, some from Russia, and many of people neither my mum nor I knew. The ones we looked at longest were of her and her siblings. I didn't say anything, but the first group picture they took all together, after my Uncle Phil died, was at her wedding. She chose that one for the wall and chuckled at how thin and young she and my dad had been. Then she picked the one she wanted of my Uncle Phil. It was his air force photo. He wore a stiff collar and cap. His eyes drooped at the sides and his nose was wide at the base, a trait he shared with Carrie. She picked it out by herself, and without a word put it to one side.

'You should keep that one,' I told her.

She nodded, and reached out to pat my hand. The next day, she would polish her nails opal pink, but right then, her hands looked naked, worn. I watched her straighten each of the photo piles like decks of cards and secure them with elastics – this one to put away for Jade, this one for frames, this one for me to take to remind me that here, I am loved.

About the Author

Photo: Dave A. Brown

SIDURA LUDWIG was born and raised in Winnipeg, Manitoba, and lived in Birmingham, UK, from 2001 to 2004. Her short fiction has appeared in several magazines and anthologies in Canada and the UK (with two stories in *Are You She?*, published by Tindal Street Press in 2004), and she is the recipient of the Canadian Author and Bookman Prize for Most Promising Writer. She lives in Toronto, Ontario, with her husband and two children.

Acknowledgements

I would like to thank The Jewish Foundation of Manitoba and the Arts Council of England, West Midlands, for funding the research, development and writing of this book.

I am indebted to members of Tindal Street Fiction Group for their early readings of my chapters. I would especially like to thank Annie Murray for the workshop that first inspired this novel. Thanks to Anna Nicole for her helpful steering; to my father for his later valuable comments; and to Martha Brooks for her many years of lessons.

Thank you to the Jewish Heritage Centre of Western Canada and Selkirk Avenue Walking Tours for help in my research.

Chapter Eight of the novel originally appeared as the short story, 'Holding My Breath Underwater', in the anthology, *Going the Distance* (Tindal Street Press, 2003).

Thank you to those who told stories: Marvyne Jenoff, Priscilla and Mel Guberman, Jay Kronson, Paul Kronson, Marion Moglove, Mel Hornstein, Rabbi Charlie Grysman, Maylene and Rael Ludwig, Sora Ludwig and Bertha Ludwig (z'l).

My sincere gratitude goes to my editor Janie Yoon at Key Porter Books, Canada for her coaching; and to my agent, Denise Bukowski for her belief in the manuscript; and to staff at Tindal Street Press.

Finally, for their love and support, I thank my parents-in-law, family and friends; and for their nurturing of my writing I am indebted to my parents and my husband, Jason.

Are you a keen reader of contemporary fiction?

Want to discover some more excellent writing from the English regions?

Become a Friend of Tindal Street Press

Ten of a total of 33 Tindal Street titles in eight years have achieved national prize listings.

By becoming a Friend of Tindal Street Press for a year, you can choose FOUR from a selection of titles that includes:

DISTINCTIVE LITERARY FICTION

Clare Morrall	*Astonishing Splashes of Colour*
Anthony Cartwright	*The Afterglow*
Austin Clarke	*The Polished Hoe*
Grace Jolliffe	*Piggy Monk Square*
Ed Trewavas	*Shawnie*
Jackie Gay	*Scapegrace*
	Wist
E. A. Markham	*Meet Me in Mozambique*
	At Home with Miss Vanesa
Will Buckingham	*Cargo Fever*
Daphne Glazer	*Goodbye, Hessle Road*
	By the Tide of Humber
Catherine O'Flynn	*What Was Lost*

SHORT STORY ANTHOLOGIES

Her Majesty
Mango Shake
Loffing Matters
Are You She?

NOIR CRIME FICTION

Mick Scully	*Little Moscow*
Alan Brayne	*Jakarta Shadows*
David Fine	*The Executioner's Art*
Nicholas Royle (ed)	*Dreams Never End*
John Dalton	*The City Trap*
	The Concrete Sea

As a Friend of Tindal Street Press, you will be supporting a unique publishing operation focused on literary fiction with a regional and contemporary edge. And you will enjoy special discounts on our varied fiction list.

For £25 you can enjoy a fine selection of original regional fiction. Send your cheque to Tindal Street Press, with a list of your preferences and interests, to 217 The Custard Factory, Gibb Street, Digbeth, Birmingham B9 4AA. We will then dispatch your choice of four titles (subject to availability).

By supporting Tindal Street in this way you will also join our **Friends of Tindal Street Press** mailing list, where we will keep you up to date with launch invitations, events, readings, forthcoming publications, prize listings and author information.

See our website *www.tindalstreet.co.uk* for our full range of titles

'If you want originality these days, look to the independent presses. Tindal Street Press is one of the best (and certainly has the best address – The Custard Factory, Birmingham) The Times

PRIZEWINNING FICTION

Hard Shoulder (eds Jackie Gay and Julia Bell) *Raymond Williams Community Publishing Prize 2000*; **The Pig Bin** (Michael Richardson) *Sagittarius Prize 2001*; **A Lone Walk** (Gul Y. Davis) *J. B. Priestley Fiction Award 2001*; **Whispers in the Walls** (eds Leone Ross and Yvonne Brissett) *World Book Day Top 10 2003*; **Astonishing Splashes of Colour** (Clare Morrall) *Shortlisted for Man Booker Prize 2003, British Book Awards Newcomer of the Year 2003*; **The Polished Hoe** (Austin Clarke) *Overall winner of Commonwealth Writers Prize 2003*; **The Afterglow** (Anthony Cartwright) *Betty Trask Award 2004; shortlisted for James Tait Black Memorial Prize 2004, John Llewellyn Rhys Prize 2004, Commonwealth Writers Prize (Eurasia) 2005*; **Piggy Monk Square** (Grace Jolliffe) *Shortlisted for Commonwealth Writers Prize (first novel) 2005*; **Meet Me in Mozambique** (E. A. Markham) *Longlisted for the Frank O'Connor International Short Story Award 2007* ; **What Was Lost** (Catherine O'Flynn) *Longlisted for the Orange Broadband Prize, Man Booker Prize and Guardian First Book Award 2007.*